TIJARAN TALES
The Girl From The Sky

Book Six

F. T. Barbini

Text Copyright © 2017 F.T. Barbini
Cover Copyright © 2017 F.T. Barbini
Cover Design by Jay Johnstone

First published by Luna Press Publishing, Edinburgh, 2017

www.lunapresspublishing.com

ISBN-13: 978-1-911143-18-5

TIJARAN TALES SERIES:

Book 1 - White Child
Book 2 - The Oracle Of Life
Book 3 - The Nuarn Rift
Book 4 - Tijara's Heart
Book 5 - The Guardian's Trail
Book 6 - The Girl From The Sky

CONTENTS

The Power of Imagination makes us infinite.
Imagine.

THE GIRL FROM THE SKY

Mah Gira stepped out of his home, and stretched his aging joints in familiar, reassuring movements. The white mane covering the entire rear side of his body from head to heel, shimmered in the lights of the street lamps and the purple glare of their Strullium encasings. The Arneshian occupation had prevented him from doing regular exercise, but because of his status as Supreme of the Mahini, Ambassador T'Rogon had showed him some leniency, allowing him to remain in his house and most importantly, ordered him to knock some sense into any hot-blooded "furcoat" that dared step out of line.

'*Furcoats*,' muttered Mah Gira, starting to get a bit worked up. 'How dare they? Awful people, with grey skin and bad manners. Constantly complaining about the snow or the rain or our underground city. Who invited them here, anyway? I did not invite you here.' He shook his head indignantly and slowly walked over to the edge of his tiny, slate yard. Looking at the bench, he negotiated a way to sit that wouldn't hurt too much. Eventually, he placed a hand on the stony seat and used it as a lever to turn and lower himself. Out of habit, he bent forward to check that the smooth black rock was still under there, completely tucked away in the right corner. It was, and he smiled to himself.

When he looked up, a couple of soldiers were just leaving one of the local's home, before walking past his gate. They didn't even glance at him, but strutted on as if they *actually* owned the place, rather than being intruders.

As well as scaring the daylights out of the Mahini, showing up as they had in the first place and proving that there *was* life beyond

Mah, the Arneshians had invaded their city, enslaved their people, killed those who rebelled and stole the only precious thing that the planet had to offer — Strullium. As a matter of fact, thought Mah Gira, he hadn't even realised that Strullium was so precious outside of their world — here they only ever used it for decoration, from lampshades to toilet bowls.

The ground beneath his feet trembled, not for the first time that day. Mah Gira, and everyone else on Mah, was getting used to these short episodes. Not knowing what caused them was the alarming part, but the Arneshians had never volunteered an explanation, so they had stopped asking. He smoothed the fur on his left arm distractedly, as he continued his reflections on the past months of occupation. The rate at which the Arneshians were mining, the veins would be dried out soon. And then what? They'd probably leave, abandoning them to certain death. They had destroyed all their greenhouses; the sole means of sustenance they had. The Mahini could rebuild them, of course they could — their Chief Engineer, Ruxshin, was very skilled and could definitely set up new winter gardens in a short enough time — but it would take months before the crops could grow in enough quantities to feed the whole city. However he looked at it, the situation was grim and getting grimmer by the day.

Just then, as if summoned, the voices of Ruxshin and Khavar drew closer to Mah Gira's home. It was one of the Supreme's jobs to spend time with the teenage Mahini, until they reached their fifteenth birthdays. It created important bonds between the older generation and the younger ones, making for a more stable and caring society. Both Ruxshin and Khavar had showed leadership skills right from the start, becoming focal points among their peers for very different reasons — there was nothing that Ruxshin couldn't grow, and there was nothing that Khavar couldn't hunt with his bow. Hutan had been another youth of such quality, with his knack for growing unusual berries to brew into weird and marvellous concoctions. Alas, he was dead now, killed by an Arneshian while defending Ruxshin. His heart ached at the memory and he pushed it away, into the place where all his dearly departed were remembered.

The Supreme waited for the pair to come into view before hailing them softly. It looked like they had just come from their day shift, as they were still wearing the protective leather suits they used above ground, which was handy, as they would shortly need to return outside. As soon as they saw him, the slender frame of Ruxshin and the bulky one of Khavar rushed over to the Supreme's feet, and knelt deeply before him, their right hands gently touching his knees as a display of respect.

'Mah Gira!' said Ruxshin, plainly happy to see him out of the house.

'Dear girl,' he answered, patting her hand, which was covered in short red fur. 'See, I still have the strength to walk about.'

'Of course you do!' stated Khavar. 'You are our leader. You'll always be strong enough.'

'Bless you, Khavar. Full of life as always. Come, both of you. Sit by my side.'

It was evident from the surprise on their faces that they hadn't expected this request, but they quickly obliged.

'I hear some of the soldiers have been misplacing their boots lately,' he started, to no one in particular.

Ruxshin suppressed a grin and looked down between her feet.

Khavar scratched his dark brown mane, blushing ever so slightly. 'They're very distracted, Mah Gira,' he replied.

'So it seems. Let's make sure they *remember* where they left them soon, yes?'

There was no anger in his voice, and perhaps even a hint of amusement, but Khavar got the message right away. 'Of course.'

'And make sure the other jokers know that too, please.'

'I'll see to that,' he answered.

'Good,' said Mah Gira, satisfied. 'Not that I object to a little fun, but these people don't seem to share our sense of humour.'

'Among other things,' added Ruxshin, ironically.

Mah Gira nodded. 'It won't last forever, you'll see.'

'Let's hope there's someone left alive to see that day, then,' blurted out Khavar. 'I wish there was something we could do to get rid of them … before it's too late.'

'We have no food of our own left,' said Ruxshin dejectedly. 'Nothing has survived — no seed, no soil, no compost. The land around Mahin is either frozen or flooded. From the moment they go, it'll be a countdown for us.'

Mah Gira leaned over to Ruxshin in a conspiratorial way. 'What if you had the chance to build a small nursery … in secret? Would that help?'

Ruxshin's eyes widened. 'If I could start the seeds now, then yes, it could. We may still need time, but it would give us a fighting chance.'

'But where can we build it?' asked Khavar. 'The Arneshians have the whole place under surveillance.'

'I disagree,' said Mah Gira, smiling. 'Follow me.'

Khavar offered him his arm, to help him stand easily and threw a curious glance at Ruxshin, who didn't seem to know any more than he did.

The Supreme opened his front door and ushered them into a small lounge; a sofa, a table and a wooden chest comprised the only furnishing in the room. A passageway opened out to the right, leading to other areas of the house. 'Close the door,' said Mah Gira to Khavar.

'What's going on?' asked Ruxshin, once they were safely alone.

In reply, the Supreme moved towards the chest and placed himself on its left side. He leaned over it and began to push.

Quickly, Khavar stepped up. 'Let me,' he said. He then leaned his body weight against it and pushed it easily along the wall, revealing a rectangular hole beyond.

'Goodness!' exclaimed Ruxshin, hurrying forward.

The cavity was large enough to allow an adult through and it opened onto a tunnel, carved into the rock. A cold breeze filtered into the room, bringing with it the smell of pine trees.

'It leads to the back of the house, outside. I've never told anybody about this … gateway,' said Mah Gira, with a cheeky little smile. 'It's a secret handed down from one Supreme to the next. Understand, had circumstances been different, I would not have disclosed this to you.'

'Of course, Mah Gira,' said Ruxshin. 'We will not tell anybody.'

'You're doing us a great honour sharing this with us,' added Khavar, bowing his head.

Mah Gira knew they wouldn't betray his trust. 'Let's cover this up while we talk.'

*

The snow crunched under their boots, while new flakes quickly filled the depressions left by their feet. To their right, far beyond the line of trees, were the ruins of their once great winter gardens, reduced now to skeletal frames.

'Are you sure this is the place?' asked Ruxshin, shivering. Dusk was setting in, soon to be replaced by the moonlit night.

Khavar stopped. They had emerged from the mouth of the tunnel and then walked quietly for about five minutes between thick trees. 'Mah Gira said that he buried the box by the White Glade, under a thin fir. We should be coming up on it soon.'

'I'm just conscious of the time, that's all,' she muttered.

'Don't worry Rux. We'll head back before they even know we've gone. Besides, it's our downtime. They'll think we're resting or something.'

Ruxshin looked around. The snow-laden firs and bushes grew along the base of the mountain — the only vegetation on the icy planes of Mah and, right now, their only shelter from the vigilant eyes of the soldiers. 'All right, but let's hurry.'

Khavar nodded.

Having him making decisions for her had been easy in the last few months. Since Hutan's death, she had become quieter — *withdrawn* was perhaps the right word — and unwilling to look past the end of the day. Working on the translator device for the Arneshians was all that took up her time. Not that she believed communicating with these people would do them any good, but what was the alternative? Her supervisor, A'Krad, was impressed enough by the work she had done on the *dictionary* to treat her with less contempt, especially since the day of shame — the *Memory*, as she had come to think of it — and the time spent in the holding cell. The excited face of the boy Michael as he had watched K'Ssander lowering the laser razor down on her back again and again in long steady strokes, removing clumps of her red mane; the hands of the guards pinning her, face down, on the floor - the images swirled around her mind. *No!* she screamed inside her head. *Stop it*. Those memories were poisonous and only made her weaker. She took a deep breath and unclenched her fists.

'Look!' said Khavar, pointing ahead. 'The White Glade.'

Glad for the diversion, she looked to where he was pointing and saw a wide empty circle in the forest, delineated by trees. It was the only place where the light was able to touch the ground, reflecting off the snow and bouncing onto the surrounding trunks, making them appear white. She looked at Khavar, and nudged him to go on ahead.

Khavar stepped cautiously into the area, checking that the coast was clear. He walked along the perimeter, looking behind every tree and peering into the snow laden bushes. Then he stopped, examining the base of a thin trunk. An X was engraved there, with the design of a bow and arrow, pointing to the right. He motioned for Ruxshin to join him and hunched down.

'What are you doing?' asked Ruxshin.

In reply, Khavar peered behind the tree, where a thick evergreen bush grew. Delicately, he began to move the branches out of the way, creating an opening large enough to fit his gloved hands. 'There's something in here,' he told her.

Ruxshin helped him pull back some more foliage, so he could dig deeper.

'It's a container of some sort,' he said, stretching his arms forward. He drew his hands back out and began to snap the twigs directly behind the tree, freeing up access to the under-bush.

Ruxshin bent forward, and poked her head into the hole they had created. 'It's ... a tiny greenhouse!' she squealed excitedly. Removing her gloves, she pushed her head further in, ignoring the branches catching the fur on the back of her head and the snow melting against her neck, trickling beneath her coat.

Khavar tried to free a passage for her as fast as he could but, in her excitement, Ruxshin wasn't paying him any attention.

'Bless you, Mah Gira!' she exclaimed. 'There are at least twenty plants in here — all healthy and growing!'

'I cannot believe that the old man went back into the ruins to gather the seeds,' said Khavar.

'That's why he's our Supreme,' she answered proudly.

'So, what do we do now? Bring it in?'

Ruxshin thought for a moment. 'This box has been here for months now, surviving the soldiers and the weather. I need to talk to Mah Gira before we move it.'

'All right. Let me cover it up again,' he said, gathering the broken branches from the ground.

Ruxshin stood up, a smile on her face for the first time in who knew how long. The memory of the tender leaves between her fingertips brought back a spark of hope, a precious treasure these days. Her mind had already switched to working mode — her *real* work, that is — and she had started mentally listing all the nutrients she would need to take the plants to the end of the snow season and through the wet six months that would follow. Putting her gloves back on, she walked to the side of the bush; she was so taken by this new project, that she didn't notice the object sticking out of the ground. Her foot caught it full on, sending her flying into the snow, face first. 'Oomph!' she exhaled, as the air was knocked from her lungs.

'Did you say something, Rux?' asked Khavar, from over his shoulder.

'Mmph,' came the reply.

'What was that?' Khavar stood up and turned around, then looked down in surprise.

Ruxshin sat herself up, snow capping her face and mane, and massaged her ankle. 'Not a word,' she admonished him.

Khavar refrained a smile and offered her his hand.

'Where is that dratted thing?' said Ruxshin, ignoring his help and checking the ground.

The snow had been pushed further back by her shoe, revealing what appeared to be the tip of a metallic blue object. Ruxshin moved towards it and poked it with a finger. When nothing happened, she looked up at Khavar, who quickly knelt in front of her. Together, they began to clear the snow away, their curiosity growing by the minute. 'It's a box,' she said, eventually.

'A long one at that,' added Khavar, perplexed.

Once the metal frame had been freed, Ruxshin used both hands to wipe the snow off a portion of the surface. 'Glass ...' she mused. She placed her face close to it, trying to look through it. A few seconds later, she screamed and fell back, scrambling away.

'What is it?' cried Khavar, retreating in panic.

Ruxshin pointed at the box, her hand shaking. 'There's ... there's *someone* in there!'

'What?' Khavar's eyes widened and he returned quickly to the box.

Ruxshin watched as he lowered his nose to the glass and placed his palms around his eyes to shield out the light.

'It's a girl,' he said, surprised. 'Come, look.' He started to briskly wipe more snow off the box.

Ruxshin joined him cautiously and leaned forward, eyeing it with suspicion. The girl inside looked perhaps a couple of years younger than her - maybe eighteen - and she seemed to be sleeping peacefully. Her long black hair framed delicate features, and her skin was as light as the snow. She was clothed in a white, full-length robe, which was wrapped around her body, right side over left, and held fast with a sash; a pair of sandals lay at her sock-clad feet.

'Is she one of them?' asked Khavar.

'An Arneshian? I don't think so,' replied Ruxshin. 'Her hair isn't white and her skin isn't grey. She looks more like the boy, Michael, than the rest of the soldiers.'

'Hmm …'

'What is it?'

Khavar shook his head. 'Don't you think it's strange that out of two species we meet from outer space, they both look remarkably like us?'

Ruxshin observed the girl. Like their invaders, she had no fur that could be seen, but her body was the same shape as hers. Of course she had noticed the similarities — it had made the Arneshians look less threatening when they had first arrived. 'Maybe that's all there is out there.'

'Maybe.'

'I'm more concerned with how she ended up here.'

Khavar looked around, then upwards. 'Some of those branches have been snapped,' he said.

'What are you saying: that she fell from the sky?'

'Nastier things have fallen from our sky recently,' he replied.

'Hey, look at her necklace!'

'That's a Strullium crystal,' said Khavar. 'How did she get that?'

Ruxshin shook her head. She examined the blue frame of the box, sliding her fingers under the lid. She stopped the moment she felt a little depression with something like a button in it, which she pressed. There was a loud click, and the lid popped up. When she pushed it aside, it moved without any resistance.

'Now, that is something else,' said Khavar, clearly impressed.

Ruxshin agreed — it was pretty astonishing what they were seeing. The girl was protected by a sort of transparent cocoon that swayed in the breeze, reflecting the shapes and the colours of the objects around them. Ruxshin removed her gloves once more, and gently touched it. Suddenly a screen popped into life above the girl's midriff, giving both of them a massive fright.

'It's like those Arneshians' weird machines,' said Khavar, recomposing himself.

Ruxshin nodded, and examined the screen. On it, the girl in the box was sitting on a bed, laughing. She wore blue clothing, very different from her current ones, and her expression was one of happiness. Two other voices could be heard around her: a female and a male.

'I can't understand what they're saying,' said Khavar eventually.

'Yes, well, if she is one of them there *is* a way around that,' replied Ruxshin.

'The translator?'

She nodded. Her hand returned to the cocoon and she pushed through, until she touched the lilac stone. The air inside the layer was warm on her skin and she didn't like it — the girl might look like she was merely sleeping, but Ruxshin knew full well that it was the permanent kind of sleep, never mind the fact that she was clearly in a coffin. 'Close it, Khavar. We have to hide her until Mah Gira decides what to do.'

Khavar slid the lid back into place, until it clicked shut. Then, with Ruxshin's help, he began to shovel snow onto it, trying to cover every bit of the blue metal. 'Do you think it's safe to leave her here?'

'They haven't found her so far. Besides, she's not going anywhere.'

CLASS OF 2861

Julius woke with a jolt, drenched in sweat, the bed sheet tangled around his legs. He stared at the blue sky of the scenery screen before him, waiting for his breathing to settle. Since returning to his old room on Zed, the dream had become more regular. No matter how much meditation he did before going to bed, he still ended up in the sickbay of the Mazda, holding Morgana's body. On those nights, he ran along the corridor that led to the infirmary, believing that she was waiting for him, hurt but alive. Instead, it was the blood on the floor that told another story. As he buried his face against her neck, the darkness rising up to meet him, he would try to believe that he was about to wake up, only to find that the terror was real and his nightmare had become reality.

When he looked to his right, Skye was watching him from the bathroom archway — he was almost as tall as the door. Julius registered that his hair was combed back and distractedly wondered why.

'Mazda again?' asked Skye, tucking his shirt inside his white trousers.

'I preferred it when all I dreamt of was Eneamar.'

'Farrah's imaginary place?' he asked, buckling his belt.

Julius nodded. 'It was her hideout when she was in the hospital. I was hoping it could be mine too, instead of …' he trailed off. That was when he finally realised that there was something odd going on. He focused on Skye again. 'Where are you going?'

Skye glanced at him sideways, while buttoning up his white jacket. 'Graduation ceremony, remember? That thing at the end of school, where they send you off into the big bad world with a handshake?'

Julius fell back in his bed and pulled the sheet over his head. It had completely slipped his mind.

'You have thirty minutes to get ready. I want you to join me and Faith in the garden.'

The garden — Julius knew why. 'I'll be there,' he replied quietly. After a few seconds of silence, he heard Skye walking past his bed to leave the room.

His friend's request had sounded pretty matter-of-fact to Julius, like someone who has grown tired of talking to a whining kid. He had noticed this progressively over the summer, and could tell that his downcast mood had had an effect on their relationship. But what was he supposed to do about it? He couldn't just pretend that Morgana was still with them. He opened his PIP under the sheet and saw that it was nine in the morning. His parents would already be on Zed by now, probably at the reception breakfast that was organised by the school for the families. Grudgingly, he pulled himself out of bed and headed for the toilet. After a quick shower, he laid the ceremonial suit on his bed and, with a heavy heart, began to dress.

The fitted jacket had the Gold Star embroidered inside an ivory shield badge on the chest, to the left. It was the class symbol for captains and, since Julius had only just started down this career path, the star only had one line underneath it. He combed his dark hair back and straightened his suit. The ceiling light made his white, varnished shoes gleam, lending him an air of legitimacy. Julius looked at the smiling picture of Morgana, stuck to one side of the mirror. 'How do I look?' he asked. He buttoned up his jacket and sighed. 'You would have looked great.'

*

As Julius crossed the mess hall, he was vaguely aware of the small clusters of 6MS students dotted around the room. Their anticipation at the impending ceremony was visible to his eyes in the form of green threads floating up from their heads. He had the painful suspicion that for most of them the memories of the Battle of Uruplatus were beginning to fade, replaced by the thrill of life and an exciting future ahead. To Julius however, it seemed like yesterday, and at the same time felt like he was stuck in the longest and bleakest summer of his life.

Leanne, Barth and Lopaka were huddled to one side, just before the garden door. They were so happy and loud that Julius was able to hear every word they were saying.

'My parents have booked us a great holiday,' said Lopaka, buzzing.

'Where to?' asked Leanne. She was holding Barth's hand tenderly.

'Out to Terra 2, actually.'

'That's amazing, Lopaka! I so want to go see it and-'

'Shhh,' said Barth, blushing, as Julius drew near.

'Hi Julius,' said Lopaka, a lot less energetically.

'Hi there,' he replied, but didn't stop. He had seen a lot of those guilty expressions since returning to Zed. It was as if his friends had moved on, except for when he was around — his presence was the painful reminder of what they were trying hard to forget.

Julius stepped into the garden, feeling the warmth of the artificial sun on his face. The oak tree stood green and imposing by the stream, a point of continuity for the Tijaran pupils. Skye was chatting to Faith, and leaning against the tree trunk. Faith had had his mechanical skirt painted cream for the occasion and Julius could see that the usual extra panel had been added to the bottom rim to cater for his growth. He walked over the soft grass, heading their way and, when they saw him, they both turned, showing the class symbols on the fronts of their ceremonial jackets. Skye had the Globe, the sign of those who were embarking on a career in politics, and Faith had the Tool of the Tinkerer, the emblem of engineers; a class which contained many sub classifications, such as navigators, like Barth. Their symbols had also been underscored with a single line.

They looked pleased to see him, even a little surprised he had come at all, but said nothing. He knew full well why they had wanted to meet here and, although it hurt, it had to be done. Three years before, Zed had left the Moon to rescue the kidnapped people of Earth. Before boarding Moonrising, Skye had placed a metal plaque at the base of their favourite tree, engraving the caption, "The Skirts were here", followed by "Skye, Faith, Julius and Morgana". Looking at it now, fixed to the oak trunk, it felt more like an epitaph to Julius.

'Fifteen,' said Faith. 'It seems like ages ago. Even me handwriting was different.'

'The last three years have flown by,' added Skye. 'Our life in school is over.'

Her life is over, period, thought Julius.

Faith dipped his hand inside his jacket and retrieved an origami lilac rose, which he laid on the grass at the base of the oak.

Julius wondered where he had got it from and was about to ask him when Faith put his left arm across his shoulders. He just stood there, watching the flower for a few moments.

'Guys,' called Siena from the garden door, breaking the spell. 'It's almost ten.'

Julius waited for Faith to move his arm away and, after glancing at the rose one last time, he headed back.

When Faith reached Siena, he kissed her on the forehead. Then, with his arm around her waist, they headed towards the Assembly Hall. Julius couldn't avoid noticing the intimacy of their relationship; although he was happy for them, his heart ached all the more. He forced himself to look elsewhere and kept his eyes on the small crowd of students on the concourse as they made their way to the ceremony. When they reached the entrance, Master Cress asked them all to wait outside while he adjusted the students' uniforms at random, making sure that they looked as pristine as he was.

Peering into the Hall, Julius was taken aback by the brightness of the room. Although the sliding roof was completely retracted, it was impossible to see the stars beyond it with all the spotlights turned on. Even the black walls were somehow glowing, as if the light was emanating from within them. In front of him, the floor was packed with parents and young children, all looking at their best, being ushered towards the rows of seats by the Mizki Seniors in Tijaran uniforms. There was a definite feel of euphoria in the crowd, which Julius could understand even in his current mindset. These people had been freed from captivity and their sons and daughters had returned home after two very long and tough years. Most of them, anyway. Flags were hanging all around the room, each of them representing one of the graduates' countries. Branches of green luxurious ivy snaked their way all across the walls of the Hall, some of them bearing large flowers of different colours. Julius couldn't smell their scent in the air, and began to wonder if the vegetation was in fact holographic. They extended to the far wall, behind the main stage. There was a new flag above the podium, which Julius had never seen before: a planet, easily identifiable as Earth, was enclosed in the centre of a white oval space, surrounded by eight golden stars.

'Here, McCoy,' said Master Cress, from his right.

Julius turned to him, startled.

'Your last button is undone,' he said, fastening it.

Julius could tell that Cress was just as excited as any of the parents that had come to the event. His students were his life and Julius would not have been able to find fault with him in all his years at Tijara — especially considering the amount of times he himself had caused the Master's temper to rise.

'What are you thinking about?' Cress asked, straightening Julius' jacket for good measure.

'Nothing, sir,' he answered. Then a thought occurred to him, and he added, 'The Solo ring. I need to give it back.'

'You can keep it a while longer, you know?'

'I'd rather give it back, if it's all the same to you, sir.'

'Very well.'

Julius pulled the black metal band off his finger, wiped it with the corner of his jacket, and handed it back to Cress.

'When will we find the likes of you again, McCoy?' he said, with a hint of a smile.

'It'll happen,' he replied, feeling a little sad.

Cress looked at him intently. 'The Grand Master and I agree that your parents should be told about Michael. *Today.*'

'Why?' he answered sceptically. 'Do you think they'd be able to change his mind?'

'For starters, they are his parents and they deserve to know. Besides, this burden you decided was yours to bear is only dragging you down, even if *you* can't see it.'

'I don't know ...' he said, unconvinced.

'If you won't, *I* will.'

Julius realised that there was no point in arguing, so he just bowed his head and moved over to the left, where he allowed the various conversations to distract him.

'Have you packed your bags?' Isolde was asking Manuel Valdez.

'All ready to be moved into our temp dorms,' he replied.

'I didn't even know there was a floor -7!' Dhara Sundaram piped in.

Neither did I, thought Julius distractedly. But there it was: the floor of the graduates, where they would stay for a few more days before leaving the academy for good.

'It's almost time,' whispered Isolde to Yuri Slovich, who nodded vigorously. 'They're all seated, look!'

Julius turned along with them and saw a sea of combed hair and colourful hats.

'*Mizkis*,' said Cress, telepathically.

Julius turned to face him and saw that Grand Master Freja had just joined their group. Behind him were the Tijaran teachers in their ceremonial uniforms – even Lao-Tzu and Chan had ditched their tunics for the occasion. He noticed that their class symbol wasn't like any other he had seen so far. Regardless of what they taught at the academy, they all wore a rectangular gold label with their name and the school name on it, which Julius assumed was a teacher's privilege to wear. Freja had GM Tijara embroidered on his golden shield, and Cress had M Tijara on his.

'*As we rehearsed, Mizkis,*' continued Cress. '*Once the last two teachers have entered, you'll follow in alphabetical order, two by two. The line behind Professor Clavel will be seated in the first two rows on the right side of the hall and the line behind Professor Morales will do the same, on the left. Get ready.*'

Julius knew he was the sixth student after Lopaka Liway, so he waited for him to take his place before standing behind him, with George Lowet to his left. What he really didn't have any desire to do was to turn around and see Morgana's empty place. Morgana's roommate, Mariam Richards, would have to face the audience's gazes alone, since everyone knew why she was walking into the Hall by herself.

As Freja entered the room solemnly, rolling drums began to beat the cadence of the steps, while the low murmur of the crowd turned to loud applause, which did not die down until the last two students had finally been seated. As he walked up the aisle, Julius turned to his right and saw Jenny and Rory applauding as hard as they could, expressions of pride on their faces that followed him all the way to his seat. He loved them for that, despite the hurt and the absurdity of the situation and, most of all, given that the war hadn't actually been won.

Once all the teachers had taken their seats on the stage, Freja stepped up to the podium, using his hands to gently hush the audience.

'Welcome to Zed,' he began, smiling warmly. 'Thank you all for being here with us today, to celebrate the graduation of our Mizkis.'

A brief applause greeted his words.

'The Class of 2861 has already made history,' he continued. 'Since their very first year on Zed, the growth and development of these students has gone hand in hand with the resurgence of the Arneshian threat, as you all well know. The events of the past few years have seen drastic changes to the way we live. Since many of you were kidnapped from Earth and eventually safely returned, many things have changed. We have new environmental laws, better relationships between countries and even a new part of the population, made up of those Arneshians who decided to turn their lives around. We have also achieved much in fostering alliances, by strengthening ties with new friends, far from here.'

Julius watched as Freja turned around and pointed at the starry banner on the wall.

'*That* is our future,' he said. 'The Galactic Federation of Earth is now a reality, made up of Zed, the colonies, Buruwang and the Halls of Ahriman; each one represented by a golden star, surrounding our planet.'

Murmurs of assent spread throughout the room, from parents and students alike.

So that's what it is, thought Julius.

'Hey,' said George, leaning over towards him. 'Freja mentioned four places, but there are eight stars on that flag. I don't get it.'

'It's because the colonies have five stars: Terra 1, 2 and 3, plus Colonial 1 and 2. With Zed, Ahriman and Buruwang, it makes eight.'

'Ah!' said George, satisfied. 'I like it.'

Julius couldn't match his classmate's enthusiasm; he felt largely indifferent about the entire thing in fact, just going through the motions, with no great expectations for the future.

'We have plenty reason to celebrate,' resumed Freja, bringing the audience's focus back to him, 'but we also have many reasons to grieve.' The GM's eyes darted to Morgana's empty seat for a moment. 'Your sons and daughters have endured a great deal, especially in this past year. But, as you know, there is one family in particular among you who has given more than anyone could ask for our cause.'

Freja took a moment before continuing while Julius, knowing what was coming, simply wanted this moment over as soon as possible.

'Morgana Ruthier is not here today. She will not collect her diploma and she will not toast to the future with us at the end of this ceremony. By no means the only loss that Zed has suffered, but she is *our* loss and nothing will ever heal that wound.'

Julius, not willing to linger on Freja's words, stopped listening and turned his thoughts instead to the conversation he would have to have with his parents.

'Mr and Mrs Ruthier have not come today but, as do you, they too know that we haven't yet reached the end of the road. Their other daughter, Kaori, has already started life as a Zed Officer, just like your children will do from today. It is one last sacrifice that we ask of you. Be strong for them in this final leg of the journey. We won a great battle at Uruplatus, but to win the war we must deliver the finishing blow. Rise now, Mizkis, and proclaim who you are.'

The students stood and prepared for the school salute.

'You will soon leave these walls as men and women of Zed,' said Freja solemnly. 'You will bear the mark of Tijara in your hearts for the rest of your days. You will live, fight and die with that name etched in your souls. Show us your commitment. To your earth!'

'TI-JA-RA!' cried the Mizkis, as one voice.

The audience, carried by the emotional strength of Freja's words and the impact of their children's proud cries, erupted in thunderous applause, which even brought several parents to tears.

As he sat down again, Julius knew that something was really wrong with him. For the first time in his life he felt nothing at that rallying cry — no stirring or shivers — just a flat state of being.

Freja was shortly flanked by Master Cress, who was now getting ready to hand the certificates to each of the students.

'Zolin Acalan,' called Professor Farshid, from the podium.

Julius watched his classmate from Colonial 1 walking proudly towards the stage. There, he shook hands with Freja and Cress, before receiving a ten-by-six inch frame, containing a certificate and a still unfolding, recorded feed of the ceremony. Faith had explained to them that, once put on display in the individual's home, the video would be replayed on a loop, with the graduate in question as the focus. Julius knew he wasn't giving his best smile at all and wondered what his folks would make of it.

Farshid continued calling the students up one by one and eventually reached George Lowet. Julius was asked to stand beside one of the ushers, since he would be up next.

'Julius McCoy,' she called, smiling proudly.

Julius let the applause shield him from the audience as he walked to the centre of the stage. There, he stood before Freja, waiting for his diploma. However, when Freja looked into his eyes, he hesitated, as if he had seen something behind them that worried him deeply. Julius held the GM's inquisitive gaze without faltering.

It was Master Cress who got things moving again, nudging Freja's arm with his elbow and handing him the frame.

'Congratulations, Julius.'

'Thank you, Grand Master,' he replied taking the certificate and bowing.

'Siena Migliori,' called Farshid, moving on.

*

After the ceremony had ended, Julius knew he didn't want to meet anybody or waste time with niceties. He grabbed his parents and whisked them away from the Hall and the buffet, making a straight line for Tijara's garden. The benches were all empty, so he sat them down on the closest one he found, before proceeding to tell them Michael's full story, from his betrayal, to Buruwang. Incredibly enough, as the words left his mouth, crashing like waves against his flabbergasted parents, a sense of relief swept over him. Master Cress had been right.

'What I don't understand is why you didn't tell us sooner,' said Rory McCoy, visibly upset.

Jenny looked as if she was in shock, like her brain was trying to digest the enormity of the situation, but failing miserably.

'I didn't see the point, Dad.'

'You *what*?' fumed Rory.

'Don't go giving yourself a heart attack, all right?'

Rory stared at him for a few seconds, his anger barely contained. He paced briefly, back and forth, in front of the bench, before sitting down, breathing deeply. 'Bear with me, lad' he said in the broadest Scottish accent Julius had ever heard him use. 'You just told me that my youngest son is a two-timing, back-stabbing traitor; a killer of his own people and, potentially, the future leader of Arnesh. Forgive me, but I think a heart attack is the least of my concerns right now.'

Julius nodded, worried about his dad's purple face and the way his right eyelid was twitching.

Jenny broke from her stupor. 'Don't be mad at Julius now, Rory.'

'I'm not mad at him, woman! I'm furious at that wee screwball of a scumbag we call our son!' he said, standing up again, hands flailing.

At that moment, Julius spotted Faith and Skye by the garden entrance, rooted to the spot and staring at them. They were followed by their own families who, no doubt, they'd wanted to introduce to the McCoys.

'*Please guys, not now!*' he told them with his mind quickly.

'*Do you need a hand?*' asked Skye, visibly worried.

'*Just tell Nurse Primula to be on standby, will you? I think Dad is having a fit.*'

'*Call if you need a hand,*' said Faith, before turning and ushering everyone out of the garden.

'Dad, you need to calm down now,' said Julius, walking up to him. He put his hands on his shoulders, realising how much taller than his dad he now was. 'I've got this.'

Rory looked his son in the eyes for a few seconds. Then, a little calmer, he sat back down, and allowed Jenny to take his hand.

'Julius will take care of this,' she told her husband. She looked up, with an uncertain smile on her face. 'Zed wouldn't hurt him, would they? I'm sure it's not his fault and deep down you know that too. What if the Arneshians made him act like that? You must find him and bring him back to us!'

Julius chose to ignore part of what his mom had just said. That was the mother in her talking, trying to reassure herself more than anything else. 'If I bring him back, he'll be in prison for the rest of his life.'

Jenny's eyes widened. 'They can't think it's his fault! He's only a child!'

'To you he'll always be one, Mum. But that's not who he is anymore and I'm done covering for him.'

Jenny buried her face in her hands and began to sob. Rory let her head rest on his left shoulder, while he patted the bench to his right, inviting his son to sit.

Julius did that, and grabbed his father's hand, now older and marked by age.

'You'll do what needs to be done, son.' His voice was steady and under control once more. 'I trust you with all my heart.'

Julius felt the mixed emotions of that morning bumping around uneasily in his mind. As long as Michael was left unchecked, they could have no peace. He knew that, as he knew that he needed to solve this, for everyone's sake. The problem was that he didn't know exactly *how* to do it or even where to find the strength to get back on the saddle. The loss of Morgana had left him feeling ineffective and unsure, filled with guilt for her death and searching for a way out that he just couldn't see.

Freja had just brewed a fresh pot of coffee. The smell was strong and had spread throughout his office. Savouring the intensity that he would soon taste, he filled three cups, which were resting on a red tray. He added one teaspoon of sugar for himself, half for Cress, and then stopped. 'Still two sugars, JD?'

'Shouldn't you know by now?' replied Kelly, with a little frown.

'I don't like to assume,' said Freja amiably. 'Not even with my own blood.'

'Two will do.'

Freja took the tray over to the coffee table, leaving his son and Cress to help themselves. September was underway and a fresh batch of 1 Mizki Juniors had just finished their first week at Tijara. The Grand Master liked that time of the year and being back in his Zed office was having a positive effect on his spirits. He felt recharged and optimistic — more than he had in the last year, anyway — and he was determined to take advantage of this period of calm before the storm. 'Gentlemen,' he said, 'before the last stretch, we have two problems to resolve: Mah and McCoy.'

'I went through the Curia archives several times,' said Cress dejectedly. 'There's no record of a planet or a constellation called Mah. Even Professor Brown, who's a Spaceology expert, has never heard of it.'

'I sent out a message to all fleet captains,' added Kelly, scratching the scar on his left cheek distractedly, 'but no one has come across such a place. I even checked with the Colonies, but no joy.'

'In the footage from the hideout,' said Freja, 'Farrah clearly says, "Mah". One reason I have for believing that this place exists is that McCoy asked me about it after he won his powers back.'

'When was this?' asked Kelly.

'During his medical, on Buruwang. He asked me if the name Mah meant anything to me. In fact, he mentioned another name as well, but I can't remember what it was.'

'We'll just ask McCoy then,' offered Kelly.

'That leads us to the second problem, JD,' said Freja. 'He's not in a good place right now.'

'Morgana's death has hit him harder than we thought,' explained Cress. 'We believed that the thirst for revenge would be enough to recharge him, but it's not happening.'

'We need to *steel* him for this last task,' said Freja.

'You need to be careful, that's what,' said Kelly. 'Bend him too much and you risk breaking him.'

Freja nodded. 'He's no longer the boy who joined the academy. We have changed him beyond repair — the Arneshians and us. And you're right: it's not about how hard he can hit, but how much he can take and still go on. Resilience is all he's got left.'

'Then let him come with me,' cut in Kelly. 'He needs a change. He can wait for the battle plans on the Mazda.'

Freja agreed that it was a good idea — too many memories in Tijara — besides, he knew Julius liked being with Kelly. Maybe it would shake him out of his daze. 'I have no objections to that. McCoy has signed up for a captain's career path and you're more than qualified to start his training. His year group will be able to leave Tijara by the middle of the month. You can have him then.'

*

It was Monday the 8th of September and the graduates were about to start their last week in Tijara school. To distinguish them from the regular students, they had already been allowed to wear officer uniforms, which comprised of the usual items of jumper over tee, combat trousers and boots, but of a deeper shade of blue, almost black, instead of the usual navy ones. That morning they had been sent a document titled "Leaving Procedures", which contained a particularly busy schedule for the next seven days.

Julius sat having breakfast with Skye, Faith and Siena, going through his appointments. As well as plenty of paperwork to be filled out, he would have to spend a long time in the Infirmary for his PIP and shield upgrades. Under normal circumstances, the mere words "Leaving Procedures" would have filled him with excitement. Instead, all that was to come — from finding T'Rogon, to beginning his career — had been locked away in a padded room in his heart; a buffer space that tinged everything in grey tones, sucking the joy and anticipation out of it. Whenever he tried to break it open, he was overwhelmed by a feeling of impotence and despair.

Just then, a small young boy stopped by the table, looking awfully shy. He was a 1MJ.

'You all right, kid?' asked Faith.

'Are you guys the Skirts?' he said, in a little voice.

'Guilty as charged,' said Skye pleasantly.

'I just wanted to say that you're awesome,' he said, breaking into a smile. 'Can I have your autographs please?'

'Sure, little man,' he said, grabbing the pad and stylus that the boy was holding. He signed and passed it on to Faith. When he was done, Siena took the pad from him and handed it over to Julius.

'Won't you sign too?' asked the boy, looking at her.

'Oh,' she said, startled. 'I'm not a Skirt. Morgana Ruthier is, not-'

'Morgana is dead!' cut in Julius. 'And so are the Skirts.' With that, he stood up, taking his tray with him.

The boy looked a mixture of frightened and disappointed. 'I'm sorry,' he said. 'I didn't know.'

From the food counter, Julius heard Siena telling the Junior that it wasn't his fault, but he also heard a sort of annoyed grunt from Skye. *Who cares*, he thought. *Games are over anyway, whether he likes it or not*. He headed for the 6MS common room, looking for a quiet place to work. A few students were already there and, as he walked in, he was aware of a few hushed comments directed his way. He chose to ignore them and went straight to one of the tables at the back, where he opened his PIP screen and activated his holographic keyboard. There was a new folder in his inbox called "Captaincy — a leading career". He touched it with his fingertips and it opened up, revealing a dozen files within. He sighed, wondering who in their right mind would ever consider taking orders from him right now.

Around midday, Faith and Skye came to find him.

'Cress wants our whole class to talk to the 1MJs this afternoon,' said Faith. 'Thirty minute slots each.'

Julius closed his PIP and leaned back in his chair, stretching. 'About what?'

Faith showed him a list of topics on his own screen, the majority of which had been scored off, with only two left.

'I'll take "Hologram Palace",' said Skye coolly, 'since it's quite obvious you don't want it anymore.'

Julius could tell that he was still annoyed with him, but had no intention of apologising. 'It's all yours,' he answered, equally coldly.

Faith raised his eyes skyward. 'That leaves the two of us to talk about "Safety on Zed" … even though I could think of *more qualified people* to teach about this particular topic …'

Julius couldn't agree more. In fact, it would be easier to just tell the Juniors about their adventures on Zed and then tell them to do the opposite. 'I take it we have to.'

The words had barely left his mouth when Skye turned on his heels and stormed out, looking very much like he was restraining himself from saying something harsh.

'Yes, McCoy,' said Faith. 'Part of our last duties for this week. I'll meet you at the end of lunch by the Grey Arts lift. *On* time.'

'I know, I know,' said Julius, noticing the impatience in Faith's voice as well. A little ashamed at his indifference, he realised that his sense of duty was unravelling fast, like a thread slipping between his fingers.

*

After lunch, Julius made his way downstairs; he knew he was late for the event, but still didn't hurry. When he reached floor -1 he saw that the Mizkis were gathered in the third classroom to the left and that the door had been left ajar. He couldn't remember receiving these kinds of talks when he was a first year student, and wondered when they had introduced them. As he reached the door, he stood to the side, listening to what Faith was saying, taking care not to be seen.

'And that brings us to curfew times.'

'Is there a curfew?' came the heartbroken voice of a boy. 'Why? What can possibly happen to us in here?'

'You'd be surprised,' replied Faith, clearly enjoying himself.

Julius closed his eyes and thought back to how Morgana had been kidnapped by Red Cap, right inside the Zed perimeter, during their Gassendi trip. He had cried her name out so hard that his voice had gone. He remembered thinking then how he would never forgive himself if anything happened to her … and then, that day had come after all. No, there was nothing for him to do here. Quietly, he returned upstairs.

*

At the end of the event, the 1MJs left the room in high spirits, talking mostly about Faith's hovering skirt in absolute, deferential awe.

Faith was gathering up his things when, unexpectedly, Freja stepped into the class and sat on one of the desks in the front row.

'Grand Master,' said Faith, surprised. 'Err … you just missed McCoy.'

'I appreciate your loyalty, but you don't need to cover for him.'

Faith blushed and turned off the last piece of equipment. 'He didn't come.'

'How is he?'

'I think he hit rock bottom around the end of June.'

'How so?' asked Freja, concerned.

'He was disappearing every night, so in the end we decided to follow him. He was in Satras, using the Sim-dating programme to talk to Morgana. We told him it wasn't healthy and eventually he stopped.'

'You did well,' nodded Freja. 'And now?'

'Aside from the nightmares, he eats and sleeps,' answered Faith with a shrug of his shoulders. 'He seems normal enough, but inside it's like he's waiting for something — waiting to see what the end will be.' Faith hovered towards the GM. 'It feels as if he's already left.'

Freja, who was looking past Faith to a point on the far wall, remained immersed in his own thoughts for a few more seconds. 'Mr Shanigan,' he said eventually, 'since the passing of Morgana, have you ever seen Julius cry?'

Faith thought long and hard. 'Now that you mention it, sir, no I haven't, and Skye would have told me if it had happened at night. He's probably the only one who hasn't shed a tear — not even *that* day, when he entered sickbay. I was a mess meself, but I noticed it.

At the time I thought he was in shock.'

Freja brought his eyes back to Faith. 'Julius is lost right now.'

'No offence, sir, but this isn't the right time to be lost; not now that we need him more than ever.'

'He's struggling with guilt. Even with his new powers, he wasn't able to save her. A burden like that could squash the hardest of men.'

'Whatever you want me to do, sir, I'll help you. I can't stand seeing him like this anymore. And Skye is ready to punch him in the face … which theoretically could make him cry for a bit.'

Freja smiled. 'I believe that, but it's not the kind of tears he needs to shed. Do you still have a copy of Miss Ruthier's Death Mail?'

Faith's eyes widened. 'Do you think it would help?'

'We've both seen it, Mr Shanigan, and I'm sure you are also aware of its potential impact. Morgana left us the only absolution he needs. If she can't make him see sense …'

He didn't complete the sentence, but Faith knew exactly what he meant. He bowed to Freja, and left the room.

*

That evening, Julius headed back to his new dorm for a shower before dinner. When he stepped out of the lift, he halted at the sight of Faith, Siena and Skye, deep in conversation outside his room. From the looks of things, Faith was trying to reason with Skye, without success. Julius could see an angry red thread lifting up from Skye's head. 'What's going on?' he asked, walking forward.

Skye turned his way and squared up to him.

'Stop it,' said Faith, trying to grab his arm, but Skye shook him off easily.

'Why did you chicken out this afternoon?'

'What? I didn't *chicken* out,' he replied bitterly. He could feel his own temper rising — if Skye wanted a fight, he might just get it.

'Is this how you're honouring her death?'

Julius' face betrayed his surprise at those words. Then his anger got the better of him and he moved forward, an inch away from Skye's nose. 'Don't you dare,' he hissed.

'You think you're the only one grieving?' Skye pressed.

'Maybe I am, you know,' he replied, the stress of the summer finally bubbling up to the surface. 'It seems that folks around here forget easily enough.'

Skye pushed him to the side, his right forearm pressed against Julius' collarbone, pinning him against the wall. 'I've had enough of your moping. We risked our lives to get your powers back for you, and you've been dragging your heels all summer, instead of helping us find your brother. Stop feeling guilty and stop feeling sorry for yourself!' With that, he let go and stormed back upstairs.

'Skye,' Faith called after him. 'You promised you'd be there!'

Skye dismissed him with a brusque wave of his hand before he disappeared from view.

Julius tried to move away from the wall, but found that he couldn't. Suddenly, the anger that had built so quickly inside him faded from his heart, and was replaced by a sense of hopelessness. Siena must have noticed this change in mood, because she went quickly to his side.

'I miss her,' he whispered. 'I miss her so much, it hurts. Laughing feels wrong; doing things — eating, feeling, living — everything feels wrong. Like I have no right to keep doing any of it.' It wasn't easy saying these things but, now that he had started, he couldn't stop. He didn't *want* to stop. 'I … I had no time to say goodbye. One minute she was there and the next … She can never forgive me.'

Siena grabbed his trembling hands and held them tight.

'You're to blame as much as *we* are, for that matter,' said Faith. 'We were there too, remember? Besides, if Morgana heard us talking about blame, she would give us a piece of her mind and you know that. But it doesn't matter me telling you this. You need to hear it from her.'

Slowly, Siena opened one of Julius' hands and placed a microchip in it. 'We think you should see this.'

Julius looked at them, feeling completely shaken. 'What is it?'

'Morgana's Death Mail,' she answered.

Julius stared at the chip resting in the palm of his hand, stunned. His heart was beating furiously as he thought about its content.

Then Faith showed him something else: a small, square case, containing a holographic programme. Written on it, in Morgana's handwriting, was "My holo-dream place". 'Skye got it from your rucksack.'

Julius looked at them both and nodded, finally willing to be led and helped. Together, they went back upstairs and, once on the concourse, they headed for the White Arts block. Faith was sure Professor Lao-Tzu wouldn't mind letting them use one of the Meditation classrooms. They found an empty one right away and went in. The control screen was by the door and Siena activated all the right switches, as she had done many times before. After this, she opened the case, slotted Morgana's chip into the simulator slot, and pressed the activation button.

At first, Julius didn't move, but stayed where he was with his eyes closed. He felt the air grow fresh and the void of an empty space behind his shoulders, instead of the door. An eagle screeched high above him; there were no other sounds. He recognised familiar smells —pine trees, heather bushes and even water. Morgana had taken him home.

Julius opened his eyes slowly, to find himself at the top of a hill overlooking a loch.

'Where are we?' asked Siena, marvelling at the panorama.

'It's Loch Achray,' answered Julius, 'in the Trossachs area. Her family took all us kids here for Morgana's tenth birthday.' He pointed at a chalet on the shore of the lake below them. 'We ate there, before climbing the peak behind it: Ben Venue.' Julius had clear memories of that day, like stills from a movie.

'We'll take a walk,' said Faith, patting him on the shoulder. He took Siena's hand and moved down the hill, towards the water.

Julius breathed deeply. From his position, he could see a myriad of multi-coloured leaves, showing that autumn was underway. It was gorgeous. The grass was still thick and soft, so he decided to remain where he was. He lay on his stomach facing the lake, prepared his PIP screen and pressed PLAY.

Morgana is sitting on a sofa, her legs gathered under her. Her long black hair is dancing, because she cannot stop laughing.

'Will you be serious already?' says Faith, out of shot. 'Siena, don't even start.'

'Sorry babe,' she says, somewhere off screen, to the right.

Morgana sits, adjusts her uniform, and her hair. She

throws a last wink at Siena before looking straight at the camera.

'Right,' says Faith, 'let's start. Death Mail test, Take One.'

Morgana bursts into laughter, echoed by Siena. The camera tilts.

'Death Mail?' says Siena. 'You ought to find another name, you know?'

'Can we record please?' says Faith, sounding exasperated. 'I'll think of something. Just roll with it, OK?'

'Sorry,' says Morgana, stifling a last giggle.

'Death Mail test, Take Two. Action.'

Morgana smiles. 'Hi, my name is Morgana Ruthier and if you're watching this, it means I'm dead.'

'Go on,' says Faith quietly.

Morgana tries to remain serious, but her lips are betraying her. 'I'm a 6MS at Tijara School, Zed, Moon, Earth, Solar System, Milky Way, and I'm a heck of a pilot.'

'That she is,' confirms Siena from the sideline.

'It's my last year at the Academy and soon I'll graduate. I hope the war with the Arneshians will be over by then.'

'Don't go too video-diary now,' Faith directs.

'Oh-oh! Excuse me for living!' she replies, giggling again.

The camera tilts to one side.

'OK, OK,' she says. 'Ahem. If you're watching this, it means that I have left behind someone very precious to me. He's the man of my life, my destiny, my perfect half.' Her eyes grow serious, like when a cloud obscures the sun. Then she smiles again. 'Julius McCoy, leaving you behind is the biggest tragedy of all. You're probably in total depression right now, going all "woe to me" on the others, mourning the loss of your beloved Hana-Chan.' She giggles. 'Don't be sad, my love. Your life must go on, brilliant and exciting! You'll be leading the fleet through the stars, exploring new galaxies and meeting new people. It's in your nature. Be a captain and a leader!' She opens her arms wide. 'Live big and hunt hard!' Now she's quiet again. 'Never forget me,

Julius. If you do ... I'll be really gone. Forever.' Morgana looks hesitantly at Faith.

'Wow,' he says. 'That was good.'

'I love you, Julius McCoy!' shouts Morgana, blowing kisses to the camera.

Siena jumps onto the bed next to her. 'We love you Julius!' she cries.

The camera is placed down on something and Faith enters the shot. In a broken, deep voice, he joins in, 'We-lo-ve-you-Ju-lius-Mc-Coy,' his arms bent rigidly, moving up and down, like a robot.

In the chaos, Morgana moves towards the camera, her hands stretched forward as if to touch the lens. Behind her, Faith and Siena continue their joyous chanting, improvising a waltz. She looks into the camera one last time, her eyes sparkling. 'I love you,' she whispers.

Fade to black.

Julius hadn't realised it but, as he watched the video, he had finally begun to well up. It felt as if the dam inside his heart was on the brink of bursting. He had taken in every word she had said, every movement she had made, craving to hear and see more, wanting to walk into the video and hold her in his arms. One of his hands closed around a clump of long grass and he pulled hard at it, as if looking for support. With her last words to him ringing in his ears, he dropped his forehead onto his arm, unable to resist the rising waves of tears. He let them flow, and take with them some of the layers of sorrow and despair that had been haunting him since her death. As he lay there, a strong hand gripped his right shoulder and he was amazed at how much relief it brought to him.

'You're not alone,' said Skye gently. 'You'll never be.'

THE MESSAGE IN THE DREAM

Freja's suggestion had worked. Morgana's Death Mail hadn't solved Julius' problems, but it had given him some much needed perspective back. As he went to bed that night, Julius reflected on how his tears had helped wash away so much of the lingering pain that had been eating at him. It still hurt but, strangely, he felt a renewed sense of purpose now. In the video she had told him to be a leader — was he at least prepared to follow her advice? He forced himself to examine the war situation, focusing only on the positives. Morgana had helped him regain his powers, enabling him to reclaim his place in the fight. Farrah had brought them a step closer to T'Rogon and his circle, giving them a location. Her sacrifice had also destroyed part of the Arneshian repository of knowledge, striking an important victory for Zed. Julius was now left with one clear goal: find his brother Michael and stop him once and for all. That was his objective. If he focused on that, the pain could be kept at bay, at least until his mission was over. After that, he could worry about his sanity, or what was left of it. And as for K'Ssander … his days were numbered.

*

On Tuesday morning, Julius awoke refreshed and hungry. Skye had left him to sleep a little longer, for which he was grateful. For a change, he hadn't had the usual recurring nightmare, but a welcome deep, restful sleep instead.

After a quick shower, he headed for the mess hall, where the others were waiting for him. He sat at their table with a full Scottish breakfast.

'Are you following Skye's diet?' asked Faith, stealing a strip of crunchy bacon.

Julius grinned and tucked into the haggis. The atmosphere was much lighter between them, even compared to the day before, and the appreciation of this had him in a good mood. He knew his problems hadn't just disappeared, but it was a start. 'So, what's the plan today?'

'Infirmary,' said Skye. 'All day. I bet you're in rapture about it, Faith.'

'I'll be *ruptured* all right, by the end of it,' he said, making them all chuckle. 'I don't know though: maybe it's because it's the last time, but I'm not too bothered about it.'

'Last time on Zed, you mean,' said Siena.

'Yeah. I'm sure they'll find the time to download new stuff into me body at a later stage.'

'True that,' she said.

At 09:00 hours, the school-leavers began to head off for their appointments.

'That's us,' said Skye, stealing the last strip of bacon from the plate.

Julius threw him a dirty glance, before returning his tray and following the others.

Dr Walliser gathered them all in the waiting area of the Infirmary, surrounded by his assistants.

Julius saw Nurse Primula and gave her a wave. She winked back, delighted to see him.

'Gather round, officers!' called the doctor.

'No one else has called me an officer since graduation,' commented Siena proudly.

'Welcome to Mr Shanigan's favourite hangout,' continued Walliser, drawing laughter from the crowd and bowing to Faith, who grinned back. 'It seems like yesterday that you came in here, as Juniors, to get your first PIP implant. And look at you now, ready to leave Tijara for good, though you will never leave our thoughts.'

Julius could tell that he was speaking genuinely, thanks to the fuzzy, warm aura surrounding his body.

'Today, your PIP implants will be connected to the Officer Network. Its most important feature is your personal account, which will reflect your career path — assignments, promotions and the like — and will be accessible to all employers in the GFE. Keep it up to date and make it count. The majority of the other features are similar to what you had in school, but I'll leave you to discover them. And, FYI, Zed Officers get some really good discounts in the federation

'— a perk of the job that you'll want to keep in mind when shopping.'

'Sir,' said Isolde, 'will Buruwang's network be available as well?'

'Indeed. Anyone belonging to the GFE is part of the network. It's only the permissions that change, according to your rank and role.'

Julius thought about Daku Derain and Walamai. He would have liked to see them again; however, he had no intention on setting foot in their town for a long time, where his memories of Morgana were at their strongest and most intimate.

'This upgrade will be quick and you'll get it either before or after the ones for your shields. Let's begin.'

The first ten students on the register were called up by the nursing staff and led into the private rooms.

Dr Walliser moved over to a wall station and activated it. He dragged two chairs over and sat down on one of them. 'Can I have the next in line please?' he called.

Julius stood and moved over to him.

'Sit here, McCoy.' Walliser patted the chair.

Julius did so and, knowing the drill, placed his arm inside the transparent glass cylinder, palm up.

'It'll only take a moment,' said the doctor, inputting the information in his terminal.

Julius nodded, and watched the little green dot that had appeared on his skin. He knew it was seeking out the chip embedded in his wrist. As he glanced up at Walliser, it occurred to him that, once he left school, he may never see him again. In fact, most of his teachers would remain behind, leaving the last leg of the journey to the fleet. He wasn't even sure if the GMs could come, given that the schools were full once again.

'There,' said the doctor. 'All done.'

Julius pulled his arm out and carefully tapped his wrist to check for any discomfort. 'Thanks, Doctor; for everything.' He felt embarrassed saying it, but he had to say how grateful he was. Without Walliser's medical expertise, his stasis could have lasted a lot longer. *Try, forever long*, he thought.

'It is I who should thank you,' he answered cheerfully. 'You made me famous among my peers, with all the articles I wrote about you.'

'Then it was quid pro quo,' replied Julius, standing up.

'Such is life. Nurse Primula will see you soon. She'll kill me if you go to another nurse.'

'I'll wait,' said Julius, grinning. He returned to the sofa area, while George Lowet took his place.

'Let's check out the new interface,' said Faith, leaning over his shoulder.

Julius opened his left hand and willed the virtual screen to pop up. A personalised greeting message appeared in the centre of the screen. In the bottom left corner was the Captain class emblem.

'I bet that's your personal account menu,' said Faith, touching it.

The icon opened a list of options, showing different forms for Julius to complete. 'I'll check that later,' he said, moving the menu off his screen with the flick of a finger. Several circular icons now replaced the welcome message. 'Look, there's one for the Forum. You should have one too, Faith.'

'I think everyone has it, but yours will also have unrestricted permissions, since you're the leader. I'm the techy expert. I bet they gave me some leeway too.'

Julius touched the screen and it opened up a new sub menu. 'There's even a calendar,' said Julius. 'Do I need to set meeting dates already? We don't even know where we'll be in the next few months.'

'Eventually you'll have to. As for the agenda, I can help you get started. Zed knows some of our fleet protocols need a change. Besides, people will bring their own issues to discuss. Believe me, I don't think you'll ever have a problem filling meetings.'

Julius nodded and touched the second icon, which was titled "GFE Forum Database". A list of names appeared, seemingly going on forever.

'You have every single contact in the federation on that thing,' said Faith, in awe. 'Power-trip, anyone?'

'Wow,' said Julius, a little less in awe and more worried about the size of the file.

'It looks like fun,' said Faith, nudging him.

'It looks like a lot of work actually; and not at the right time either.'

'Hmm. Let's get this week out of the way first, I say.'

Julius closed the Forum menu and quickly checked the other icons on his screen. Maps, directories, job listings and housings were only a few of the many pages he could explore. It seemed like his future was being facilitated in more than one way. Still, he couldn't even consider buying his folks a house on Colonial 1 at the moment. As long as Michael was out there, there was no space for other projects.

'McCoy!' called Nurse Primula, from one of the rooms.

Julius closed his PIP and stood up. 'Later, Faith.'

'So good to see you,' she told him when he arrived. She ushered him inside and pointed at a small changing room to the side. 'There's an overall for you behind there. I'll be back in five minutes.'

Julius did so, and swapped his clothes for a blue overall, which he tied behind his neck and back. Barefoot, he hopped onto the bed and waited for the nurse to return.

Primula came back into the room, and tied her long brown hair in a ponytail. 'How are you?'

'Better, I guess.'

'How's your sleep?'

Julius hesitated, thinking that she had been through enough with him to not have to lie about his sleep. 'Not great, although last night was fine.'

Primula looked at him with concern. She started up the machine to the left of the bed. 'Bad dreams?'

He nodded. 'And not even there can I save her.'

'Stop,' she said, putting her hand on his arm. 'Don't do this to yourself. If you really must blame someone, blame the bastard that killed her and use your anger to find him.'

Julius was taken aback hearing her speak like this. It must have shown on his face, because Primula removed her hand, and blushed.

'When you were in stasis,' she said, continuing the preparations, 'Morgana came to see you every day. No matter how bad a week she was having, she never lost focus on her priority — to find a cure for you. I have never met anyone so resilient, or more dedicated to a friend than she was. She did this because she believed that you had a job to finish.'

Julius saw her eyes welling up as she spoke. It had never occurred to him to ask her about those days in the Infirmary, after her death. The nurse had probably spent more time with Morgana than the boys had that year. He didn't trust himself enough to speak, as her words had created a knot in his throat, so he just nodded firmly. *'Thank you,*' he told her with his mind.

Primula wiped her eyes and smiled. 'You're welcome.'

*

Julius woke up in the Infirmary bed late that afternoon. They had had to put him to sleep before they could implant the new shields. He stretched, feeling groggy and thirsty. 'Ouch,' he said, flinching. His hand went to his head, to a spot behind his right ear. There was a plaster there.

'Don't touch it yet,' said Primula, entering the room.

'What is it?'

'Your last ever implant: the core of the other four chips. It's linked directly into your brain, to activate your shields quicker, among other things.'

Julius was still feeling too out of sorts to really understand the mechanics of it.

'The dizziness will pass,' she told him kindly. 'By the way, they won't be activated until you leave school. Get dressed now and go get some dinner.'

'Dinner? How long was I out for?'

'Most of the day, I'm afraid. It's almost nine in the evening.'

Julius didn't like losing time like that without knowing. It reminded him too much of his stasis. However, he thanked her and slowly climbed out of bed.

When he returned to the waiting room, Siena and Skye were chatting away on the sofa.

'There you are,' said Siena. 'Faith won't be out for another hour or so. We should go eat.'

Julius had no objections to that and headed for the mess hall with them.

With the exception of a few Seniors, there were mainly leavers in the room, all looking tired. On her way to the counter, Siena stopped to wake Astra Evangelou, who was just about to slump into her soup, face first.

'That's how I feel,' muttered Skye, watching her stand and sway out of the canteen like a zombie.

Julius nodded. 'I just hope that the tiredness means no dreams tonight.'

They had a quick nibble and decided to go straight to their dorms. After leaving Siena, the boys made their way down to their room.

'So, what's the schedule for tomorrow?' asked Julius.

'In theory, leavers should apply for their first assignment. But with the mission still on, who knows what Freja will want us to do?'

Julius nodded. 'Given the choice, I wondered how many in our class would pick active duties. And we still don't know where to go.'

'Faith and I will be there, McCoy. Don't you worry about that.'

What remains of the Skirts, thought Julius.

*

Julius was walking through Eneamar, navigating the streets with the confidence of a local. Everything around him was clean and tidy as it always was and he felt refreshed. He made his way toward the metal sphere at the centre of the square and sat on a bench, watching the people walking by. The soothing music in the air and warmth of the sun made him feel relaxed and, after several minutes, he decided to close his eyes for a while.

He couldn't tell how long he rested for, but when he woke, Eneamar had changed. He stood up, realizing that the sun had gone, leaving behind a light mist and drizzle. There was a chill in the air and the music had stopped, while all the people had disappeared, taking all other sounds with them. Julius shivered. Gradually, one noise resurfaced — the water in the canal had begun to flow towards the globe. He took a step forward and saw that it was rushing into the square, as if it were a mountain torrent. Anxiety gripped his heart and he knew that he had to reach the hill, where the statue of the Archer stood.

He turned right, following the stream back to its source. The leaves in the trees above him had turned dark, as if autumn had suddenly arrived. Julius saw the water change colour, from clear to dark red. Scared, he ran towards the hill, trying to ignore the river of blood now gurgling by his side. As the slope approached, he didn't stop, but spurred himself forward, scrambling upwards. Just as he reached the summit, his foot caught on something; he fell forward, and landed hard on the ground. Winded, he looked up, only to recoil in horror. The grassy hilltop was strewn with bodies; their backs were covered in fur. They had burn-wounds and dried blood all over them. The statue of the Archer was gone, replaced by one of K'Ssander holding Morgana's lifeless body in his arms. The arrow that used to be perched, cocked in the bow, was now protruding from her chest, pointing at the sky. Blood gushed from her wound, cascading into the canal and forming the stream at their feet. That was when Morgana's eyes flew open and she slowly raised her hand, a frightening crackle from her stiff joints accompanying the movement. She pointed into the far distance and said, 'Mah.' As the air flew back into his lungs, Julius opened his mouth and screamed.

*

'Julius! Wake up!'

The voice arrived from afar, growing closer. Julius forced himself to focus on it and suddenly there he was, back in his bed, on Zed.

'Shh. It's me. Calm down.'

Julius looked up, panting, and saw Skye sitting on the bed, holding his arms. 'What …'

'Just relax. It's over now.'

Julius lay back down, his skin covered in sweat. A hurried knock at the door made him flinch.

'It's fine,' Skye said, before opening the door.

Freja entered the room, followed by Doctor Walliser. 'Mr Shanigan,' he said, turning towards the corridor, 'send the others back to their rooms, please.'

'Yes, sir,' came Faith's reply from outside.

The doctor took Skye's place on the bed and passed his handheld medical scanner over Julius' head and chest.

'What happened, Mr Miller?' asked Freja, worried.

'He had another dream, sir. Only … this time it was really bad. I was woken up by his screams and couldn't get him to stop. The whole floor heard us and that's when I told Faith to call you.'

'You did well. Have a glass of water.'

'Don't mind if I do. He scared the heck out of me.'

Walliser closed his device and gave Julius an injection in the side of his neck. 'It's a R.E.M. inhibitor. It'll get rid of all dreams for the

'Hypnosis, sir? Will it work?'

'The way we do it now, yes.'

'Miller and Shanigan,' said Freja, 'could you please sit over here.'

Julius took his place and got comfortable, while his old teacher sat by his side.

'This will help you slip into a trance in a few minutes, without falling asleep,' said Walliser, injecting him in the neck.

Julius flinched, but the pain was short-lived. He watched as the doctor dimmed all the lights in the office, before taking a seat next to Freja. From his position, all he could see was the empty wall in front of him.

'Close your eyes now,' began Lao-tzu. 'I want you to focus only on my words.' His voice was calm, soothing and it felt to Julius like it was coming to him from afar. 'Turn your thoughts to Buruwang. I want you to remember the place and its sounds.'

Julius remembered them all, although, in his present state, the images were out of focus. His head felt heavy and couldn't even lift his fingers.

'Can you see it?'

'Yes,' he answered.

'You are there,' said Lao-tzu.

At those words, Julius felt a cold spot in the middle of his forehead and all the images appeared in sharp definition. He saw the ocean and heard the waves and the seagulls, but felt nothing, as if it was someone else there, walking on the sand.

In the office, the empty wall had become a screen, showing the images from Julius' brain. They all saw him standing on the beach.

'It is the morning of your medical test. You have just woken up. Where are you?'

'I'm in my bed,' answered Julius quickly.

The screen showed him inside the hut. There was someone else under the sheet, next to him.

'Who is that there with you?'

'Morgana.'

There was an embarrassed shuffling of feet at the back of the room, followed by a little cough from Faith.

'Did you dream?'

'Yes.'

'What did you see?'

'Eneamar, where Farrah used to go when she was in hospital.'

Lao-tzu turned to look at Freja, puzzled, before resuming his questioning.

'Describe Eneamar.'

'It's a clean city, built beside the ocean.' As he spoke, the images on the wall reflected his descriptions. 'The people are friendly and elegantly dressed. You are safe walking its streets. It is very green, with hanging gardens everywhere. Even the glass buildings have gardens on their balconies.'

'What do you do in Eneamar?'

'I start to walk and I reach the main square. There's a fountain that looks like a planet. I know it's Earth.'

Skye and Faith exchanged a quick glance. Even Freja sat up. The globe did look like Earth, with the bas-relief showing the familiar continental shapes.

'I see water flowing into the square and I want to know where it comes from. I walk along the canal and it takes me through a field, beneath tall trees. There's a hill at the edge of the forest, covered in grass. I begin to climb up it, wanting to see the view from its top.'

'What do you see?' asked Lao-tzu, peering at the screen.

'I see a statue. It is an archer, ready to shoot an arrow into the air. It has fur.'

Freja stood and quietly walked over to the screen.

'Is he wearing the fur?'

'No, only short strips of suede. The fur grows on his skin, all over the back of his body.'

'Wha-' began Skye, but Freja hushed him with a raised hand. He also looked mystified and pointed at the fur on the back of the statue.

'Is the Archer from Eneamar?' asked Lao-tzu.

'No. He comes from beyond. The arrow points to it.'

'Where does it point to, Julius?'

'Mah. Eronan says so.'

The name made Freja turn to Julius suddenly, as if he had just remembered something. 'Who is he, Julius?'

'Eronan can reverse the effects of the Chemical War. He's Marcus' friend.'

The statement about the War took everyone by surprise, leaving them to ponder its meaning.

'Marcus Tijara?' asked Lao-tzu, after a few moments. The surprise in his voice was plain even to himself, so he steadied it. 'Is he a friend of Marcus Tijara?' he continued.

'Yes. He wears a red tunic and he looks just like he did in Marcus' office.' An image of the office promptly appeared on the screen.

Lao-tzu turned to Freja, who motioned for him to continue. 'Julius, when did you see Tijara?'

'When I was on the Guardian's Trail. I saw Eronan come to see Marcus on Zed and tell him to go to Eneamar. Mah points to Eneamar and Eneamar points to Mah.'

Lao-tzu took a few seconds, as if he was thinking about how to put the next question to Julius. 'I want you to remember what they said about those two locations, in Marcus' office. Word for word.'

The screen now showed Eronan and Marcus sitting opposite each other, on either side of a desk.

'He doesn't look right,' whispered Skye, pointing at Eronan.

Everyone examined the stranger's facial details for as long as Julius' view stayed on him. His eyes were far from those of a human.

When Julius began to recall their dialogue, the view drew back to include both Eronan and Marcus. His voice had no emotion.

' *"And what other choice do I have, pray?" says Tijara.*

"You could come with me to Eneamar and leave the others to their squabbles," Eronan tells him.

"Leave our solar system?"

"We're only a wormhole away – the closest one from here. It's so well hidden that no one would ever find you. You can join me later, if you prefer. Once you're through it, it's only a matter of looking for the Archer, on the highest peak of the tallest mountain of Mah. He will show you the way."'

'Is there more?' asked Lao-tzu, after Julius had gone quiet.

On the screen, Julius walked towards Eronan and tried to touch his face, but his fingers went right through his skin. On the sofa, he became agitated, as if he was having a bad dream.

'We need to bring him back,' said Walliser.

Lao-tzu nodded. 'Julius, I want you to follow my voice and focus on your body. Now.'

On the screen, everyone saw Julius lying on the couch, as if there was a camera looking down on him from the ceiling.

'I am going to count to three, and when I say the word "Awake", you will leave the trance and come back to reality. One … Two … Three … Awake.'

Julius opened his eyes and the room sprung back into focus. He saw Freja standing at the foot of the couch. 'What happened? Did it work?'

'Take a look for yourself,' answered Freja. The GM pressed a button on the wall-screen and rewound the film back to Eronan's entrance.

Seeing his face plainly on the screen startled Julius, and more so when he saw Tijara sitting in the office. The scene was familiar, but he couldn't quite place it. 'Is this from the Guardian's Trail?'

'It appears so.'

Doctor Walliser turned to Skye and Faith. 'We are aware that the Trail left no clear memories with either of you or Mr McCoy. However, since you were his guides, do you recognise the encounter with Tijara from any part of your experiences?'

'Yes,' replied Faith. 'I was in that room as Julius' guide. When I saw it on the screen, it felt way too familiar, and so did Eronan. I just don't know how I could have forgotten about it.'

'Doctor,' said Freja, 'how sure can we be that Julius' recollection was genuine?'

'One hundred per cent, actually. We have just unpacked a memory that had been stored away.'

'Very well. Master Cress, you have an undiscovered wormhole to find.'

Cress bowed and hurried out of the room.

'Professor, what do you make of the message?'

Lao-tzu thought about it for a few seconds. 'Aside from the directions for reaching Eneamar from Mah, it seems to me that he was offering Tijara a way out. Judging by Marcus' facial characteristics, I would also place this event around the time of his death. It is likely that the "squabbles" Eronan mentioned referred to the situation with Clodagh.'

'Yes, I agree with that timeline. Julius, you said that Eronan can reverse the effects of the Chemical War — what does that mean?'

'I'm sorry, sir,' he said, shaking his head, 'I don't know.'

Freja nodded, and grew thoughtful. 'There must be a reason Eronan appeared when you were on the Guardian's Trail. And if he can really help us, then we must find Eneamar before we deal with T'Rogon. McCoy, your first assignment as a Zed Officer will be to discover all you can about Eronan. Miller and Shanigan can accompany you, if they don't have other plans.'

'Wha-' said Faith, shocked that the Grand Master would even think of separating him from Julius. 'I'm seeing this through to the end, sir.'

'I couldn't do anything else, sir,' added Skye firmly.

'I thought as much, but I had to ask. All of you will need to go to the Curia Archive.'

'To Ahriman?' said Julius, surprised.

He nodded. 'A transporter is leaving at lunch for Colonial 1. They'll drop you off on the way. The new teleportation system will make it a very quick trip — especially thanks to the Shanigan Relay.'

Faith grinned and immediately blushed.

'Once you get there, I want you to dig out everything you can on Eronan. Start from March 2628 — the time of Tijara's death — and work your way back to the present. Doctor Walliser will send you a still of Eronan's face from the video we just watched. In the meantime, we'll get the fleet organised. Please understand that time is of the essence. As soon as Cress and his team discover the wormhole, you'll be recalled, even if your assignment is unsuccessful.'

'Understood, sir,' replied Skye.

'Good. That will be all. McCoy, a word if you please.'

Julius thanked Professor Lao-tzu for his help.

'Here, McCoy,' said Walliser handing him a small tub of pills. 'If you wake up from another cracker like last night, take one of these. But only if it's *that* bad.'

'Thanks,' he said, putting the container in his side pocket.

'We'll start packing,' Faith told him, as he left the room.

Freja walked towards the window as the door slid shut. He touched a button which let light back into the room and the glass of the window became clear. He crossed his arms in front of him and looked quietly outside for a few moments. 'When JD was nine, my wife Kathryn died suddenly, in her sleep.'

Julius was taken aback by this unexpected disclosure.

'Every night I gave her a goodnight kiss, but not *that* night. The Zed shield was malfunctioning and, even though it wasn't an emergency, nor was I an engineer that could fix the problem, I felt I had to go and check nonetheless. Duty, above all. I spent a whole year in utter dejection before being able to look at the world again with any interest, and before some of the guilt, for not being there, finally left me. The people around me bore the brunt of my sadness; especially, I regret to say, my son.' Freja took a deep breath and turned around.

Julius thought about his last moments with Morgana. Before they left the hideout, she said she would never leave him. He had kissed her lips then, for the very last time. The memory made his stomach tighten. It had been too brief. He had to swallow before he could speak. 'How did you manage to recover, sir?'

'Mostly through time and friendship — though it never really leaves you. You just … *adapt*. We all grieve in different ways, McCoy, but I'm afraid you don't have the luxury of time. Friendship, *that* you have, but not time.'

Julius nodded, painfully aware of the pressure he was under.

'I need you back. I want you to use your grief to get you back in the race, because you are our champion and we believe in you. I don't know why, but you've been chosen to lead our mighty fleet through this chaos. I don't intend to leave this war as an inheritance to my granddaughter, and I need your help to make it so.'

Julius was deeply moved by Freja's words. Over the years, he knew that the Grand Master had supported him above and beyond expectations, believing in his abilities. To be told all this openly, along with such personal details of his own past, made it all the more powerful and true.

'I won't let you down, sir.'

*

'Where are you guys going?' asked Lopaka. It was midday and he had just arrived in the dorm corridor, in time to see Julius and Skye leaving their rooms with their rucksacks shouldered.

'First assignment, my friend,' replied Skye. 'Off to Ahriman.'

'Oh. You'll miss the graduation party in Satras.'

'I know, but there's stuff to do before *the mission* starts.'

Lopaka nodded and Julius realised that the "mission" now meant only one thing for everyone — the end of Arnesh.

'I'll find you in space then,' said Lopaka. 'I'll be in an engine room somewhere.'

'For sure,' said Julius. 'Stay safe.'

'Yeah. You too. Hey, speaking of engines, where's Faith?'

'He's been saying goodbye to Siena for the last four hours,' said Skye, grinning.

'Who could blame him, right?'

I couldn't, thought Julius. He smiled too, though — Faith's happiness was as important to him as his welfare was. He couldn't really sulk about the fact that *his* girlfriend was still alive.

After leaving Lopaka, they made their way to the main entrance, where Faith and Siena were waiting, cuddling on one of the couches. They stood up quickly when they heard them approaching, but not quick enough to go unnoticed.

'Tut tut, naughty Irish boy' said Skye, pretending to be shocked.

'Don't you even start,' Faith admonished him, finger raised.

Siena giggled, then went over to Skye to say goodbye.

'We won't be gone long, you'll see,' he told her, giving her a peck on the cheek.

'Look after each other,' she said, moving to Julius and hugging him.

She remained at the top of the stairs that led to the Zed underground until they had disappeared from view. The boys lingered a bit as they walked through the hustle and bustle of the hangar, reminiscing about the times spent in there. To recall them from their reveries was the vision of Captain Foster, standing on the main platform. When he saw them, he waved them his way.

'This here is your lift to Pit-Stop Pete,' he said, pointing at a Stork behind him. 'Good luck out there, boys.'

'We'll make our own luck, sir,' Julius told him, shaking his hand.

'That's the spirit, McCoy.'

'And don't let your guard down with the Juniors, sir,' added Skye. 'They're pretty pesky this year.'

'After you, Miller, everyone's a doddle.'

As they climbed aboard, it didn't escape them that Foster was actually smiling.

'Now I've really seen it all,' remarked Faith.

The shuttle took them to the Zed docking station, where they registered at the arrival desk. They had only a few minutes to spare before the transporter would leave, but Faith insisted on touching base with Pete, his inspiration and mentor. By one o'clock, they were seated in a small passenger lounge, heading for the first of the portals which would take them to Ahriman in a series of skips.

Later that afternoon, the transporter entered planet Funesto's orbit over a strip of desert, which they immediately recognised as the eastern plateau. The search for Tijara's crystal had started there, by the Seffira Cave, over a year ago.

Julius looked out of the shuttle window, wanting to see what had changed since the Arneshians had been expelled, and he wasn't disappointed. The Halls had been completely revamped. A new atmosphere shield, like the one on Zed, had been built to encapsulate the main complex, removing the need for using an EMU while on Curia ground. The central building, where Julius had met his brother Michael for the first time after his stasis, was now completely restructured and brought back to its original splendour. The whitewashed walls had been cleaned and repaired, the iron doors polished, the fountains refilled and new plants potted. Earth had definitely left its stamp.

As the shuttle landed gently outside the main entrance, Julius saw the square filled with Zed Officers and Curia workers walking around looking busy. When he stepped outside, he had to force himself not to think about the fact that it had been Morgana who made that landing on their last visit. Fortunately, a distraction arrived in the form of a short man, who was waving and walking quickly in their direction. When he reached them, he snapped to attention and bowed low, catching Julius and the others off guard.

'Welcome to Ahriman, sirs,' he said obsequiously. 'I am Milan Todorov, Secretary to the Curiates.'

'*Sirs*?' whispered Faith sideways. 'Is he talking to us?'

'Thank you, my good man,' said Skye, stepping forward. 'Take us to your leader. Our business cannot wait.' With that, he let the man go ahead, raised his chin and followed him theatrically.

'*Take us to your leader?*' repeated Faith. 'Has he gone insane?'

'A long time ago,' replied Julius wryly.

They followed Skye through the large main gate. Its light-coloured metal had been restored like the rest of the building and shone brightly in the sun, revealing the stylised stars that decorated the two doors. The gate led them to a large atrium, its marble floors polished to reflect the sunlight shining through the glass roof. Wide arches opened onto the main area, showing the many doors that opened onto the different sections of the building. Directly opposite the gate, a central staircase began, branching out into two thinner sections, curling their way up to the mezzanine on the first floor.

The guide halted at the foot of the staircase and looked up, towards the stout woman who was descending towards them. 'Curiate Alohalani Kaula will organise your stay in the Halls.'

'Great news,' whispered Skye. 'She's a really nice lady – from Tonga. And she likes me.'

Julius had never personally met any of the other Curiates; only Aldobrando, their leader. Knowing that this particular member of Roversi's council was an easy-going person heartened him, as it would make their job much easier. The woman had long, wavy hair, gathered in a ponytail that reached down to her waist. Its colour was matched by the deep brown shade of her eyes. On her uniform, she sported the class emblem – the globe on a grey shield, completely boxed in by four lines. Only Roversi, as the Curio Maximus, was allowed to have a gold shield, to distinguish him above all others. Curiates also wore three pale blue stripes on the sleeves of their jackets.

'Good day, officers,' she said kindly.

They bowed to her promptly.

'Curiate Kaula,' said Skye, 'it's a pleasure to see you again.'

'I was very pleased to hear that you would be working with us again, Mr Miller.' She turned to Julius and Faith, smiling. 'He has worked so hard in his placements that Colonial Affairs has already offered him a position.'

'You don't say,' commented Faith, with a cheeky wink to Julius.

'Once the mission is over, I will be only too glad to accept it,' replied Skye.

It was a fleeting moment but, right then, Julius realised that life would not necessarily keep them together forever, and that their friendship would have to go through the test of distance as well as time. It made him sad thinking about it, but it was inevitable.

'Follow me, please,' said Kaula, heading across the square. 'Lodgings have been arranged for you within the main complex. Todorov will send you the blueprints for the building shortly.' When she reached the last door in the south-west corner, she stopped and turned around. 'Grand Master Freja has explained your mission. Mr Todorov will be on standby to attend to your needs. He will give you access to the records you seek.'

'Thank you, Curiate Kaula,' replied Julius.

'Your mission concerns us all, Mr McCoy. You have our full support.'

They bowed to her and let Todorov usher them inside the archive.

Back on Earth, Julius had visited the National Museum of Scotland many times, passionate as he was about history. There was a special section in the basement, with a perfect replica of a vast library from ancient times. Once paper books had gone out of fashion and the world had fully switched to digital, Britain had decided to save some of them for posterity. Walking along the aisles, between high shelves loaded with colourful tomes of all sizes, had been something quite wondrous. Julius' eyes would travel along the hundreds of titles printed on the spines, wondering about the secret worlds they contained. By contrast, the archive of Ahriman was very different from the basement of the museum – bright and light, furnished with desks and terminals – and rather disappointing, thought Julius.

'All the records from 2628 have been made accessible to you. We have a mixture of sources, from official documents to news bulletins. The classified material has already been searched by our own people, but there was nothing there.'

'Can we access files from Earth and the colonies as well?' asked Faith.

'It's all there – the entire written history of humankind.'

'A walk in the park then,' said Skye, sighing.

'I will return at dinner time and escort you to your quarters,' said Todorov.

'Thanks,' answered Julius, heading towards the closest table to dump his rucksack. 'We don't have much time. We must make this search as efficient as possible,' he said, activating his terminal, before opening his PIP to retrieve Eronan's picture. Faith and Skye took their places at terminals either side of him, ready to start. 'In the video, Eronan looks like he's in his forties maybe? We should limit ourselves to going back as far as 2580, I'd say.'

'Sounds good to me,' said Faith. 'I'll do '28, Julius can take '27, and Skye '26. Then, after that, '25 for me, '24 for Julius, '23 for Skye and so on.'

'Deeply convoluted, but OK,' said Skye. 'How do we start?'

'Use the search box – top right corner,' said Julius. 'Enter your year, and in the key word field, type "Eronan".'

'Good idea,' said Faith. 'I would also add, "alien".'

'If people knew about an alien on Zed, surely we wouldn't be here,' commented Skye.

'Yes, but perhaps a journalist noticed his weird features. And on that note, add "crystal eyes" too, for good measure.'

His eyes were certainly peculiar, agreed Julius, but he doubted those key words could really help. *I'll start with his name*, he thought. As he hit Enter, the screen began to scan a thick list of names. The whole process took a few seconds, but the result brought back a blank screen. 'Not found,' said Julius.

'Same here.'

'Yup.'

They repeated the process a few more times, ending on the same blank screen. Eagerly, they kept going, until a search of every year back to 2580 was completed.

'No sign of Eronan,' said Faith, leaning heavily back in his chair.

'No sign of his name, you mean,' Skye added. 'We need to check pictures next.'

'Yes,' agreed Julius, opening the search field again. 'Faith, go for pictures containing unnamed people. Skye, you search for a combination of unnamed and people of the Curia, and I'll look for unnamed pictured with Marcus Tijara.'

They all agreed, put their heads down and trawled through the records once again.

It was close to 20:00 hours before they had a breakthrough.

'Come check this out,' said Skye eagerly.

Julius and Faith moved to his station and, from over his shoulders, peered at the monitor.

'This is from the opening of the Lunar Perimeter, in 2620,' explained Skye. 'There's Tijara, with Clodagh to his left.'

'There he is, behind her …' said Faith, astonished.

Julius immediately recognised him. Eronan was standing a few steps behind the front row, in his red tunic. He was wearing a pair of dark shades, and smiling at someone beside him. Although dated, the digital picture had retained the vibrancy of its original colours. 'Look at his neckline.'

Skye clicked on Eronan and magnified his head and neck as much as possible, without losing any definition. 'Is it … *glowing*?'

'Well, I'll be air-locked,' said Faith, looking closer. 'Could it be an effect of the light?'

'Probably,' replied Julius. 'Weird though.'

'They all look so young,' said Skye, bringing the zoom over the faces of Marcus and Clodagh. 'They must have been very happy back then. Way before she went cuckoo.'

Marcus had loved her very much; Julius was sure of that. No matter what she had done to him, he had still loved her. They had been destined for each other. Morgana's face floated up to the surface of his consciousness – it was never too far away. Had she been his destiny? The silence that followed in his mind made his heart ache.

'Hey, Jules,' said Skye, tapping him on the shoulder.

'Huh?'

'Todorov is here. Let's go get some food.'

*

The following morning, after a quick breakfast, they returned to the archives with renewed energy. Finding proof of Eronan's presence on Zed had given them hope of discovering more evidence, so they decided to stick to their plan until they had searched every year. In the middle of the morning, Julius took a coffee break, during which he sent the link over to Freja, to share the findings. He was hoping to receive good news from him as well, but there were none – the wormhole was still eluding the scouts.

When the second day of searches was brought unsuccessfully to an end, Julius began to grow restless. What if they never found out who he was, or Mah's location? Farrah had told him that Michael was there and he believed her. *Perhaps tomorrow* … he thought. As it turned out, it took them another three days before a new clue was discovered.

'Golly,' said Faith one evening. His eyes were red from staring at the screen for so long. 'Reading about the aftermath of the Chemical War isn't pretty.'

'Chemical War?' said Skye. 'Why are you looking so far back?'

'At this point anything goes, quite frankly.'

'Did Eronan look 80 to you?'

Julius could tell they were getting tired from their stroppy chit-chat – maybe it was time to call it a night.

'I'll tell you what then: I'll do a last search for Eronan of … forever, shall I?'

'And waste time we don't have?'

'Dinner?' Julius cut in.

Unperturbed, Faith said, 'All history – Eronan. Search. Dinner it is.' With that, he got ready to leave.

Julius stretched in his chair before standing up. 'Faith, wait up.' He turned his terminal off and headed for the door.

Skye was about to follow them when a tiny beep sounded in the room, rooting everyone to the spot. 'It found something,' he said, staring at the terminal.

Julius and Faith quickly joined him, their eyes fixed on the monitor. There were two entries on the screen, dated 2431 and 2020.

'Open the first link,' Faith commanded the terminal.

The computer obeyed and an article appeared, titled "Inauguration of the orbital aereodock". Below it was a picture of a plump man in a fluorescent green suit, holding a bottle of bubbly, amidst a small, cheering crowd. Standing to his left, applauding, was a man in a red tunic and shaded glasses. The caption read, "Mr Jankowksy seals the deal with his new associate, Mr Eronan."

'It's him,' said Faith, astonished.

'It can't be,' replied Julius. 'He would have been 197 when Tijara died.'

'I'm telling you, it's him,' insisted Faith. 'Look at his neck.' He moved the cursor over the man's head, magnifying it several times. The line created by his tunic against his skin was glowing almost imperceptibly, but unmistakably.　　　'He kinda does look like Eronan too,' added Skye.

'Open the second link,' commanded Faith once more.

The picture was from a small American newspaper. This time it showed a crowd standing in front of a shuttle plane. There were ordinary women, men and children with suitcases at their feet. On the side of the plane, in red letters, were the words "Mahin Space Enterprise". Two men stood in the foreground, shaking hands. The caption read, "Captain Gorghinian and his sponsor, Mr Eronan, before leaving Earth." The *sponsor* was wearing the usual red tunic and dark glasses. He even had the same unusual glow at the base of his neck. To all effects, he looked identical to the man in the previous two pictures.

'So now he's 278,' blurted out Skye. 'And what does it mean, *leaving Earth*? In 2020 there was no colonisation of other planets, or space stations open to civilians.'

Julius was at a loss for what to say. Common sense told him that it was impossible for that man to be Eronan, but gut instinct told him otherwise. 'Freja will find it hard to believe.'

'Well, this is all we have,' said Faith. 'Send him the links and let him decide. We'll keep looking in the meantime.'

FINDING THE WAY

Push, Ruxshin. Come on!' grunted Khavar.

'I … am … pushing!'

The coffin was heavier than it looked, and carrying it from the snowy glade to the secret tunnel had taken over an hour. Thankfully, Mah Gira had been able to provide them with a long strip of sturdy leather to slip underneath it. Whenever they got stuck, they used it to lift the front of the box upwards and overcome the obstacle. The tunnel, however, was posing a different set of problems.

'Why can't this tunnel be straight?' moaned Ruxshin. 'I can't get past the last corner. I think we're stuck.'

Khavar looked around and assessed the situation. 'All right, go ahead and prepare a space in the house with Mah Gira. I'll take care of this.'

Ruxshin knew his friend enough to know that he would. She stepped over the coffin and headed towards the concealed entrance. A chest of drawers was blocking the access, so she knocked lightly against it. Soon after, hurried steps were heard coming her way, followed by the sound of someone loudly clearing their throat. 'It's us – open up,' she said.

Mah Gira started to push the chest to one side, helped by Ruxshin from within the tunnel.

'Where is it?' he asked her, worried.

'Khavar is handling it – the box is awkward to steer. Where will we put it?'

'Under my bed, I'd say.'

'Are you sure?'

'Young lady, at my age, death is always nearby anyway.'

She grinned at him. Then she heard a noise coming from the tunnel. 'Here he is. Watch out.'

They moved aside, leaving as much space as possible for Khavar to enter. Somehow, he had heaved the coffin onto his shoulders and walked with it for the last stretch. His face was red from the strain and big pearls of sweat wet his brow. He was carrying the leather strip between his teeth.

'This way,' said Mah Gira, grabbing the leather and showing him to his bedroom.

Ruxshin followed them inside and, once Khavar had placed the coffin down on the bed, she helped him lower it onto the floor, where Mah Gira had placed the leather like a rug.

'Dizzy,' muttered Khavar, sitting down heavily on the bed.

'Well done,' said the Supreme. Eagerly, he bent over the coffin to look at the girl inside, compassion on his face. 'What a pity to die so young.'

'We need to know what her message is about,' said Ruxshin. 'Do you think she's one of them?'

'Like Michael, yes. And *he* speaks the language of the Arneshians.'

'I must get hold of a translator then. I can do it this afternoon.'

'I'll do it,' said Khavar seriously. 'If they catch you … they already-'

'I'm the only one that can do it,' she interrupted. 'I work there.' She could see in his eyes that he was thinking about what K'Ssander had done to her – it was sweet of him to worry, but pointless.

Mah Gira patted Khavar on the shoulder. Although he was also concerned, she really was the only one that could enter the building in broad daylight without raising suspicion. 'Be careful,' he told her.

Ruxshin nodded. She kissed Mah Gira's hand and headed out.

*

Ruxshin pushed the door of her workplace open and walked inside. As foreseen, the guard by the entrance knew who she was and let her in without thinking twice. Her face betrayed no emotion but inside her heart was thumping hard. *Stay calm*, she thought.

The building was comprised of a corridor with four rooms, two on either side. Her team worked in the first one to the right, which was now empty, as her shift had ended at lunchtime, while the second team was always in the room opposite hers. She could see them right now sitting around a large table, compiling the dictionary, unaware of her presence. 'Good,' she whispered, moving along swiftly.

Her goal was to reach the second room on the left, where the translators were stored. Unfortunately, that meant having to pass in front of her supervisor A'Krad's room. The odds of him being away from his desk were zero, so she thought of a quick excuse, in case he saw her. Stepping as lightly as she could without looking conspicuous, she took the plunge and walked right to the end of the corridor, without looking back. Her trembling hand was stretching towards the touchpad that released the door lock, when a small cough made her jump and made all the hair on her body stand on end in panic.

'I didn't mean to scare you, Ruxshin,' said A'Krad, looking surprised. 'What are you doing back here?'

He was wearing the translator around his wrist, allowing this conversation to happen. Digging out her best smile, she shook her head affably. 'I'm sorry, I should have come to see you first. It's just that I forgot to close today's log at the end of the shift and I didn't want to disturb you.'

A'Krad held her gaze for a moment, before his face relaxed. 'But of course. Please continue.'

Ruxshin watched as he turned back towards his office, feeling a little faint after that sudden adrenaline rush. Taking a deep breath, she stepped inside the storage room and waited for the door to slide shut behind her. A few boxes were stacked against the walls, ready to be shipped out to the Arneshian troops. She knew this because she had prepared them herself, over the course of the last week. She accessed the terminal log and quickly removed one device from the stock, as if it had never been packaged. The transaction required her thumbprint identification in order to be authorised, so she went ahead and pressed her finger against the screen. 'There,' she whispered, satisfied. Opening the box nearest to her, she collected one translator wristband, or Unilogus, as A'Krad had renamed them. It had taken the Arneshians over a year, but they had managed to transform the original box-shaped device into this slimmer, portable model. It worked much better than its prototype; the translation was indeed faster, but not quite simultaneous, much to T'Rogon's annoyance and Ruxshin's secret delight. Carefully, she closed the box and turned off the terminal, quickly exiting the storage. When she reached her supervisor's room, she stopped at the door. 'Thank you, A'Krad. See you tomorrow.'

'Goodbye, Ruxshin,' he replied from his desk.

Had Ruxshin not been in such a hurry to return to Mah Gira, she might have noticed the live feed monitors in A'Krad's room. Each of them showed one of the four rooms of that building, including the storage area. Unknown to her, A'Krad had watched her every move as soon as he had returned to his office. He couldn't understand why she would steal a Unilogus, but he was determined to find out, so he followed her cautiously.

*

... she moves towards the camera, her hands stretched forward as if to touch the lens. Behind her, the boy and the other girl begin to dance together. Morgana looks into the camera one last time, her eyes sparkling. 'I love you,' she whispers.

Fade to black ...

Ruxshin's eyes were moist with tears and she wiped them lightly. The words of the girl called Morgana had made her heart ache. And what of her lover, Julius? Did he know she was dead? If he was the one who had put her in that coffin, why would he let her go, away from him?

'I don't think I understood half the things she said,' said Khavar, shaking his head. 'What's a *6MS*?'

Mah Gira leaned back in his chair, struggling to take in all the words he had just heard. 'I couldn't say, but her world is at war with the Arneshians too, that much is clear.'

'She said she was a pilot at Tijara school,' added Ruxshin. 'If they know how to fight against them, maybe her people can help us.'

'Even so, where do we find them, and how?' said Khavar. 'We can't exactly leave Mahin.'

Ruxshin, however, wasn't bothered by that. The message she had just watched had acted like a catalyst, strengthening her resolve to act against her captors 'This school, Tijara, is somewhere … in one of these places she talked of – these systems and ways. We just need to find them!'

'I'll tell you what: why don't we make A'Krad take us there in one of their flying machines?'

Ruxshin gave him a look, as if to say, *I just might*. Carefully, she pushed her hand through the cocoon layer, reaching for Morgana's Strullium pendant.

'What are you doing?' asked Khavar, grabbing her wrist.

She looked at him, a serious expression on her face. 'If I don't, her story will be forgotten.'

Khavar threw a quick glance at Mah Gira, who just nodded, so he let her continue.

Ruxshin shivered when her fingers touched the girl's neck – her skin was cold as marble and there was no give when her knuckles pressed against it. Deftly, she unclasped the pendant and pulled it loose, trying not to mess her hair up. She gathered the delicate silver chain inside her cupped palm and put it away safely inside her coat. 'We need to go back to A'Krad,' she told the others. 'He'll know where these places are.'

Khavar looked thoughtful. 'How do we get him to talk?'

Suddenly, a shadow blocked the light from the open window, making them turn. An arm shot inside the room and pulled the curtain aside, revealing A'Krad's stern features.

Ruxshin yelped, while Khavar instinctively threw himself in front of her and Mah Gira. They were far too surprised to speak. The fact that the Arneshian had his palms opened towards them, charged and ready to fire, had also rooted them to the spot. Even without the Unilogus, they knew they were in big trouble.

'I'm curious,' said A'Krad, swinging a leg over the low window ledge to get inside, 'how did you plan to make me talk exactly?' He was now inside the small bedroom, readjusting his aim, while crackling energy sparked from the disks under his skin. He advanced slowly toward the coffin, motioning for the Mahin to move away. 'Back! Back!' he barked at them.

They scampered against the wall, which gave Ruxshin an opportunity to glance into the lounge. Thankfully, the chest of drawers was back in place. *The tunnel is safe*, she thought. That single moment of relief helped her to refocus on her current situation. There was no way they could allow A'Krad to report back or take the coffin. 'A'Krad ...' she started, almost pleading. Her supervisor, however, hushed her unceremoniously, while his eyes never left the object on the floor. Ruxshin couldn't tell what he was thinking, but he looked as stunned as they had been when they had found the coffin.

'Zed … This is impossible,' he muttered. 'How did you …'

'So you *do* know of Tijara!' said Ruxshin.

A'Krad didn't reply, but kept staring at the girl in disbelief. His hesitation was not long-lived, but those few seconds turned out to be more than enough for him to lose the upper hand.

Khavar jumped forward, planting his right shoulder in the man's midriff, winding him. The momentum of his lunge carried them both over the bed and beyond it, where they tumbled onto the stone floor.

As this happened, Ruxshin shook herself from her daze and, grabbing Mah Gira's blanket, she threw it, with her on top, over the struggling men, hoping to hinder A'Krad somehow. Instead, the Arneshian fought back harder. An electric shock scorched through the blanket and struck the ceiling. The hot flux missed Ruxshin's head by an inch, but it still burned a patch of skin and hair away from her right temple. She screamed, but kept her weight over the wriggling mass below her, not caring about the kicks and elbows that her body was receiving. Out the corner of her eye, she saw Mah Gira running to close the window and the curtain, before he too joined the fight.

He grabbed the lamp from his bedside, which was made from an intricate – and heavy – block of Strullium. 'Uncover him!' he cried at her.

A'Krad shot out a hand from underneath the blanket, grabbed the Supreme's ankle and pulled, causing Mah Gira to fall hard on his back, while the lamp tumbled noisily to the floor. Then the Arneshian curled his hand into a fist and punched the twitching shape of Khavar under the cover. The Mahini man cried out in pain as the wrestling resumed.

The wound on Ruxshin's head was burning, making her wish for the cold snow outside. But there was no time to think about that, as Mah Gira was struggling back to his feet and reaching for the lamp. He held it high above his head and nodded to her. Ruxshin pulled the cover back, revealing A'Krad's head. 'Now!' she cried.

Mah Gira brought the lamp down, striking him on the side of the head, bringing the fight to an abrupt end.

Khavar was sweating heavily, and let his head rest between the Arneshian's neck and shoulder, overcome by fatigue.

'Are you okay, Mah Gira?' asked Ruxshin, temporarily forgetting her wound.

The old man placed the lamp back on the stand and sat down on his armchair, exhausted. He nodded though, reassuring her that he wasn't hurt.

Ruxshin climbed off the heap on the floor before helping Khavar to his feet.

'We need to tie him up,' he said. 'What can I use?'

'In the kitchen,' said Mah Gira. 'There are bindings under the sink. And bring a wet cloth for Ruxshin.'

Khavar disappeared into the room to the right, while Ruxshin moved over to the window to check outside. Thankfully, all was quiet in the street and no one seemed to have notice what had happened in the Supreme's home. She turned and looked at her unconscious supervisor. 'This is bad. When T'Rogon finds out, he'll be after you.'

'You needn't worry about me,' he replied. 'We wanted A'Krad's help and now we have it.'

She could tell that Mah Gira was worried just as much as she was. This unplanned fight had pushed them into a corner, with not many choices left. 'If he doesn't tell us where to go, he'll have to come with us.'

Khavar returned to the room just then, carrying a bundle of thick leather strips. He passed a wet sponge to Ruxshin, which she used to gently dab at her wound. He then turned A'Krad onto his back, grabbed his wrists, and positioned his palms together. 'Tie him while I hold him.'

Ruxshin nodded and proceeded to wrap the leather around his wrists, and all the way down to his fingers. It was a clever idea, she thought, realising that the man's weapons were now neutralised.

'If he tries to use them,' said Khavar, 'he'll fry his own hands first.'

Ruxshin used one last binding to gag him, before taking a step back. 'So, it turns out that this was the easy part.'

'You can't leave him behind,' said Mah Gira. 'He could lie about the location of Tijara, and you need a pilot.'

'But how do we get him out of here?' asked Khavar. 'The city is crawling with soldiers, and we would never make it past the lifts.'

'Use the tunnel then. You'll have to go behind and around the hill of the White Glade, but the trees and the snow will cover you until you reach the Arneshian aerodock.'

'We wait for darkness then,' said Khavar. 'In the meantime, we drag this scumbag back into the tunnel, where he can't call for help.'

They agreed that it was a good idea so, while Ruxshin helped Mah Gira free the tunnel entrance from the chest of drawers, Khavar scooped up A'Krad. The Arneshian was a big man and it wasn't easy to manoeuvre him out of the room – Ruxshin noticed his head banging against the wall one too many times to be just accidental, but found that she didn't really care.

Once in the tunnel, Khavar put him down, checked that his restraints were still holding, bound his feet and pulled one of Mah Gira's pillowcases over his head.

'There,' he said. 'Let's hide Morgana now.'

They discussed if it was sensible to leave the coffin under the bed, after what had just happened. In the end, they agreed to carry it back into the tunnel, where no one could find it, even if they searched the house.

An hour later, with the tunnel concealed once again, Mah Gira heated up a thick broth for them to eat and served it along with a generous handful of nuts.

'We can't take your rations,' said Khavar. 'Hand-out day is two sunrises away.'

'You're about to spend the night in the snow; you'll need this more than I do. Besides, if I'm really starving, I'll go to your house and take yours,' he replied.

Khavar chuckled. 'If you say so.'

A knock at the door made them all jump in their seats.

'Mah Gira, open the door.' There was no mistaking K'Ssander's voice.

Ruxshin's hand began to tremble, making her spoon rattle against the bowl. She had to put it down on the table, for fear it would give her away.

Mah Gira stood up. 'Be calm,' he told them quietly. 'We'll be all right.' He went to open the door, his head held high.

K'Ssander had brought three guards along, who were standing behind him and trying to peer suspiciously into the house.

'What is it?' asked the Supreme briskly.

K'Ssander looked at the old man with disdain, as if he were an insect. 'Where's the red-fur girl?'

'There's no one here by that name, young man. However, if you're looking for the Mahini's Chief Engineer, Ruxshin, then she is sitting in my house.'

The Arneshian didn't seem to enjoy being patronised by a slave, so he pushed the man aside and stepped inside. Ruxshin and Khavar were on their feet in an instant, and moved over to their leader protectively.

'Where is A'Krad?' asked the Arneshian.

'How should I know?' she replied.

K'Ssander stretched his hand forward and grabbed her by the front of her coat, moving her over to the opposite wall.

Khavar tried to stop this, but the guards immediately surrounded him.

'Where is he?' repeated K'Ssander.

'I don't know,' she answered, managing somehow to keep her voice steady.

'Why did you go back to his office this afternoon?'

Ruxshin could feel his eyes burning into her, trying to catch her out. 'I had forgotten something. He helped me with it, and then I left and returned here.'

'He followed you here; the guards saw him.'

'He never came here, I swear.'

'She's telling the truth,' said Khavar, trying to sound convincing. 'We came to visit our leader, and that was all. No one else was here.'

'You can search my *vast* dwelling, if it pleases you,' said Mah Gira. 'Although I doubt you'll find what you seek.'

K'Ssander motioned for his men to search the place, something they did pretty quickly, on account of the lack of hiding places.

Ruxshin was secretly thankful that they'd decided to move the coffin into the tunnel, and hoped that A'Krad was still out cold, and unable to hear their voices.

'Nothing, sir,' said one of the soldiers, returning to the front room.

K'Ssander paused for a moment, not looking pleased. 'Guards, take the *Supreme* away.'

'No!' cried Khavar and Ruxshin together, stepping forward.

'Stay where you are,' Mah Gira ordered. 'This is all a misunderstanding and I am sure the Ambassador will see that.'

Ruxshin was torn, but realised that he was right. If they reacted and were also taken, their chances of leaving Mah would disappear in an instant. She backed down.

'The quicker A'Krad returns,' said K'Ssander, looking at her, 'the quicker *he* gets out.'

They waited for the Arneshian to leave with Mah Gira, then locked the door.

'I hate him so much,' said Ruxshin, throwing herself onto the small couch. Just hearing his voice made her shake with anger, never mind having to talk to him. 'I have never met anyone so … *broken* in my whole life.'

'We can't waste any more time,' said Khavar. 'We must leave now, before they come back.' He went to the chest and pushed it out of the way. 'Quickly now.'

Ruxshin fastened her coat and entered the tunnel, pleased to see that their prisoner was still unconscious. She turned back to the opening and helped Khavar drag the cabinet back into place, making absolutely sure there were no gaps. 'This is the best we can do from this side.'

'Yeah. Come on, let's see if this one is ready to walk.' He adjusted the rope around A'Krad's ankles, giving him enough slack so he could walk in small steps, then shook him by the shoulder, and heaved him up. The Arneshian began to regain consciousness and low muffled noises could be heard coming from under the hood. Khavar pulled it off.

Surprise mixed with fear was spread all over the supervisor's face. His eyes darted from Ruxshin to Khavar, to his surroundings, clearly unable to tell where he was. 'Mmph …'

'I wouldn't bother,' Khavar told him coldly. He moved closer to A'Krad, pulling the meanest face he could muster. 'Let me tell you how it is: you're going to come on a night walk with us and you're going to behave. If you don't, I'll knock you out again, and drag you by your feet. We're going to board one of your ships so you can take us to Tijara. Understood?'

A'Krad tried to move back, and made a grunting noise in reply.

Khavar grabbed him by the collar and pressed his knuckles into his neck, deep enough to stop him breathing. *'Understood?'*

The man was visibly struggling for air and had no choice but to give in. He nodded his head vigorously.

Satisfied, Khavar let go and pulled the hood back down. 'Grab his other arm,' he said to Ruxshin.

Slowly, they walked out into the open, careful that their prisoner wouldn't trip and fall. With the cold night air enveloping them and thick snow crunching under their boots, A'Krad hesitated, but the Mahini pulled him forward.

'Lift your feet!' Ruxshin ordered.

Khavar took charge of steering. Being an experienced hunter, he knew the land better than most. He followed the path in the direction of the White Glade and, after ten minutes or so, he veered to the left, up a smaller trail that was sheltered by snow-laden shrubs.

An hour passed and the night grew darker. A series of small tremors accompanied the group on their trail. It was unusual to have more than one in any given hour, let alone several. At one point, the ground shook hard enough to halt them in their tracks.

'You wouldn't know anything about this now, would you, Arneshian?' asked Khavar.

'Our leader is restless,' he said.

'Who are you talking about?'

'*She* knows him – the same one who had the great idea to give you that hair trim.'

Khavar hit him on the side of the head. 'Watch your mouth, *ferech*.'

Ruxshin stepped forward, stunned. 'Michael? *Leader*?'

'Surprising, isn't it? He may be young, but oh so powerful. You'll all see. They're testing his latest creation tonight.'

Ruxshin looked at Khavar, perplexed. Whatever could he mean? A boy like him, with untold powers, could only spell trouble for Mah. Uneasy, she motioned for Khavar to keep moving, eager more than ever to reach their destination.

When they reached the hill summit, Ruxshin stopped to catch her breath. She glanced towards the lights stretching out on the plane below her, and looked at her city. The round elevator shafts appeared like bright eyes opening onto the surface of Mah, revealing the powerful reflectors that had been installed underground by the Arneshians. There were people working in the mines day and night, and they would continue to do so until all the Strullium had been removed from their land. Spiralling columns of smoke wafted upwards from the Mahini dwellings, glowing now in the surrounding lights. *I wonder if my fireplace has been lit yet*, she thought, feeling a little melancholy. The soldiers staying in her home were used to that small comfort and soon they would be wondering why there were no logs burning brightly, and where on Mah their "maid" had gone. That worried her. 'We need to hurry before they realise we've left.'

Khavar must have noticed the edge to her voice, or at any rate shared her fear, because he nodded right away. 'This way,' he said, grabbing A'Krad by the elbow and leading the group down a new path. 'The trail will lead us past the ruins of Greenhouse 4.'

'What about guards?' asked Ruxshin, walking carefully but briskly on the other side of A'Krad.

'Not so many at this time.'

Ruxshin didn't look too convinced.

'Look,' said Khavar, 'there will be guards every way we go. Other paths would take us too far away from the aerodock. It makes sense.'

'I know,' she said. 'It's just that …'

Khavar stretched his arm behind A'Krad and over her shoulders. 'We'll make it,' he said reassuringly.

They walked for most of the night, struggling to find sure footing in the soft snow. The gentle fall of flakes turned into a storm on a couple of occasions, forcing them to seek shelter; once by a group of trees and the second time at the base of a long, low rock formation. They huddled against each other, all three facing inwards and downwards, to keep the swirling flurry at bay. Ruxshin and Khavar had to press against the pillowcase over A'Krad's head to keep it in place – given the situation, the Arneshian didn't complain about their proximity, probably welcoming the short-lived cosiness it created. Despite the brighter white clouds in the sky, the night had grown increasingly dark, hiding both path and obstacle. They couldn't risk carrying torches for fear of being spotted by patrols, so they endured the struggle as best they could, pushing and pulling their prisoner along.

Ruxshin's stomach was beginning to grumble but, in the hurry to leave Mah Gira's home, they had packed no extra food. 'How long?' she asked, shouting over the wind.

Khavar stopped to get his bearings. 'Once we get to the bottom of the hill, it will be about half an hour to GH4. From there, maybe ten or twenty minutes more to the acrodock.'

'Will we make it before sunrise?'

'We have to.'

Ruxshin sighed and started walking again, ignoring the fact that she could barely feel her legs. Fur or not, the icy cold night had no mercy to dish out.

*

The prison block was tucked away in a corner of the underground. It had been hastily built by the Arneshians using the local resources. To K'Ssander, anything involving wood and mechanical locks should have been kept inside a museum, but they hadn't had any choice. Glumly, he headed to the holding cell where Mah Gira was being kept. He hooked the fingers of his left hand over the lower ledge of the little window that was cut into the door's surface and began to tap his fingers lightly on the wood. For some reason, he couldn't sleep and he didn't know why. Uneasy, he peered inside the room.

Mah Gira had spent the night locked in the small cell in the company of a high-backed chair, a cup of water and a bowl of reconstituted food. He had complained at first, and even asked to speak to T'Rogon. Then he had drifted off with his chin resting on his chest, and was now snoozing peacefully, emitting a low snoring.

In K'Ssander's mind, the man looked far too frail to act as a leader for these people, though he did have charisma – he had to grant him that. The way the Mahini worshipped him, bowed, and even kissed his hand, was an unmistakable sign of respect. The temptation to get rid of him was strong, but the Ambassador had forbidden anyone to harm him. And he was right. The murder of the Supreme would surely cause an insurrection; even if the Arneshians out-powered them and could squash them all in an instant, it would gain them nothing. No Mahini meant no miners and no knowledge of the subterranean tunnels – it would slow their operation down and they had no time to lose. Zed was still a problem that needed resolving and the Arneshians required Strullium to deliver the final blow. If this wasn't enough, there was the matter of A'Krad's disappearance to deal with. K'Ssander had better things to do than play detective or babysit geriatric citizens, but T'Rogon had insisted, so he adjusted the Unilogus on his wrist and switched it on – it was time to wake the old man up.

He unlocked the door with a long iron key and stepped inside. There was a spare chair in the room and he dragged it noisily to in front of the prisoner, meaning to wake him up; it worked. Mah Gira looked startled and it seemed to K'Ssander that, for a second there, he hadn't been too sure where he was. 'You're not telling me the truth, Supreme,' he began, hoping to catch him off guard.

Mah Gira regarded him with a puzzled expression, then brought his finger to his right ear, tapped it and shook his head.

'Have you gone deaf now?'

The old man pointed at his empty wrist and said, 'Unilogus.'

K'Ssander understood the word, but wondered what he meant by it. 'He lifted his own wrist, showing the bracelet. 'You don't need one - I have mine.'

Mah Gira shook his head again.

'Great,' muttered K'Ssander. His Unilogus must have stopped working. Frustrated, he stormed out, slamming the cell door behind him. He barged into the technician's office, making the brown-haired Arneshian jump out of his skin. 'It's broken,' K'Ssander growled at him, taking the band off his wrist and throwing it into the man's lap. 'Fix it.'

'Yes, sir. Right away,' he replied quickly. He took a hand-held tool and began to scan the device. He tinkered with it for a few more minutes, opening panels and tightening dials, before returning it. 'I can't fix it. I'm sorry,' said the man, positively worried about having to disappoint his superior. 'It's missing a part.'

'Well, where did the part go?'

'It was never there. A mistake in the assembly line probably.'

'Excuses! It worked just fine today.'

'It … it couldn't have; this Unilogus was never activated.'

It was K'Ssander's turn to look confused. He stood there, speechless, feeling a sense of unease resurfacing slowly, but surely. That very afternoon, he had talked to three Mahini using this very wristband. His men hadn't been wearing one – of that he was sure. Then it dawned on him, and the surprise in his eyes was replaced by a cold realisation: the only way to explain the conversation was if one of them had been wearing a Unilogus too, a thing which was strictly forbidden for any furcoats. As he turned on his heels and stormed out of the room and into the corridor, he knew beyond doubt that Ruxshin had been the one wearing the band – that had to be why she had returned to work and why A'Krad had followed her back to the underground. When he passed Mah Gira's holding cell, he stopped briefly and leaned inside. The Supreme must have felt the change in him, because he shrank in his seat. 'I'll get you for this,' he said coldly. 'Ruxshin better be home and have some answers, or I'll do far worse than just give her a *shave*.'

*

'This is worse than I thought,' said Khavar, peeking over the edge of a large metal crate. He pointed at two groups of guards, stationed at either side of a small transporter.

Ruxshin nibbled her lower lip anxiously and nudged A'Krad. 'Why is there only one ship?'

Her former supervisor shook his head and remained silent.

She scowled at him. 'There's no way we can get aboard that ship unseen.'

'We need a diversion,' said Khavar. 'Something to-'

A blaring siren broke the still of the night, making all three of them jump.

'What's happening?' cried Ruxshin over the noise.

In reply, Khavar grabbed A'Krad's forearm in a tighter grip, readying him to sprint. 'I don't know, but it's the diversion we were looking for. Come on.'

Ruxshin held the Arneshian's free arm and followed, keeping herself low enough to hide behind the odd crate. The soldiers had moved forward as one, and they were now huddled around a newcomer. She squinted her eyes, trying to work out who it was through the falling snowflakes, and when she did, she gasped out loud. 'It's K'Ssander! Khavar, he knows!'

'We can't go back now. This way!'

Ruxshin's heart skipped a beat but she kept moving along the shadowed perimeter. Under their leader's orders, the soldiers were spreading out in different directions, but still two of them remained on the landing pad. K'Ssander wasn't far from them, and was carefully searching the aerodock. She heard him bark something, a single word, and four powerful spotlights flooded the pad as if it was broad daylight.

'Get down!' ordered Khavar, crouching suddenly and dragging the others down with him. When A'Krad made a noise, trying to communicate, he quickly removed the gag. 'What?'

'You won't make it,' said A'Krad, gloating.

'Shut up, or I'll *make* you.'

Ruxshin could see the shuttle clearly, only a hundred feet or so away. Its hatch was yawning open invitingly, but just out of reach.

'Listen carefully,' whispered Khavar. 'I'll backtrack, as far away as possible from the shuttle. From there I can distract the guards while you two get on board.'

'No way,' replied Ruxshin. 'Too risky. You'll never make it in time.'

Khavar grabbed one of her hands. 'If I don't, no one will get on that transporter and you know that. You and A'Krad must leave now and look for help, or we're all lost.'

Ruxshin felt her throat closing and tears welling in her eyes. What if they caught him? K'Ssander would kill him without hesitation. Still, how much more pain could her people endure before the Arneshians crushed their spirits?

'If he's here,' continued Khavar, trying to reason with her, 'it means that he knows something and that Mah Gira is in danger. Very soon everyone else will be too. Go and bring back help. Zed is the only hope we have.' He squeezed her hand. 'Look at me - you can do this.'

Ruxshin saw the urgency in his eyes and felt the last of her objections crumble. 'Promise you'll be here when I return.'

Khavar smiled. 'I will.'

She let go of his hand and watched him sneak back the way they had come. Soon the snow hid him from view, as if he had never existed. Ruxshin readied herself and A'Krad to sprint towards the shuttle.

'You'll fail,' he told her coldly.

'Shut up!'

'K'Ssander will kill your friend and your leader. As for you-'

'Shut up!' she growled in his face, her hatred resurfacing, fuelled by the memory of her humiliation at their hands.

'You don't even know how to pilot that ship, let alone make it to the wormhole.'

Ruxshin bit her lip, storing the word "*wormhole*" in the back of her head. It would surely help her later. A'Krad had kept quiet throughout the night, obviously waiting to be alone with her to rattle her cage. She wouldn't let him, however. It was true that she had never piloted a spaceship before, but she still knew a thing or two about engines. Besides, she had learned a very useful word when working on the dictionary. She looked at the man assuredly. 'Autopilot.'

A'Krad flinched at that.

'You thought I'd forgotten, didn't you?' she mocked. 'Your ship will take me to Zed, whether you help or not.'

Just then, Khavar's cry echoed in the darkness: 'Over here, you naked *ferechs*!'

Immediately, a flood of electric discharges shot out from the guards.

'Get them!' shouted K'Ssander, charging in the direction of the voice.

Ruxshin knew this was her moment. As soon as the guards left their post, she leapt up and ran onto the pad, dragging her prisoner behind her. She could tell he was purposely slowing her down. 'Move!' she yelled, yanking him forward by his arm. There were still sixty feet to go to the shuttle but, at their speed, the distance seemed greater. Then A'Krad stumbled and fell flat on his face. Ruxshin was pulled to the ground, and her shin banged against his bent knee. Pain shot up her leg and she had to stifle a cry for fear of being heard. 'Get up!' she ordered, struggling to get back to her feet.

'Make me,' shouted A'Krad cruelly.

'Be quiet! Up!' she hissed, fearing that someone would hear

them. 'I said UP!' He wasn't budging though. In fact, he had relaxed his body completely, and become almost impossible to shift. She was now a sitting duck beneath the spotlights.

Two guards materialised right behind them, at the edge of the pool of light. 'STOP!' they cried.

Frantic with terror, Ruxshin saw one of the men start running towards her, while the other bellowed their position to the whole landing area. Time was up. She looked at the useless Arneshian on the ground, then at the open hatch of the shuttle. She had no choice. 'I can do this,' she said, letting go of A'Krad's arm. Just then, K'Ssander appeared in her field of vision.

'Grab A'Krad,' he told his men. '*She*'s mine!'

Ruxshin hesitated for only a couple of seconds, then turned and ran, adrenaline pumping through her veins. A couple of lightning strikes zipped past her, and fizzed into the snow ahead of her. A third one grazed the outside of her left thigh; searing pain spread across her skin. There was no time to check how bad it was but, since she was still able to run, she ignored it. Thirty feet now … Twenty. A flurry of electric fire charged the air all around her, charring the outer layer of her winter suit. Snow sprayed up to either side of her. Ten feet … a bolt whizzed right between her legs, striking the ground in a blinding flash. The hatch was close now and Ruxshin readied herself to jump. A few steps from it, she leapt forward and landed nimbly inside. She whirled and saw K'Ssander advancing, his palm open, pointed at the shuttle. Catching her breath, she ordered, 'Autopilot, engaged.'

The shuttle came to life, its panels lighting up all at once.

'Lock the door!' she cried, still amazed that it had worked.

The hatch began to close, all too slowly.

She flattened herself against the back wall, hypnotised by the sight of the Arneshian running at her and the outer light decreasing as the gap diminished. K'Ssander fired a shot through the opening. Ruxshin jolted to the side, a second too late. The bolt sunk into her left calf. She cried out in pain and fell to the floor, clutching her wound.

'Door locked,' said the on-board computer calmly. 'State your destination.'

A mighty thump on the side of the shuttle made her scream again.

She was so scared that she even managed to climb back to her feet and move painfully over to the pilot chair, ignoring her injuries.

'Open the hatch!' growled K'Ssander, banging against the metal. 'I'll kill you. I swear I'll kill you for this!'

Terrified, Ruxshin stared out the windscreen and saw a handful of soldiers converging on the ship. Time was running out. 'Computer,' she said, steadying her voice as best she could, 'take me to Zed!'

'Location not found,' replied the machine.

Ruxshin panicked. What else had Morgana said? Her focus was all over the place, especially now that drilling noises had replaced the pounding on the outer hull – they were breaking in. 'Think,' she told herself, trying to recall the recording. After mentioning Zed, the girl had talked about a system. She couldn't begin to guess where it was, but given that the coffin had made it to her planet, it would surely have to be close enough. 'What is the nearest system to Mah?' she asked, changing tactics.

'The Solar System, in the Milky Way Galaxy.'

'That's the one!' she cried, recognising the name. 'Go! Now!'

'Calculating route. Please fasten your seatbelt.'

Ruxshin did just that, before clutching the armrests of her seat and taking a deep breath. Even if the destination was wrong, she needed to get out of here before they breached the hull. Just as the shuttle began to lift-off, K'Ssander appeared on the ground in front of her and looked up. There was so much hatred in his eyes that she recoiled in her seat. Then a soldier came into view and held up a light fur coat for her to see. It was Khavar's snow jacket. Ruxshin's heart sank. As tears gathered in her eyes, the front of the shuttle began to lift, pushed upwards from beneath. She felt the engine burst into life and a pressure growing in her chest, as gravity pinned her back against the seat. She closed her eyes and hoped with all her might that Khavar hadn't been killed.

The ascent seemed to last an unbearably long time. She was scared to bits about being inside a flying machine, piloted by a computer and heading for an unknown destination. She didn't know the first thing about space, or how she would survive if she ended up on another planet. But what choice did she have? She was lost in these thoughts when the shuttle was struck by something and tilted to the right. 'What's happening?'

The computer replied as if all was normal. 'The craft is under attack. Do you wish to halt and negotiate?'

'Wha- No! Don't you dare!'

'Understood. Maintaining course. Wormhole locked on ideal trajectory.'

That word: *wormhole* ... A'Krad had told her about it – whatever it was. 'I'm on the right course,' she said, allowing herself to hope. Another wave rocked the craft. 'Can't we go faster?'

'Affirmative.'

'Well?' she pressed, seeing as there was no change in speed.

'Do you wish to go faster?'

'Yes! I damn well wish to go FASTER!'

'Velocity increasing.'

'And while we're at it, see if you can lose them!'

'Affirmative.'

Honestly, thought Ruxshin. *Who created these machines?* Still, she counted her blessings for, without this autopilot, her race wouldn't have even started. She saw a handlebar attached to the panel in front of her and guessed that it was the steering mechanism for the real pilot. It was jerking in all directions, and she was thankful that someone else was doing the driving. Unable to do anything else except panic, she clutched the armrests, stiffening her body during the sharp bends they were making, to avoid whiplash.

'Wormhole proximity increasing. Entry on ten ... nine ... eight ...'

'Here goes nothing,' she said, not knowing what to expect. Her eyes were fixed on something that looked like a giant orb, slowly filling the screen of the shuttle. Its surface shifted, as if it wasn't really part of the space surrounding it. *Will it hurt?* she thought suddenly. For the second time, she closed her eyes and hoped for the best.

THE WORMHOLE

'Coochy coochy coo! Who's me favourite snuggle bunny?' cooed Faith, holding Elian's baby girl carefully. His index finger wiggled over her perfect little button nose, making her giggle.

'Faith, you're a splendid babysitter,' said Elian, watching them in delight.

'With such an angel, who wouldn't be?' he replied, not taking his eyes off her. 'Isn't that right, little Savannah? Coochy-coochy-coo!'

Julius grinned, surprised at Faith's paternal instincts. He had been lulling Kelly's baby for almost an hour without showing any sign of tiredness, and it seemed that her mum was also appreciating this unplanned moment of rest – she looked tired out from a recent spate of sleepless nights. The rhythmic bouncing of a ball brought his attention back to the basketball match underway in the Ahura Mazda's rec-bay, where Kelly and Skye were taking on a couple of officers from engineering. Julius watched as Kelly leapt into the air before slam-dunking the ball in the basket.

'Show them who's the daddy, babe!' hollered Elian, clapping for her husband.

Kelly bowed to her before giving a high five to Skye. 'And that, my friends,' he said to the other team, 'is the end of the game.'

'Well played, Captain,' said the officers, before saluting quickly and leaving.

Kelly moved towards the large steps around the field, drying his face with the bottom of his t-shirt. He caressed his daughter's cheek with the back of his finger, before going to sit by his wife.

Skye, who was a bit red from all the exercise, plonked himself down next to Julius. 'I haven't run like that in a while,' he said, panting.

'Glad to see you still can,' said Julius.

'Very funny,' he replied, nudging him.

Julius stretched out on the step, resting forward on his elbows and forearms. He could feel the vibration of the ship through the palms of his hands and body. He loved the soothing sensation of it. As a matter of fact, being on the Mazda was always a sure way to rid him of the blues, at least in part, and he was glad that Freja had sent his son to fetch them from the Halls. They had explored the archives as much as possible and there was really nothing left to do.

'Now, Savannah,' said Faith, propping the baby in front of a window, 'see that marvellous place over there that looks like a daisy?'

Savannah cooed with delight.

'That, me lovely, is Pit-Stop Pete, your uncle Faith's true home.'

Elian looked at Julius sideways and chuckled, while Kelly and Skye shook their heads.

'And see that absolute marvel – not you this time – parked right underneath it? That is me own baby. Isn't she gorgeous?'

Savannah giggled, patting the reinforced glass with her tiny hand.

'And what's your baby's name, Faith?' asked Elian.

Faith looked immediately at Julius. Although it was supposed to have been his birthday present to name Faith's first ship, they had decided to go with Morgana's choice in the end. '*Tranquillity*,' he said, proudly.

Kelly went to stand by him and looked at it. 'She truly is a beauty, Faith. If ever the Mazda decides to pack up on me, I know what model I'd want next.'

'Really?' he said, visibly touched.

'Yeah,' he said. '*Tranquillity* … it's a good name. Though, I'd feel more tranquil if we found that bloody wormhole. We scouted everywhere around Earth and all available charts, but nothing. And what you guys found, those pictures with Eronan, don't make things any clearer.'

Julius nodded. If anything, tracing the alien back to 2020 had only made things worse. How was it even possible? Then he thought about another impossible find. 'Hey, what's the story with the Mahin Space Enterprise? I mean, those people didn't really leave Earth, did they?'

'That picture you recovered,' said Elian, 'it really surprised me. The MSE has been a regular ghost story of the fleet for almost 900 years.'

'Ghost story?' asked Skye.

'Space colonisation didn't really begin until Marcus Tijara's time, around 2600,' explained Kelly. 'In the 21st Century, Earth had the International Space Station up and running, plus several probe missions with the use of robots, but no space travel as we know it. A lot of private companies began to experiment with space tourism and, for a while, people did think that it would work, but it didn't. Earth was overridden by economic crisis, global warming, conflicts and epidemics and, in the end, the governments decided to reroute the funds into the betterment of the planet – which didn't really work for a long time, but that's another story. Then, one day, this newspaper article appears, saying that a group of willing humans, led by Captain Gorghinian, is all packed up and ready to leave Earth.'

'People thought it was a hoax,' continued Elian, 'or the latest bunch of space crazies, ready to follow the whims of some unknown rich corporation – and it had to be filthy rich to have anything that could take people up when the governmental agencies couldn't.'

'Who were these folks who left?' asked Skye.

'Mostly they were fans of a TV series about space exploration: "Mahini 2.5". Apparently it was very famous back then.'

'Oh yes, I forgot about that,' added Kelly. 'They loved the show so much that they'd learned to speak one of its made-up languages as well. Anyhow, their shuttle was filmed taking off from Earth without a hitch, but thirty minutes into the flight they lost all contact.'

'What do you mean?' asked Julius who, like Skye, was now sitting up, captivated by the story.

Elian shrugged her shoulders, looking pensive. 'They just vanished. Off all radars. Either their shuttle crashed back into the ocean – which is why it was never found – or they actually left.'

'I'd like to think they made it,' said Faith in a hushed tone.

Elian stood up and walked over to him. Savannah was sleeping peacefully in her soft white blanket. 'Good job,' she whispered. 'I'll take her to our room now and see if I can squeeze a nap in there too.'

Faith handed the girl to her mother, looking pleased with his effort.

'What do you think, Captain?' asked Julius.

'I used to believe they just crashed, but since you found that picture with Eronan in it, I'm a bit iffy. And if he's the same guy from Tijara's time, then we have a bigger problem than-'

'Bridge to Kelly,' a voice said over the ship's computer.

Savannah woke with a start and began to cry.

'Damn it,' said Elian, hurrying out of the bay.

The captain touched the com-link on his chest. 'Go ahead, Lieutenant Steele.'

'We've detected a strange anomaly a few light years from here, sir. It's expanding.'

'On my way,' said Kelly, standing quickly. 'Come along.'

Julius and the others followed him, exchanging puzzled glances among themselves.

Kelly entered the bridge and went straight to his pilot, a fragile looking individual, who was analysing the steady flow of data. 'What is it, Lieutenant?'

'I think we've just found the wormhole.'

A wave of excitement washed over Julius.

'Can you give us a visual?'

Lieutenant Steele did so and, as the orb appeared in its fullness, the entire bridge was stunned.

Julius had travelled through a wormhole before so he recognised its shape immediately. 'How could we have missed it?'

'Send a message to Freja immediately,' ordered Kelly. 'We'll go take a closer look.'

'Captain, there's something else in there.'

Kelly turned back to Steele's screen, trying to interpret the readings. 'It can't be.'

'What is it?' asked Skye, still staring at the wormhole.

'There's a ship coming out of it.'

'Make that four, Captain,' added his lieutenant.

Kelly ran towards his chair, ordering a tactical alert. Immediately, the main lighting system dimmed while the power was rerouted to more important parts of the ship. 'Action stations on the double. Faith, go to engineering. Julius and Skye, lower war-deck.'

'Yes, sir,' replied Julius, sprinting out of the room. He knew the path to the war-deck as if it were his own home, as did Skye. A few minutes later they reached their post and took position at two free catalysts, surrounded by the ship's veteran fighters. Like all war-decks, its walls and ceiling could turn transparent, showing the outer space beyond, overlaid by a grid with important information.

Julius had never fought from the lower deck, but he knew that it was the floor that disappeared there, something not all fighters could stomach. He grabbed the handles of the catalyst and prepared his mind to call upon the energy needed to fire it.

An eerie silence fell among the soldiers as they waited to hear from the bridge. Shortly after, Steele's voice began to report. 'Four crafts confirmed. The first will enter visual contact in 30 seconds.'

'Fighters on standby,' said Kelly.

'Ready, Captain.'

The reply was from a rough looking man, a couple of catalysts to the left of Julius. He knew him as Lieutenant Velasquez, a veteran fighter with many years of experience. On his chest was the Cougar emblem, which was the symbol of pilots and fighters.

'Here they come,' said Steele.

Everyone stared at the screen, holding their breath.

'It's an Arneshian craft!'

'Lock on target,' ordered Kelly. 'Steele, scan for bio-signs.'

'There's one, sir; a bio-signature.'

'At least they haven't sent holograms this time,' said Skye.

Julius nodded, and then spotted three more crafts emerging from the wormhole, all Arneshian. To their surprise, the latecomers opened fire on the first ship. 'They're not here for us, Captain,' cried Julius. 'They're chasing that shuttle!'

'Affirmative,' confirmed Steele. 'And all bio-signatures are human, sir.'

'All right,' said Kelly, 'let's save number one. Any enemy of the Arneshians is a friend of mine. Disable the other's engines. If they shoot back, blow them out of the sky. Steele, get us closer. I want the lower war-deck crew on that first ship to beam her in.'

Julius locked onto the craft that was furthest away, knowing that only his range was broad enough to reach it. Using the overlay grid, he identified its engine, drew on his powers, and waited to get a clear shot before unleashing on the target. 'Just a little closer,' he muttered, following the ship with the catalyst. 'Now.' A yellow beam hurtled out of the cannon and crashed into its target. The ship slowed and turned its weapons on the Mazda.

'Now you've done it,' said Velasquez. 'Fire at will,' he ordered.

Julius let loose. It was a brief battle. The three crafts were no match for the Mazda and, within a few minutes, they had been destroyed.

The first ship was the only one left standing now, and was soon enveloped inside the protective yellow cocoon of the Mazda's tractor beam. It was drawn towards them, before disappearing from view below the hull.

'Velasquez,' said Kelly, 'take your team to Bay 2.'

'Aye, sir. Let's move, people.'

Julius and Skye followed them, curious to find out who was piloting the shuttle and why the Arneshians had been in pursuit. When they reached the bay, Kelly was already there, pointing his Gauntlet at the shuttle hatch. He signalled for the fighters to do likewise, so Julius readied his weapon.

Faith was stationed behind a console, his fingers lightly tapping at a control panel; a secondary energy field sprung to life around the craft. 'Ready, Captain,' he told Kelly.

'Release the hatch.'

Slowly, the door began to open, revealing a crouched figure, with both arms over its head in a protective gesture, clutching something in one hand that looked like a metal band.

Julius shifted to the side, trying to get a better view. Whoever they were, they were shaking uncontrollably. The thick coat they were wearing had burnt patches in several places, which he recognised immediately as ones that must have been made by an Arneshian's palm-weapon. The pilot was sporting a larger wounded area along their left leg, which would need to be tended to by a doctor.

Kelly moved forward cautiously. 'Who are you?' he asked, not unkindly.

The figure made a little noise, and lowered its arms, bringing the metal strip to face-height. 'Help me ...' It was a woman's voice. She slowly raised her head, revealing herself to her rescuers. Loose strands of red hair escaped from under the hood of her coat, framing bright green eyes. She tried to stand, propping herself against the shuttle for balance. 'Julius McCoy ...' she said, speaking through the strange metal band; they all saw her lips moving, but the words were quite clearly coming from it – her own words were unintelligible.

Julius stepped forward hesitantly. When she spotted him, it seemed as if a shadow had slipped from her features. Mustering her strength, she spoke again: 'She says you have a fleet. She says you can save us …'

'Who told you that?' he asked.

'The girl in the box…' That was all she could manage, before fainting.

Kelly jolted forward, and caught her just in time. 'Velasquez, alert sickbay and get engineering to analyse this shuttle. Faith, get that language gizmo and check it out. Julius, follow us.'

Julius was completely baffled and couldn't understand how she knew his name. As he hurried alongside Kelly, with Skye in tow, he looked at the girl lying in the captain's arms, trying to remember if he had seen her before, but to no avail. At the same time, a painful thought occurred to him: he hadn't been to the sickbay since the day Morgana had died, and that was exactly where he was heading now. He was struck by a horrible sense of déjà vu just then, but forced his mind away from it.

'Was she talking about Farrah?' asked Skye.

While it was true that Farrah had been kept contained inside a glass tank, it just didn't add up that this was who the strange newcomer had been referring to. On the other hand, how many "girls-in-a-box" did Julius know? 'I don't think so. I mean, why wouldn't Farrah have told us there was someone looking for us ... for *me*?'

'We'll just have to ask *her* then,' he answered.

When they reached sickbay, the boys stood to the side, allowing Kelly to enter first.

Doctor Bato was the Mazda physician, a jovial middle-aged woman, of Filipino descent. 'What do we have here, Captain?' she enquired, motioning for the girl to be placed on the medical bed.

'She just fainted,' he replied, shaking his head. 'I'm not sure about the rest.'

Bato examined the wounded leg immediately, but didn't seem too worried. 'Leave her with me.' She gently pulled back the injured newcomer's hood and, as she did so, it revealed her unusual hairline.

Kelly shifted the coat away from her neck, marvelling at how it grew all the way down the back of her head and down between her shoulders.

Julius, who had stepped forward to take a closer look, gasped at the familiar sight. 'The statue of the Archer …' he said, trailing off.

'The one on Eneamar?' asked Skye.

'Yes.'

Kelly nodded as well. He had been told about the hypnotherapy session. 'Can you check her DNA, Doc?'

Bato took a device against the skin of her neck and pressed a button. For a few seconds it analysed the result, while the room went completely quiet. She raised an eyebrow. 'It's human.'

'Are you sure?' asked Kelly.

'Positive. There are some minor modifications to her genetic structure – possibly accounting for the fur – but other than that, she's as human as us.'

'Check for mind-skills too.'

'I will, Captain. Give me an hour.'

Satisfied, Kelly led Julius and Skye out of sickbay and back to the bridge.

When they got there, Elian was leaning against the Captain's chair, deep in conversation with Faith.

'Any news?' asked Julius, upon entering the room.

'The shuttle is definitely Arneshian,' replied Faith, 'and this device is a translator.'

'From what language?'

'None we've heard before. Sounds harsh though, guttural.'

'Did the Arneshians make it?' asked Kelly.

'Oh yes. It's got their tech-magic written all over it. I want to take it apart to study it, but I figured you might want to use it with our guest first.'

Elian looked at her husband worriedly. 'How's the girl, JD?'

'Bato is taking care of her now. She's human, apparently.'

Faith's eyebrows shot up in surprise. 'Did I miss something during Spaceology classes? Whenever did we colonise space, pre-Tijara?'

'You were never awake in Brown's class,' replied Julius. 'But it still doesn't make any sense. She has fur like the Archer – how can she be human?'

'Fur?' said Faith. 'Then, couldn't she be from Mah?'

'What makes you say that?' asked Kelly.

'The Archer is in Eneamar, but the people of that city, as Julius told us already, look nothing like fur-covered folks – they're more like Eronan, you know?'

Skye nodded in agreement. 'I think you're right. The statue points to Mah and maybe that's where she's from too.'

Julius seemed troubled. 'How do you explain the DNA then?'

'Don't forget the people of Buruwang,' said Elian. 'We didn't know about them, but they exist – humans on another planet.'

She was right, of course, but to Julius the thought created more questions than answers. 'Aye, but this is getting ridiculous. I mean, have we been leaking humans left, right, and centre for the last few centuries without knowing?'

'It certainly looks like it,' said Kelly. 'What bothers me though is that those Arneshian crafts have come out of the wormhole we were looking for. Since she was inside one of *their* shuttles, it is likely that they've landed on her planet. And if it is Mah, then T'Rogon has beaten us to it.'

'Is this why she wants our help?'

'You can bet your fancy Draw it is.'

Julius was uneasy and, like everyone else, he could do nothing more but wait for Bato to end her examination. Kelly and Skye took the opportunity to go for a quick shower, while Elian returned to her quarters to check on Savannah. Julius followed Faith to the sickbay's waiting room and watched him play with the translator, listening in fascination to the new sounds it made when a word was spoken into it. Mercifully, the wait came to an end and, upon the others re-joining them, Doctor Bato came out to meet them.

'How is she?' asked Kelly.

'Recovering. Her leg wound wasn't serious – it will mend in a few days. The hypothermia will require my attention overnight – she almost froze to death. Captain, I know you need to talk to her, but I cannot give you more than five minutes – and I mean it.'

'It will do for now. Thanks, Doc.'

Bato ushered them back in, halting by a glass divider. 'Only the captain can go in. You will be able to see and hear quite well from here.'

Disappointed, Julius followed the others while Kelly stepped inside the room, holding the translator in his hand. He watched as the doctor moved a curtain aside, revealing the girl as she lay on the bed. Her thick coat had been removed, while a thermal blanket covered her entire body, up to her collarbones. He could see that she was wearing a green sickbay camisole. Her red hair jutted out to either side of the pillow in uneven lengths, as if someone had attempted a haircut with an axe. He wondered how old she was and how scared she must have been when the Arneshians were chasing her through the wormhole. It was a miracle that she had made it out of there alive.

The doctor walked to the top of the bed, while the captain stood by the right side of the girl, facing the glass. Bato injected something into her neck and, within a matter of seconds, she opened her eyes and stared directly at Kelly. The sight must have startled her, because she began to thrash in the bed, kicking at her blanket, clearly frightened. Immediately, Kelly placed his hands over her legs, to avoid being hit. Bato was quickly by her side, hands pressed down on her shoulders. 'Everything is fine; hush. You are safe and among friends.'

The captain made sure the device was close enough to translate their words, so as to reassure her. It seemed to work, because the girl stopped kicking.

'Hi, sweetheart,' continued Bato, full of motherly concern. 'We need to talk to you briefly, and then we'll let you sleep again. Is that okay?'

The girl looked at her suspiciously at first, then looked at the man holding the device. Perhaps she recognised him from before, because she seemed to relax a bit and nodded.

Bato looked up and whispered, 'Five minutes.'

Kelly nodded. 'Hi … my name is Captain Kelly, of the Galactic Federation of Earth. You are now aboard my ship, the Ahura Mazda.'

'Zed?' she asked timidly.

Kelly smiled, 'Yes, we are Zed. What is your name?'

'Ruxshin, of the Mahini.'

Kelly looked at the people behind the glass in astonishment.

'Could it really be ...' whispered Julius.

Kelly turned to her once more. 'What is the name of your planet, Ruxshin?'

'Mah,' she answered. She shivered and closed her eyes for a moment.

'Quickly, Captain,' said Bato.

'Is your planet under attack?'

The girl nodded. 'The ... Arneshians did ... this.'

'Was there a man named Ambassador T'Rogon?'

'Yes, he's in charge.'

Kelly let out a sigh. 'Thank you. One last question, please: who told you to look for help? For us?'

Ruxshin was evidently struggling to talk, but mustered her last strength. 'Morgana did ... she spoke of Julius.'

The silence that followed those words lingered heavily in the room. As if in a trance, Julius stepped forward from behind the glass. 'What did you just say?'

Ruxshin turned her head towards the voice. '... In my coat ...' she whispered, before closing her eyes.

'That's enough now,' said the doctor.

'Where is her coat?' asked Kelly.

Bato pointed at a chair in a corner, and Julius hurried to it. With trembling fingers, he began to search every pocket he could find, unaware that the others had gathered around him and were looking on, quite shaken by what they'd heard. His fingertips closed around something and, even before pulling it out, Julius knew immediately what it was. As his hand re-emerged, the light caught the silver chain and the Strullium lilac crystal, making them sparkle brightly.

*

Julius had troubled sleep. He spent the best part of the night reflecting on the impossibility of what Ruxshin had told them; yet, she had given him a proof that he couldn't refute. He had had the necklace specially made for Morgana, and he knew it was hers beyond all shadow of a doubt. Images of the pendant, and of the moment he had given it to her, passed in and out of his mind, condemning him to a restless night that left him tired and cranky. When the dark dawn of space arrived, he was glad to get out of bed, hoping that a cold shower would remove the last dregs of sleep from his thoughts. He had a long day ahead of him. Freja would join them at 09:00 hours for a briefing on the situation as well as for a chance to meet Ruxshin. He looked at the sleeping shape of Skye, then at Faith's empty bed, and quietly left the room, heading for the mess hall. Coffee could always make *some* wrongs right.

The ready room of the Mazda was at the front of the ship, below the war-deck. When Julius arrived, Faith was already there fitting the translator over a large metal cube. 'I didn't see you at breakfast. What are you up to?'

'I know; I haven't had the time. I'm fitting a multidirectional receiver and amplifier, so we can all be translated and heard properly. It doesn't look great, but I made it last night – no time to embellish it.'

Julius examined it closely, once again amazed by Faith's ingenuity. He took a seat, his right hand clasped around the pendant, which was in the safety of his trouser leg pocket. 'Faith ...'

'Uh-huh?'

'Is it possible that Morgana ... that the coffin travelled through the wormhole? I mean, the pendant is real enough, but ...'

Faith stopped what he was doing to look at him. 'I'd say so, yes,' he answered. 'It's built well enough to withstand that kind of pressure - it was a special one off, that coffin was. Ruxshin must have seen the death mail, Julius. You know that Morgana didn't actually talk to her, right?'

The death mail – of course. 'I was so spaced out last night, I forgot you'd put that in there with her.'

Faith smiled and continued setting up the device. 'It's true what they say – we can't really see all ends.'

Julius mulled over those words for a moment. The death of Morgana had proven to be an important link in a chain of events. Without it, or the special coffin, they would not have found the way to Mah and Michael. 'It didn't need to be her though,' he said bitterly.

Faith looked up once more. 'And what life would you have traded hers for?'

Julius felt an immediate sense of guilt at his own selfish thought and had no answer to give.

Shortly afterwards, Freja arrived at the meeting, accompanied by Master Cress. Once they were all settled around the table, Kelly called for his wife to bring the girl in. There was an excited anticipation preceding her arrival for, as well as meeting a representative of another planet, they were about to learn potentially important information about their enemies.

When she entered the ready room, Julius saw that Ruxshin was wearing clothes made of stitched leather cloths and furs, together with a pair of sturdy leather boots. A rosy complexion had returned to her cheeks and she confidently held all in the room with her gaze. As her hosts stood up, bowing their heads slightly in greeting, she returned the gesture gratefully. The fact that there was a grey wisp over her head also told Julius that she was still very anxious.

'You can sit here,' said Elian, offering the chair between her and Kelly.

When she sat, Julius noticed red fur growing along the back of her hand. His first impulse was to reach over and touch it, but of course he knew better than that. The girl turned briefly towards him, and when their eyes met, he noticed how she backed away in surprise, as if she had recognised him from sickbay. She smiled and turned her attention to the rest of the group.

'Welcome among us, Ruxshin. I am Freja, Head of Tijara, one of the Zed schools. This is my second, Cress,' he continued, pointing. 'Captain Kelly and Lieutenant Flywheel you know already. These here are Julius, Skye and Faith. I am very glad you have found us.'

'Thank you,' she replied, looking briefly around the table. 'And thank you for saving me from the Arneshians.'

'We want to do more than that, but we need to know all the facts first. Will you help us?'

'The Mahini will do anything to see *them* out of our homeland.'

There, she had used that word again: *Mahini*. Julius immediately thought of the picture they had seen of Eronan standing in front of a shuttle with the words "Mahin Space Enterprise" on it. Coincidence or not, they would need to discuss that possibility. The wisp over Ruxshin's head turned briefly scarlet. Julius saw the determination in her eyes and was pleased – time was ticking and they would work faster with a smart and resolute guide.

'We understand that your planet, Mah, is currently occupied by Arneshian troops. Is this correct?' asked Freja.

'It is. The occupation started ...' Ruxshin began to count on her fingers before answering, '... a year and a half ago. You use *years* too, right? A'Krad, my supervisor, said so.'

'We do,' answered Kelly. 'What does this A'Krad *supervise*, exactly?'

'We've been doing all sorts of work for them. Mining Strullium and-'

'Strullium?' cut in Freja.

'Yes, it's a blue metal when it's liquid. Our planet is filled with it.'

Freja exchanged a quick glance with Cress, who had been taking notes on his PIP screen since the meeting had begun. 'We use Strullium too, to run our fleet. The Arneshians will help themselves to it, believe me.'

'That has become apparent,' she replied. 'We don't even mind, to be honest, as we have no real use for it – we make furniture out of it. But unfortunately they have destroyed our greenhouses and every other means we had of creating food. Mah is not a very hospitable place as it is, and now it's even worse.'

'In what way?' asked Cress.

'Six months of snow and six months of rain.'

'Hmm,' said Kelly. 'I take it it's the snowy season now, judging by the state you got here, right?'

'It is. The rain will start on the day the Arneshians call the 1st of October, uninterrupted, for six months.'

'Sounds just like home,' muttered Julius vaguely.

'We'll make sure we plan for it then,' added Cress, matter-of-factly.

'Ruxshin,' continued Freja, 'have you ever seen or heard of a young man named K'Ssander among the Arneshians?'

The girl's facial reaction at the name was enough to confirm she did. Still, she nodded. 'He almost caught me on the landing pad. I think they got Khavar, my friend. He may be dead by now.'

'I'm sorry,' replied Freja.

'Look, it may be too late for Khavar, but Mah Gira is still alive. He's our chief and they have captured him. If we don't work or don't do what they ask, they kill us … or do *things* to us.'

Julius saw a strange wisp emanating from her aura: a mix of red and grey, indicating shame. *What did they do to her, to make her feel this way?* he wondered.

'It is very likely that your leader is still alive,' Freja reassured her. 'T'Rogon is a diplomat at heart and knows the value of negotiation. He will not kill him, especially if his life means a lot to your people.

He's leverage.'

'Death is not the worst thing they can impose on us. There are some among them who take joy in humiliating us. Like this boy, Michael, who they're now calling their *leader*.'

The room grew suddenly quiet.

'Do you know him?' asked Ruxshin, seeing the reaction she had caused.

Julius remained quiet, leaving the others to answer for him.

'We do, Ruxshin,' answered Freja. However, he did not volunteer any more information. 'When was the last time you saw him?'

'About seven months ago. I know he's still on Mah, because the soldiers talk about going to "*Michael's Chamber*" often enough, whatever that is, and of strange tests that cause the very ground we walk on to shake; but none of us have seen him since. And, quite frankly, good riddance. If there's anyone worse than K'Ssander, it's him. I would kill him with my own hands if I could.'

Freja risked a quick glance at Julius, before continuing. 'Ruxshin, we need to find a statue on Mah.'

'What kind of statue?'

'It depicts an archer; a Mahini archer. Do you know where it is?'

'I've never seen any such statue in Mahin – our city. It could be somewhere on the planet, though. Mah Gira will definitely know.'

'Another reason to find him then.'

'Will you really help me?' said Ruxshin, leaning forward. She sounded almost incredulous.

Freja nodded. 'We believe that statue holds the key to defeating the Arneshians. We must find it before we can deal with them.'

The wisp around her body turned to emerald green, as if she hadn't heard such good news in a long time. She looked at Elian and squeezed her hand, overjoyed, making the lieutenant smile.

Freja looked at Julius once more. '*Do you want to hear this?*' he asked, telepathically.

Julius knew he was going to ask about Morgana. '*I do.*'

Freja looked back at the girl. 'How did you come across Morgana?'

*

The meeting went on longer than planned, as questions on the Mahini, and their oppression at the hands of the Arneshians, began to emerge naturally, painting a very sad state of affairs, but a very useful one all the same. They were about to infiltrate the city and they would need all the information they could get.

Around 11:00 hours, they all began mapping a 4D rendering of the city of Mahin and the surrounding area. The girl proved to have a prodigious memory because she was able to relay the geography of her plateau in great detail, from trees to glades, to the position of all the former greenhouses and access lifts to the underground. Her knowledge of the Arneshian compounds, due to her work with A'Krad and her previous visit to the holding cells, proved to be very useful.

At midday, the GM sent Faith to engineering to work on replicating the Unilogus – Ruxshin had told them its name – while his son had been asked to co-ordinate the invasion with Julius and Skye.

'If it wasn't for her people, I would be inclined to nuke the whole planet,' said Kelly, pouring over their quadrant route-chart, which was now sporting a brand new wormhole.

'Amen to that,' replied Skye.

Julius could see their point, but although the temptation to get rid of Michael in such a way was strong, it was nothing compared to how much he wanted to deal with him and K'Ssander *personally*. Besides, Morgana's body was there too now. Ruxshin's story of how they'd found the coffin had caught him unprepared. He had to restrain himself from asking her all sorts of questions in front of everybody, about how she looked, or if Khavar had thought her beautiful the way he did. He was tremendously glad that she had been found by them, and that the casket had remained undiscovered by the Arneshians.

Later that afternoon, Freja came to see them in the ready room. 'Did you get our schematics, JD?'

'Yes. They look very accurate.'

'She's got a good memory. Run me through your plan then,' he said, going to stand next to Julius and Skye.

Kelly touched his com-link. 'Computer, activate Mahin 1.'

The long, glass table-top lit up green as it came to life. The familiar 4D rendering of the plateau emerged until it took centre stage. 'This, here, is Mahin,' he said, using a laser pen to circle the structure in the middle. The landing pad is to the north, next to the main Arneshian compounds. All the shafts you see dotted around are lifts to the underground – there is no other access to it.'

'All except Mah Gira's secret tunnel,' said Julius.

'That's right,' said Kelly, pointing the laser at a small forest to the south. 'Ruxshin and Khavar made it to the landing pad undetected, by skirting the city along the eastern border. If the tunnel is still hidden, it's our best bet to enter the lower level. Anywhere else would involve an attack, and I don't think it's what we're planning for, right?'

'Yes,' replied Freja. 'T'Rogon is expecting an invasion, but not an infiltration party, at this stage. However, this means that the wormhole will be guarded too. They'll detect us as soon as we enter their quadrant.'

'That's what we're counting on,' he said. 'We'll be using our Cougars as shields – not to engage, but as a diversion. They chase our fighters, we split away and land on Mah.'

'Won't they be able to detect your signatures?'

'Scan this room for bio-signs, please,' Kelly requested.

Freja looked perplexed, but did as indicated, using his PIP. 'Four people.'

In reply, Kelly looked to his right. 'Faith?'

At that moment, Faith materialised in a corner of the room, smiling brightly. 'Et voila!'

Julius enjoyed the expression on the GM's face – he looked impressed. 'We managed to cloak his signature using the Arneshian technology left behind during their visit to Earth,' he explained. 'They'll have no indication of intruders.'

'Once on the ground,' continued Kelly, 'we hit the east road and get in through the tunnel.'

'I take it a full port is out of the question?' enquired Freja.

All eyes turned to Faith, who shrugged his shoulders. 'We've never ported through a wormhole, sir,' he explained. 'Testing may take too long and I wouldn't send a soul without one.'

'Damn right you wouldn't,' mumbled Skye.

'It's kinda far, truth be told, but I can run some trials if you want me to. I've been working on a portable version of the Shanigan Relay, and it may just do the trick.'

'Yes, please,' said Freja. 'I want you to give one portal to Captain Kelly. He will release it near Mah's orbit, for us to use.'

It was Faith's turn to be impressed. 'Great idea, sir. We can start testing as soon as they drop it.'

Freja nodded. 'What happens once you get to the tunnel?'

'Computer, activate Mahin 2,' said Kelly.

A new 4D map appeared, this time of the underground level.

'This here is Mah Gira's house,' explained Skye. 'And this one, across town, is the holding cellblock. All we need to do is go to him and ask for the location of the Archer.'

Freja remained silent for a while, pondering the feasibility of the plan. 'I guess it's easy enough to replicate Ruxshin's clothing, but the rest ... if you could just turn into Mahini, then yes, it would be a perfect plan.'

'Actually, sir,' said Faith, 'we sort of can.'

Julius, Skye and Kelly didn't seem too surprised at that; in fact, they looked quite chuffed. Freja, on the other hand, looked at him with interest - when it came to Faith and his inventions, expectations were generally high. 'Astonish me then, since the rest of the room seems to already be in the know.'

'Wait for it, sir,' piped up Skye, looking excited. 'This is something else.'

'Well, so,' began Faith, holding everyone's attention, 'the two things that could give us away are the language and the fur. After downloading the vocabulary into the Officer Network, I went to talk to Doctor Bato and we came up with a throat implant – a different version of the Unilogus - linked to the PIP. So basically, when the translation feature is activated, it triggers the chip in your voice box; you open your mouth and what comes out is the language of choice. Like so.' Faith pressed a button on his PIP and began to speak.

Freja looked completely stunned at the sounds reaching his ears – so guttural and completely unlike Faith's Irish ones.

'Would you believe it?' was all he could say.

'And that's not all,' said Faith, reverting to the common speech. 'Check my back out!' And with that, he turned around and pulled his t-shirt over his head.

'Zed's beard!' Freja exclaimed, rushing over to examine Faith's hairy back. 'How …'

Julius stepped closer as well. He had already seen it and touched it plenty, but it was still amazing. 'It's just a DNA alteration, sir,' he explained. 'Dr Bato will be able to reverse it when we get back. She's a genius, by the way.'

'Unbelievable,' the GM murmured. He turned to his son. 'And how will the party get back afterwards?'

The enthusiasm quickly left their faces.

'I see,' said Freja, understanding that was no plan for that.

'Once we make it to the Archer,' said Kelly, 'and retrieve the coordinates, you'll need to pick us up.'

'Hopefully the portal you drop will work. Otherwise, we'll think of something else,' replied Freja. 'Leave that to us. Once you make it safely to the Archer, you stay put until we contact you – and bring plenty of provisions.'

*

Preparations completely took up the following couple of weeks. Julius was itching to ask Ruxshin various questions about Morgana, but he had no opportunity. The girl was either in sickbay or in long, drawn out meetings with Cress and the GM, dishing out every bit of information she possessed on Mah. And, when she was free, Julius was busy elsewhere. Part of the groundwork involved installing a trace on the Arneshian shuttle, altering the DNA of the infiltration party, implanting them with the translation chip and gearing them up for cold weather and snow. Julius, Skye and Kelly made up the entire team, while Faith would help to co-ordinate things from the Mazda. 'I can't imagine any of the Mahini wearing a skirt like mine, to be honest,' he had told them candidly. They knew he was right – no amount of camouflage could conceal his metallic hovering device.

Ruxshin, on the other hand, didn't seem too happy about being left behind. Towards the end of the second week, she took to roaming the guest areas of the Mazda like a lion in a cage, asking for updates whenever she saw an officer. It was understandable given the circumstances, but it wasn't helping either.

On Monday the 22nd, Julius walked into Bay 2 to find Ruxshin arguing with one of the technicians. By the looks of things, he seemed more uncomfortable than she was, practically hiding inside the shuttle as he worked, while she stood by the hatch, determined to convince him why she had to be in the landing party.

Upon hearing steps, the engineer shot out of the craft, looking exasperated. 'Why don't you ask *him*?' he told her over his shoulder, while hurrying for the exit.

Ruxshin fell quiet and looked at Julius, as if studying him.

'Hi,' he said. Then he remembered his new throat implant and turned his PIP on. 'Hi,' he said again. Only, this time, he could barely recognise his own voice.

'That's a pretty neat trick your friends came up with,' she said, pointing at her own throat.

'Aye, it's really strange though,' he said. 'My thoughts don't match my words. Hard to get used to.'

Ruxshin smiled. 'You all look like Arneshians, you know that, right? And you invent things, just like they do.'

Julius couldn't detect any sarcasm in her voice. She was just stating a fact. He wondered what she would say if she saw his mind-skills in action. 'We are both humans ... and so are you, apparently.'

'Yes, the doctor told me. But she doesn't know why we look different from you.'

'Neither do I,' he answered truthfully. He was toying with the idea of asking her about Morgana, when she stepped up to him, quickly and eagerly. He was taken aback, not least because he hadn't been physically close to a woman for some time, and right now he could count her freckles.

'You must take me with you,' she begged.

Julius was caught off guard, distracted by her scent – a distant reminder of pine trees and sweet resins. 'I can't,' he replied eventually.

'It is *my* home,' she continued, standing up to him. 'I know the land, the access to the tunnel and every nook and cranny of the underground. You'll look lost and out of place, and they will catch you!'

Julius could understand her feelings perfectly – he would have done the same in her place – but he couldn't afford to babysit her. Determined not to be dragged into a fight, he took a step back. 'I'm sorry, but the Grand Master has been clear about that. His word goes.'

Ruxshin tilted her head to the side, as if trying to suss him out. The fight reappeared in her eyes. '*She* said you'd be a leader. It seems to me that it's quite the opposite.'

It was like being slapped. Julius knew exactly who Ruxhin was referring to, and why she had said it. It was his turn to step up to her, barely containing his anger. He planted his index finger in the middle of her chest and stared her down. 'Don't you ever use her like that again. *Ever.*'

Ruxshin lost her edge and cowered back.

Again, the sudden change stopped Julius in his tracks. She looked scared, as if she was expecting him to hit her. Confused by her reaction and shaken by guilt at his outburst, he stepped back and walked out of the bay.

'McCoy, is everything all right?'

Kelly had just crossed his path in the corridor. 'I'm fine,' he growled.

'What was that? I can't understand you.'

Julius stopped and realised that his Unilogus was still turned on. 'Great,' he said, deactivating it. 'I just had my first argument in Mahin.'

Kelly raised an eyebrow.

'Ruxshin wants to tag along,' he explained, leaving out the rest of their exchange.

'She can't,' he replied, 'and that is that. Now, go get ready. The shuttle will leave in one hour.'

He nodded and headed for his quarters, trying to push away the discomfort of his first proper encounter with Ruxshin.

*

Elian had taken the Mazda right up to the wormhole, surrounded by the Zed fleet. Two teams had been positioned on the upper and lower decks of her ship, ready to defend the fleet if any enemy decided to pay them a visit.

'Is everyone ready?' asked Freja. He was standing in Bay 2 with the landing party, who were wearing Mahini style clothing.

'As ready as we'll ever be,' replied Faith. 'The shuttle has been cloaked.'

'Very well. Good luck, Team 1. You know what's at stake,' said Freja. 'Mr Shanigan, you can join me on the bridge.'

'Aye, sir,' he replied, hovering around the craft for one last check.

While Kelly exchanged a last minute word with his father, Julius shouldered his small backpack and did a mental check of his gear. The fur coat was really heavy and he had to leave it open for as long as he was on the shuttle, or it would be too hot. He had packed several highly caloric bars rich in proteins, fat and grains. He also carried a bottle of concentrated hydration fluid; a mouthful of it made up for a whole glass of water. The EMU device was pinned to his chest, underneath all the layers – if it was good enough for deep space, it was good enough to keep him from the cold of Mah. Satisfied, he stepped into the craft and secured his luggage in a side compartment. Then he went to the front, occupying one of the two pilot seats. A few minutes later, Kelly joined him, taking the other place, while Skye strapped himself into the seat behind Julius.

'Hey,' said Skye, grinning, 'do you know what Ruxshin told me about the female Mahini the other night?'

'Here we go,' sighed Julius, rolling his eyes.

'They tend to be quite *affectionate* people – not sure what she meant, but I intend to find out.'

'Whatever you do,' said Kelly, turning to him, 'don't you dare bring back any kittens.'

'Skye, are we going to have a problem with you?' said Julius.

'The local gals might … but it doesn't follow that they won't like it!'

'Like what?' asked Faith, his head peaking inside the hatch.

'Take a wild guess,' said Julius, nodding at Skye.

'The Miller is going *hunting*?'

'I told you,' Kelly piped in, index finger waving, 'I don't want any tiny fur balls on my ship.'

'No offense, Captain,' said Skye, 'but right now you're as hairy as she is.'

'And anyway … why did Ruxshin mention that, exactly? Were you asking her funny questions?'

'*Moi?*' he said, looking all innocent. 'Never!'

'You fancy her?'

'She's kinda hot, actually. Red hair, green eyes, those cute little freckles of hers. And she gave the slip to K'Ssander – feisty!'

'You're hopeless,' Julius told him, shaking his head.

'Not that you're wrong, mind you,' added Faith as an afterthought, 'but that's beside the point.'

'I'm only representing my people. You know: inter-space relationsh-'

The ship intercom came to life, cutting him short. 'Team 1,' called Freja, 'stand by.'

'Roger that, bridge,' replied Kelly over his com-link. 'Take your positions.'

'Good luck guys,' said Faith. 'And remember that your powers won't work through the cloak. And don't forget to eject the portal.'

'Will do. See you on the other side,' replied Julius, sadly aware that Faith wasn't going with them on this mission.

The captain closed the hatch and checked the controls. He had spent a lot of time familiarising himself with the Arneshian craft and felt pretty confident. He turned the engine on without a hiccup.

'The Cougars are in position,' said Freja. 'Team 1, ready check.'

'Bay 2, depressurising now,' replied Kelly. 'Team 1, we're good to go.'

Julius watched the port slide open underneath them, revealing the darkness below. He checked his straps again and cracked his knuckles nervously, while Michael's face appeared at the edge of his consciousness.

A NEW SOLAR SYSTEM

The Arneshian shuttle carrying Team 1 approached the group of Cougars that had been deployed to escort them through the wormhole. Five of them would be sent ahead and five more would follow the shuttle.

'We're going to have two former Solo champions in that wormhole,' said Kelly, taking his position in the convoy. 'What are the odds?'

'Is Docherty here?' asked Julius, suddenly interested. He hadn't seen him since the funeral and wondered where Kaori was.

Kelly pointed at his Cougar in reply. 'He's leading the toon.'

The tag name "Arrow" shone on the name plate on the side of that craft in the front group and Julius knew it was Bernard's.

'Arrow, Team 1 in position and ready to go,' said Kelly.

'Captain!' Docherty replied, sounding surprised. 'You really snuck up on us.'

'That's what I wanted to hear. It means the cloak is working just fine.'

Julius allowed himself a sigh of relief – they would need all the stealth they could get. He looked ahead and saw the Cougars beginning to enter into the wormhole. Kelly matched their speed and guided them smoothly inside the sphere that marked the entrance to the conduit. Since he wasn't in charge of piloting the craft, Julius gave himself the chance to observe his surroundings properly, marvelling at its beauty as he went. There were no defined edges around him, but a layer of undulating, shimmering surfaces instead. It made him think his eyes were playing tricks on him, bringing the images in and out of focus. As Kelly accelerated, the blurring increased, creating strands of light that streamed past them.

'I wish we could use our mind-skills,' said Skye, breaking the silence. 'It would make me feel much safer.'

'The only way to do that,' said Kelly, 'is by leaving the craft and surfing it to the surface.'

'Now *that's* an idea!'

'Yeah, well, let's hope it doesn't come to that.'

Julius hand wandered to the EMU button on his chest without realising it. It wouldn't be the first time he had hitched a ride on top of a ship.

The Cougars cruised smoothly ahead, flying steady and sure. Bernard's scouting group would be exposed to the enemy right from the start, and would need to fly by them quickly, as well as taking the brunt of any opposition. He had to give them enough time to-

'Atchoo!'

'What was that?' started Kelly, before being interrupted by a second sneeze.

Julius and Skye were on their feet in an instant, Gauntlets pointed towards the rear of the shuttle. They exchanged a quick, wary glance.

'Who's there?' called Skye.

There was a shuffling noise from inside one of the cabinets built into the back wall. Julius advanced cautiously and released the latch, without lowering his weapon. As the door swung open, a huddled Ruxshin tumbled out into the open.

'Don't shoot! Don't shoot please!' she cried, shielding herself with her arms, while speaking into her Unilogus.

'Shoot? What- No!' replied Skye, astonished.

'What are you doing here?' said Julius, barely able to contain his temper.

'I'm sorry! I just *had* to come, but you wouldn't listen!'

'Ruxshin,' said Kelly, over his shoulder. He sounded disappointed. 'This is not how we do things. There were serious reasons for leaving you behind, including the fact you're a wanted fugitive. You're less of a help than you think.'

Ruxshin blushed, her gaze falling to her feet. 'It's my home,' she answered quietly.

Julius lowered his weapon and returned to his seat, feeling annoyed. The way she had used Morgana that very morning had marked her in his bad books right away, and this latest stunt wasn't going to change that sentiment.

'You better sit down and buckle up,' Skye told her, helping her to her feet. 'It's going to get rough.'

'Arrow, come in,' said Kelly.

'Yes, Captain?'

'When you re-enter, please advise the GM that we have a stowaway on board.'

'Sir?'

'The Mahini girl.'

'Oh,' he replied, sounding uncertain. 'Is … there something I should do?'

'Just clear us safe passage, Arrow; that's all I ask for.'

'Roger that, Captain. Two minutes to go.'

Kelly turned to Julius. 'There's a spare EMU in my rucksack – try the inside pocket. Give it to her. Then turn on your translator, since she's here.'

Julius nodded and got up – time was short and he had to focus on the mission rather than on personal matters. He rifled through Kelly's belongings and found the EMU badge. He turned to her and showed her his own activator, fixed to his t-shirt. 'Put this on, as close to your body as possible.'

Ruxshin nodded, grabbed the badge and opened the top half of her coat. 'This good?' she said, pointing above her left breast.

'It'll do,' he replied.

She fixed it onto her chest and looked up apprehensively. 'I'm sorry,' she whispered.

Julius saw her blush when he looked at her, noticing little pink dots in her otherwise grey aura – he couldn't read them, but they made him feel uncomfortable. He nodded curtly, before going back to his seat.

'It's fine,' said Skye, trying to reassure her. 'I'll tell you if you need to use it.'

'Thirty seconds, Captain,' said Docherty.

Kelly took a deep breath and readjusted his grip on the piloting levers. 'Enter the coordinates, McCoy. The computer will alert us when it's time to drop the portal.'

Julius did so quickly. They were going to land in a hilly area east of the tunnel entrance, where Ruxshin had said there were no soldiers.

Finally, the end of the wormhole came into view and a thick silence fell over the crew.

'Arrow is out,' Docherty informed them.

Julius tensed as he watched the scouts disappearing into the new system, one after the other. Sitting there, unable to do anything but watch, made him feel restless and uneasy. He stared at the new controls which the Mazda's engineers had added, to check the vitals of all the Cougars in the party, hoping that no lights would turn red.

Kelly brought them into the open smoothly, and kept moving forward until the back group had joined them too. 'Here comes trouble,' he said, 'as expected.'

Julius saw at least ten Arneshian crafts converging toward them. The Cougars began their evasive manoeuvres by splitting outwards from their balled-up position, like sparks from fireworks. The confusion left the enemy disorganised for a few seconds, before they also split to follow the individual fighters.

With the front guard gone, Kelly decelerated slightly, allowing the rear group to move forward and surround his shuttle. They were covered once again.

Julius didn't know the pilots, but they were flying competently, shielding them from all angles. 'Enemies approaching at ten o'clock,' he warned.

'I see them,' replied Kelly. 'Shields up.'

Julius obeyed promptly, not a second too soon, as a stray shot from one of the enemy crafts found its way into the group. Their shuttle shook, but held intact. 'Docherty is coming back,' he said, watching the plane on the radar. 'He's being followed.'

'Let's hope he doesn't bring them too close to us,' replied Kelly.

'Can you see the others?' asked Skye.

'The scan range of this craft is pretty shabby – they keep passing in and out of radar,' said Julius.

'Wings,' called Kelly, 'make some white noise for us.'

'Aye, sir,' came the reply from a female voice.

Julius didn't know who the pilot was, but knew that "white noise" was a manoeuvre designed to confuse the readings of scanner sensors by way of mind-skill impulses – in this case, the aim was to protect the Arneshian shuttle even more. The Cougars where moving clockwise around his craft, each of the pilots unleashing a series of mind-pushes to confuse the Arneshians. At the same time, they all had to fly in formation, to avoid being hit.

The six planes twisted and turned their way ahead like a flock of birds, forging a path towards Mah, amidst the shimmering enemy-fire. Kelly's face was like a mask, focused on piloting and removed from all the rest.

Julius couldn't do anything, except hold his breath during the countless corkscrew manoeuvres, ignoring the odd little whimpering sounds from Ruxshin. His eyes kept creeping back to the radar, waiting for the proximity alarm to go off. 'Watch out!' he cried suddenly. Instinctively, he pushed back in his seat, as he saw an Arneshian ship chasing a Cougar, before veering away from its prey. 'He's coming right at us!'

Kelly banked sharp left, bringing them outside the safety of the group, but he had no other choice. Following the coordinates, he stayed his course, hoping that the enemy wouldn't notice.

Two Zed crafts appeared to either side of the shuttle, giving them all a chance to catch breath.

'Captain Kelly?'

'Wings, talk to me.'

'The group is scattered, but they'll keep the Arneshians distracted for as long as they can. Mah is right ahead. You can make it.'

The pilot had just finished speaking when a violent shock pushed the shuttle to the left. Ruxshin screamed in fear.

'Wings!' cried Kelly. 'Come in, Wings!'

'She's gone, sir,' came the nervous reply from the second Cougar.

As if to confirm his words, several shards of metal bounced off their shuttle, before ricocheting out into space.

'Captain,' said Julius, checking their own craft's vitals, 'our shield has been damaged. We cannot take another hit!'

'Blackie,' ordered Kelly to the remaining pilot, 'take that craft away from us *now* – our cloaking device may not last for long.'

'Roger that, Captain.'

Julius watched as the Cougar to his right flipped backwards and began firing at the enemy craft behind. It was a daring manoeuvre given their speed, but it paid off. The enemy had to take evasive action, leaving Kelly free to accelerate forward. As they sped away, Mah came into view, looking starkly bright against the darkness around it.

'Get ready to eject the portal, McCoy. We want it to remain outside the planet's orbit.'

Julius keyed in the code given to him by Faith to open the outer locker where the portal was being stored. The button went from red to green, indicating that it was ready to be fired. 'Let's hope it works,' he said, as he ejected it.

Just as they zoomed out of the fighting zone, an alarm echoed inside their craft.

'What's happening?' cried Ruxshin.

'We're losing speed,' said Kelly, testing his controls. 'Miller, check the back!'

Skye unbuckled his seatbelt and moved to the rear. He opened one of the covers to see if they had taken any damage and a plume of smoke escaped. He quickly took an extinguisher and put the fire out. 'Not good.'

'We're drifting,' admitted Kelly. I can steer, but that's about it.'

'And the cloak?' asked Skye.

'Its core engine was in the back. We probably lost that too,' he said, leaning back in his seat.

Julius ran his fingers through his hair, trying to think of a solution. He used their radar to scan for objects but, between them and Mah, there were no structures or debris of any kind - without any solid objects, there was no way he could pull them closer using his skills.

'Oh no,' said Kelly, staring at the radar.

Julius and Skye leaned forward and saw two incoming crafts heading their way. One of the Cougars had taken a long detour, bringing the enemy with it. Unable to move out of the way, there was nothing they could do but wait.

The beeping sound of the proximity alert became more insistent as the chase drew closer to their location. Then, just as it was beginning to slow again, a stray hit slammed against the tail of their shuttle, making it spin out of control and sending Skye crashing forward.

Julius tried to grab him to break his fall, while Kelly used the handles to counteract the spin. As successfully as he did this, the momentum was still accelerating them onwards.

'They've pushed us towards the planet's orbit!' cried Kelly. 'We'll land all right - gravity will see to that pretty soon.'

'Yes, but not where we want to go,' added Skye, massaging his head. 'We're heading way beyond the eastern forest.'

'Better than the middle of the city,' replied Kelly. 'McCoy, if you have any bright ideas, now's the time.'

Julius felt a sting of panic. He could see the dark patch that was Mah disappearing fast to their right, together with their designated landing spot. Ahead there was only snow, just as Ruxshin had described. No matter how he looked at it, there was only one way they could survive the one-way trip without crashing. He unbuckled his seatbelt and looked at them. 'Suit up, people.'

'Thinking of sharing?' asked Kelly, as he activated his own EMU underneath the fur coat.

'You're not going to like this.' He turned to Skye. '*You'll* certainly like this.'

'We're going out, aren't we?' Skye said gleefully.

'It ain't normal that you're this excited about it,' replied Kelly, helping Ruxshin with her suit.

'We fly down, then?' continued Skye, unperturbed.

'Er … no. If we leave the shuttle to crash, they'll know we're there.' Julius said.

'Then how are we …'

Julius cracked on. 'Ruxshin, you'll be fine,' he said to her, tightening her straps. 'Just stay there and keep the face shield on at all times – it will allow you to breathe and hear us.'

She was too shocked to say anything, so just nodded anxiously.

'We are going to act as the thrusters for this craft,' Julius explained. 'You hold on to whatever you can find in here. I open the port door and the three of us push against the ground until we slow ourselves down.'

Skye's smile fell from his face, and he looked at Kelly. 'I love this man.'

Kelly, on the other hand, didn't seem to share his enthusiasm. 'Are you insane?'

'We've done it before, Captain,' Julius answered. 'Thirty of us halted a Heron ship in its track.'

'There are three of us here,' pointed out Kelly, unconvinced.

'Yeah, but the ship is smaller. Come on, we need to secure ourselves to something – but make sure we can reach the hatch.'

Kelly raised his hands in resignation.

'There's some sort of rope in the cupboard where I was hiding,' volunteered Ruxshin. 'Although I'm not sure I understood your plan properly.'

Ignoring her last remark, Julius got straight to it. He rummaged for a few seconds, then turned around, holding a length of rope and two grapples.

At that moment, the craft jolted and gained speed. The orbital pull had sucked them in.

'Let's do this quickly then,' said Kelly.

They secured the hooks to two handles on either side of the hatch, then fastened the rope around their waists and knotted it at the base points of the grapples. They had purposely kept it short and tight, to prevent them being sucked outside once the door was opened.

'Focus on the ground,' Julius told them. 'Skye, you get the door.'

'Wait!' said Ruxshin. 'What are you doing?'

'Counting down,' continued Skye. 'Three, two, one … Unlock.'

The door didn't even finish opening before it was sucked clear off its hinges by the vacuum. Ruxshin screamed as she was dragged forward against her safety harness. The rope around their waists tightened, making them groan in pain, but they tensed their abdominal muscles and held fast.

'Take a deep breath,' hollered Julius. He could see the ground speeding up toward them. Still, they had to wait until they were in range, or there would be nothing to push against but air.

'The craft is tilting!' cried Skye. 'We'll lose sight of the ground.'

'Hit the starboard wall … as gently as you can,' replied Kelly.

Skye forced himself sideways, pointing his right hand behind him, and let out a quick burst.

It did the trick and the hatch faced the onrushing surface below once more.

'Here we go!' shouted Julius. 'Push with everything you've got.' He felt a familiar inner click in the recesses of his mind, stretched his hands forward and unleashed a powerful push towards the planet.

Three beams of yellow light shot out of the craft and struck the ground in a flurry of snowflakes. The candid white blanket turned black, as the heat scorched the grass beneath.

'Skye!' cried Kelly, as the shuttle began to tilt again, this time as a result of their mind-skills.

'I'm on it.'

Julius kept going, ignoring the sharp pain at the back of his head.

'Keep pushing!' he urged them. They were visibly losing speed and with a couple of hundred feet to go, Julius knew they'd made it. He mustered the last of his strength and unleashed a further wave, which slowed the shuttle down even more.

Skye turned to starboard and gave a last push to ensure they landed the right way up.

Now under control, the Arneshian spacecraft touched down. As soon as they eased off with the mind-push, a violent gust of snow blasted into them, forcing them all to the floor.

They had made it.

Kelly was the first to his feet and started to undo one of the knots.

Shaken, but unhurt, Ruxshin staggered out of her seat and went to work on the other one, ignoring the raging storm. She was regarding these men in a new light now: a mixture of fear and awe.

Julius' head and ribcage throbbed. He tried to loosen the rope around his waist, enough to push it down, past his hips. When he managed to wriggle free, he rushed to the front, to check the radars. The scanner sensors seemed to be working fine and there was no trace of incoming visitors. He sighed, relieved.

Skye had retrieved their bags from the locker, and handed Julius his. 'My clock says it's night time,' he added, 'but the sky is pretty light here.'

'I've noticed,' agreed Kelly. 'Can you tell what time it is, Ruxshin?'

'The middle of the day, give or take.'

'It'll do. Listen up then. The map in our PIPs will take us back toward the forest. The storm should cover our tracks well enough. Ruxshin, as soon as you recognise the area, I want you to take us straight to the secret tunnel. No point in backtracking now.'

Ruxshin seemed on the verge of asking something, but changed her mind and simply nodded.

When Julius stepped outside, the stormy wind wrapped around his body, buffeting him from all sides. He turned to the craft and was pleased to see that the snow had practically covered it already. He motioned for Kelly to move on, making sure that Ruxshin was right in front of him – the last thing they needed was to lose her. As she walked, she turned her head briefly and gave him a strange look, as if she was seeing him for the first time – Julius knew that their display of mind-skills would require some further explanation, but he would worry about that later.

The EMU turned out to be the perfect protection from the storm, keeping them cosy in a way that a regular fur coat couldn't have.

The visors allowed them to talk to each other without using their mind-skills and without the need to shout over the elements. Still, the walk was far from enjoyable, as they had to negotiate their path amidst the dips hidden under the soft white layers. Kelly, as the first in the line, was taking the brunt of all the falls and missteps, but bore it quite stoically. Skye had his PIP open as well, to double check they didn't stray from the path.

After an hour Ruxshin stopped and turned to the others. 'Do you feel it?'

A deep tremor sprung up beneath their feet at that moment.

'What was that?' asked Skye.

'One of those *Michael-tests* I was telling you about.'

'What's beyond that low hill?' asked Julius, pointing east. 'The rumbling is coming from there.'

'A valley. There's a forest, a lake, and some rocky outcrops.'

'Give me a minute,' he said to the others. 'I want to check it out.'

Kelly seemed unsure about this detour, but nodded. 'Let's go together. Come on, Ruxshin.'

The tremors intensified as they drew closer to the hill and, by the time they climbed to the top, the rumbling had become so strong that they had to scramble on all fours.

'Over here. Keep low,' Julius told them, lying down, and trying to ignore the weird sensation of the tremors in his bones.

The snow continued to fall, coating everything in white. Still, the landscape was visible enough for them to recognise the landmarks mentioned by Ruxshin a few moments before.

'I can see the lake and th-' began Kelly, before the words died in his throat. 'Look there, to the right.'

Julius did so. On top of a mound stood a group of people, surrounding a machine of sorts. An eerie purple light spread like a fog all around them.

'What the heck are they doing?' asked Skye to no one in particular.

The light around the machine grew stronger, until the lake itself was tinged with it. The small forest to the left of the water began to tremble, gently at first, as if a light breeze had just blown through the treetops, but the breeze quickly became a heavier wind, causing their peaks to bend in all directions. At the same time, a new rumbling emerged, which appeared to be strongest in the ground below the forest. The trees were shaking so much that they became a blur of green and brown. After a few seconds of this, the entire mass of land broke free from the soil below and lifted into the air. Their roots were in full view, dragging clumps of earth and stone up with them. Then, suddenly, it stopped and the forest hovered above the ground, no longer shaking.

This didn't last long before a further tremor began, this time below the lake. The water bubbled, as if it were in a pan that someone had lit a massive fire beneath. A sinister screech broke the air from the edges of the lake, as the rocks around it cracked and split, and slid over each other. As if a giant hand had scooped it up, the body of water levitated into the sky. Some of the icy liquid cascaded over the rim of this invisible field and down into the newly created hole in the ground below it. The lake, once in the air, stopped and hovered peacefully.

When the body of water and the trees moved towards each other, Ruxshin yelped in fear, shaking Julius from his trance. 'How is this possible?' he asked.

No one replied though, as the show wasn't over yet. Accelerating through the snow, the circular surface of the lake floated to the side of the forest, tilted forward and wrapped itself around the trees, like a hand gripping a bunch of flowers. The water poured over the pine needles their roots, and finally down to the ground below. With the trees grasped firmly, the watery tentacles slammed them down to the surface, sending shockwaves along the ground for miles. It took a couple of minutes before the tremors completely subsided.

'I can't believe this,' began Kelly. 'That machine tampered with every law of physics we know. If this is an indication of Michael's latest achievements, we have some serious planning to do.'

'He's practicing telekinesis and mixing it with technology,' said Julius, matter-of-factly. 'He was given mind-skills from Farrah, remember?'

'He's a fast learner then,' said Skye.

Julius nodded, a new set of worries weighing on his heart. He looked at Ruxshin, fear spread across her face, and felt sorry for her.

*

When the forest came into view, everyone drew a sigh of relief. They had been happy to leave the scene of Michael's demonstration behind them for the minute, and push on. That was a worry for another day.

Fortunately, Ruxshin had a good recollection of her journey with Khavar and A'Krad, and Kelly was happy to let her steer their course. By the time they reached the shelter of the trees, the sky had darkened considerably.

Julius had to admit that Ruxshin's knowledge of the landscape was helping them advance much faster, but he had no intention of admitting it – he was still ticked off at her.

They climbed the eastern slopes of the hills, trudging over snapped branches and ducking under snow-laden boughs. Their helmets muffled the howling of the wind, but they knew it was still blowing strong from the flurry of white all around them.

'This is the last hill,' announced Ruxshin, sounding relieved and stopping to catch her breath.

The others gathered around her, and stared down the face of a slope that was riddled with firs.

'It's about an hour to the White Glade from here.'

'We'll be quicker than that,' said Kelly. 'You had A'Krad to drag when you were coming up this way.'

Ruxshin nodded and headed down the slope.

Kelly had been right, thought Julius, as he negotiated his way down: thirty minutes in and already the landscape had changed. The tall firs had thinned, to be replaced by larger bushes and feet-entangling roots. A path began to appear in the snow, marked by flat boulders on either side.

Ruxshin must have recognised it, because there was an extra spring in her step as she completed the last portion of the path. 'We made it,' she said, turning to the others. 'The Glade is to the left, but we're going right. Not long now.'

Julius glanced to one side, trying to imagine the place where Morgana's casket had landed. He paused a few extra seconds there, trying to keep his emotions at bay, before re-joining the party.

Eventually, they reached the entrance to the secret tunnel, where Ruxshin turned and looked directly at Julius.

'What ... what is it?' he asked.

'She's in there, in the tunnel.'

Kelly and Skye appeared to have been caught off guard as much as Julius and, for a moment, were unsure how to proceed.

Julius felt his stomach tighten as a flurry of memories rushed to mind. Suddenly he didn't know which way to go. Part of him wanted to see her beautiful face again; on the other hand, he knew that even a glimpse of her would probably jeopardise the tenuous healing process that had just started to mend his heart. Ruxshin didn't need to know this, so he used his mind-skills to speak to the others instead. *'Can you go ahead, please? I don't think I can.'*

'You can both stay behind,' said Kelly. *'I'll take care of it and call you when the coast is clear.'*

Julius nodded and saw a tinge of green in Skye's aura as well - it seemed he wasn't ready for this either.

Maintaining the pretence for Ruxshin's benefit, Kelly motioned for her to join him. 'I want you boys to stay behind and watch our back. I'll go ahead with Ruxshin to check the place out.'

Once the two of them had disappeared inside the tunnel, Skye and Julius moved over to the entrance without speaking, both secretly knowing what the other was thinking. The snow kept falling, wrapping each of them in their own reflections.

It was at least ten minutes before Kelly returned and called them inside.

Julius stooped as he walked along the tunnel, using his hands for balance. His eyes scouted ahead, exploring the rocky path and wondering when he would catch a glimpse of the coffin. As he approached the light at the end of the tunnel, he realised that Kelly was standing to the right hand side, as if to block his view.

'Don't linger! Keep going straight now,' he told them.

Julius swallowed and had to force himself to focus ahead. His eyes were attracted to the shadow on his right, like magnets to iron. When he emerged in Mah Gira's lounge and was able to stand up straight again, he drew a deep, relieved breath.

Kelly stepped inside behind Skye and helped Ruxshin reposition the chest of drawers in front of the opening.

'We made it,' he said, removing his EMU.

Julius did the same and felt the new hair on the back of his body spring up. It was a strange sensation, but oddly pleasant too. He readjusted his outer clothing and fur coat, while his eyes took in the spartan room around him. As the Mahini's leader, he would have expected Mah Gira's home to be more richly furnished than this - in truth though, he preferred it this way; it made him instinctively develop a liking for the man.

'Ruxshin,' said Kelly, 'you will remain here with Skye.'

'But I-'

'You nothing!' he cut her off. 'I'm in charge. Skye has an instrument that will allow you to see Mah Gira and talk to him when we get there. You need to be content with that.'

She didn't seem to like the idea, but was smart enough to know when to let go. 'Fine,' she said despondently. 'Don't get lost, at least.'

'We'll do our best, trust me.'

'Don't worry, Ruxshin,' said Skye, 'I know how to keep you entertained.'

Kelly threw him a serious warning glare, making Skye grin guiltily.

'Err … I'll tell you all about our awesome abilities; that's what I meant! I bet you're dying to know how we stopped that shuttle in mid-air, aren't you?'

Julius shook his head, before pulling his hood up and opening the door onto Mah Gira's small courtyard.

The underground was quite different from what Julius had expected. It was cleaner and brighter, with beautiful Strullium decorations embellishing the streets. Groups of Mahini passed from home to home, their mood sombre and their voices hushed. There were also Arneshian patrols, not en masse, but enough to remind the locals that they were being watched. Julius felt anger rising in him. The Arneshian corruption had finally seeped out of their solar system to infest another. He wondered where Michael was, and what the soldiers had meant when they talked about his "Chamber". The word made him think of Farrah's glass cage - was Michael floating, suspended like she had been? A human computer; a vessel for all Arneshian knowledge? For some reason though, he doubted that.

'*We turn right here,*' said Kelly telepathically, as they crossed one of the squares.

Julius saw two guards hanging around at the corner of one the houses, overseeing the path they were about to take, and tensed.

'*Relax*,' said Kelly. '*Keep your head down and carry on.*'

Julius followed the captain's lead and kept walking, trying to act as inconspicuous as possible. Fortunately, the guards were too busy discussing their R&R plans to pay them much attention, and soon were out of earshot.

The holding block had been an Arneshian addition to the underground, and it stuck out like a sore thumb - a dark rectangular wooden structure, positioned against the natural rocks. The only hint of colour was the reflection of the many Strullium crystals protruding above it.

Julius' eyes moved immediately to the entrance, where one Arneshian was standing guard. '*Any ideas?*'

Kelly slowed and took a good look around. Then he saw something that made him grin. '*Watch this.*'

Julius saw the captain locking his eyes somewhere on the ceiling above the block, and past the soldier. He wasn't sure what Kelly was doing until he noticed a protruding crystal starting to shake in its cradle, slowly at first, but getting steadily faster. Suddenly, it popped out of place, shot off to the right, and crashed against the rocky wall behind the building.

The soldier jumped in fright, before sheepishly checking that no one had seen him. Then he opened his palms, activating the electric disks in them, and edged around the corner in search of the cause of the noise.

Kelly tapped Julius on the shoulder and nodded towards the now unguarded entrance. As soon as the guard disappeared behind the corner, they sprinted forward and sneaked inside, unchallenged.

Julius stared along the long empty corridor ahead. There were four doors on the right hand side, each with a small square window cut into the top halves of the panels. The third one, unlike the others, was ajar. Following Kelly's lead, he moved forward slowly and quietly, observing the opening mechanism for each door. They were old lock-and-key devices, which he had only ever seen in books or museum displays. He wondered how easy it would be to try and force them. The first two cells were empty, but they could hear noises from the open doorway of the next one along. They stopped.

Kelly opened his PIP and selected the camera option, and used it to take a sneaky peek inside, by moving the sensor just beyond the edge of the entrance.

Julius tilted forward to look at the image on the screen. He saw a man sitting at a computer terminal, absorbed in his work. He scanned the surface of the desk and its surroundings; something caught the light, causing a tiny glint. When Julius looked closer, he realised it was a long metal key, resting to the left-hand side of the screen, but still too close to the guard. He pointed it out to Kelly.

'*It's your turn now, McCoy,*' Kelly told him.

Julius went back to the projection on the Captain's PIP, exploring the room further. He spotted a waste bucket on the floor beyond the Arneshian, and grinned. Quietly, he swapped places with Kelly and knelt down, peering around the corner, until his eyes were locked onto the bin. He opened his left hand towards the room and took a deep breath. A small yellow orb began to form above his palm, before turning bright orange as tiny flames erupted all around it, like a miniature sun. Slowly he willed it forward, keeping it so low that it was practically skimming along the floor. The fireball moved silently ahead, dodging the chair's leg until it reached the bucket. There, it began to ascend slowly towards the rim, where it stopped. Julius released more energy and, as the ball grew, he dropped it into the bucket. Whatever was in there instantly caught alight, and the small flame became a lively fire.

Shocked, the man leapt up and hurried around the room erratically, looking for something to put the fire out with. Julius didn't have the luxury of time, so he quickly found the keys with his mind, lifted them from the desk and dragged them towards him, where Kelly was waiting to catch them. They couldn't afford to wait and see the end of the impromptu comedy sketch Julius had created so, with grins on their faces, they tiptoed to the door at the end of the corridor.

Kelly inserted the key in the lock and turned it to the right a few times, until he heard a click. Julius heard footsteps approaching the corridor. Worried that the guard would leave his room, he readied himself to unleash a barrage of mind-skills.

'You need to turn it to the left,' someone whispered from inside the room.

Startled, Kelly did as advised and the door unlocked. He waited for Julius to sidestep inside, then followed and closed the door.

An old man was standing in the middle of the room, a serene expression on his face, his fingers interlaced against his chest. 'Welcome,' he said quietly.

'Mah Gira?' replied Kelly, keeping his voice low.

The man nodded. 'I must be getting older than I thought. There was a time when I knew the faces of all my people.'

'We are not what you think,' replied Kelly, gently pushing Julius away from the door and into a corner, where they both knelt.

Mah Gira moved closer to them, as if waiting to be told a secret.

'I'm Captain Kelly and he's Julius McCoy. We come from Earth.'

'Ruxshin ...' said the man, a trace of hope creeping onto his face.

Julius nodded and opened his PIP, ignoring the stupefied expression of Mah Gira at the sight of this new technology. When the video came to life, Ruxshin's face appeared next to Skye's.

'Mah Gira!' she cried.

Quickly, Skye clamped his hand over her mouth to shush her, while Julius turned the volume down and Mah Gira broke into a fit of pretend coughing.

'Sorry,' she whispered. 'I was so worried about you!'

'My dear girl,' said the Supreme, 'you did it! K'Ssander never said a word – I was afraid you ... Well, I was wrong.'

'Where is Khavar?'

Mah Gira's eyes grew troubled and he looked at his visitors.

'We believe he was taken,' explained Kelly. 'Only Ruxshin made it to us.'

'If he was captured, they haven't brought him here. Knowing Khavar though, I doubt he let them take him without a fight.'

'We'll find him,' said Skye to Ruxshin. He even put an arm around her shoulders for good measure.

'We need your help,' said Kelly. 'We can defeat the Arneshians, but in order to do that-'

'Mah Gira,' interrupted Ruxshin, 'they need to find a statue. Is there an archer statue in Mah?'

The Supreme looked amazed once more. '*The* Archer?'

'Is it real?' asked Julius, wanting to know that his dreams had meant something.

'Yes, but ... how do you know about it?'

'It's a long story,' replied Kelly. 'Suffice it to say that this *Archer* holds the key to another planet – a place where we hope to find powerful allies.'

The old man observed them quietly, while an inner debate was obviously taking place inside his head. He looked at Ruxshin, as if looking for reassurance. 'Hope doesn't amount to much, but it's what has brought you here,' he said eventually. 'What you seek is on top of Mount Mahtab, a ten day trek from here. By the time you reach it, the rainy season will have started – it will be treacherous.'

'We can handle that,' said Kelly.

'Who put it there?' asked Julius.

'The first colony of Mahini brought it with them, when they settled on this planet. We have passed on their story from chief to chief - although, now that you've explained your reasons for wanting to reach it, it seems that there is more to it than meets the eye.'

'I'll want to hear that story when we get back, if you don't mind,' said Kelly, standing. He went to the door to check that the corridor was still clear. 'We will return – that's a promise.'

'I pray you do, Captain. My people didn't stand a chance against the invasion and still aren't able to fight back alone. We are food gatherers - some hunters, by necessity - not soldiers.'

'Hunters, huh? That's a start. They can protect your people when we help you make a stand.'

'Is there someone you can trust?' asked Julius.

Mah Gira thought about that. Then he looked at Skye. 'Young man, go into my courtyard please, and see if there is a black stone tucked under the bench.

Skye hurried to the window. He peered through the curtain, checking first that the coast was clear, before poking his head out and looking for the object. 'I can see it,' he said, being careful to keep his PIP inside the room.

'I need you to move it to the opposite side,' explained Mah Gira. 'All the way to the left.'

Skye nodded, and turned his PIP off.

In the cell, everyone waited with bated breath for a few, long minutes.

When the link came back up, Skye was once again in the safety of the house. 'Done.'

'The stone is a signal,' explained Mah Gira. 'The man I trust will know what to do.'

'Nice trick,' said Julius.

'We need to go now,' said Kelly. 'How do we get to this mountain?'

Mah Gira bent forward. 'There is an underground tunnel that passes under the plateau …'

*

They reached the foot of Mount Mahtab as the last dregs of sunlight were seeping from the sky. In the darkness they made a small camp, using a pop-up tent.

Seeing the tent, Julius thought of the Seffira Cave, when they had set up their base camp on Ahriman the year before. He remembered Morgana advancing through the desert haze like a mirage, carrying one of the larger tents, red sand and blue sky reflecting off her EMU. For a moment, he could almost feel the heat of that day warming his body, but the sensation didn't last long. The sound of the tent popping open brought him back to reality. Its surface was designed to reflect the surroundings, so camouflaging it. As he helped Kelly lay the tent on the ground, it became obvious that it was only large enough for three people. They would need to squeeze in if they all wanted shelter from the icy wind, but perhaps the extra body heat wouldn't be completely unwelcome. He ducked inside and began to remove his boots. Ruxshin entered next, followed by Skye, and they followed suit, placing all the shoes in a recess near the tent's entrance.

Kelly joined them after a few minutes. 'I've set up a protective perimeter,' he said. 'If anything comes close to us, it will trigger our defences.'

'Here,' said Skye, handing a food bar to Ruxshin. 'It will fill you up.'

Julius noticed how she hesitated. When she took it, her aura was tinged with red-and-grey specks of shame, because she knew that neither the food, nor the tent, had been meant for her. Seeing this genuine reaction from her softened his disposition towards her a little.

Kelly grabbed a cup from his rucksack and opened the tent-flap. He scooped some snow into it, before quickly withdrawing his arm.

He poured some of the concentrated hydration fluid over the melting snow and stirred it with a metal spoon. 'I hope your snow's edible,' he said to Ruxshin.

They watched him drink the content in one gulp, waiting to see how he would react.

'It ain't Martian Bile, but it'll do,' he said, before scooping up some more snow for the others.

Under the glow of a small orange tube-light, they ate and drank in silence, the howling sound of the storm muffled by the tent. From the moment Kelly sealed the entire structure by activating the electromagnetic field, the wind simply washed over it, without even causing a ripple. One by one they lay down, trying not to take up too much space.

Julius was on the edge of the mat, with Ruxshin between him and Kelly. He was tired from the long walk, but sleep didn't seem to be forthcoming. He rolled onto his back as gently as he could, but his movements were hindered by the many layers he was wearing. He decided to deactivate his EMU suit and that gave him more breathing space, although he definitely felt cooler than he would have liked. He began to stroke the fur growing on the backs of his hands; it was soft, long and comforting. He found it strange how easy it had been to get used to it.

The light breathing of Ruxshin caught his ear and he turned towards her. She was lying on her left side with both her hands gathered to her face. She seemed peaceful, save for a little crease between her eyebrows. Julius could see her eyes moving beneath the lids and wondered what she was dreaming about. He knew nothing of her, her family or friends. It was obvious that Mah Gira trusted her deeply, or he would not have sent her on such a rescue mission. She definitely seemed a resourceful sort of girl, not easily put down. But then, why did she hate Michael so much? It was clear that something serious had happened between them, something that had scared her. Should he tell her that Michael was his brother?

Ruxshin made a little noise. The dream was obviously agitating her and the furrow on her brow grew deeper. Delicately, he placed his right hand on her shoulder. 'Shhh,' he whispered. 'Shhh.' She stopped fidgeting almost immediately and her breathing became calm again.

A wave of deep sadness washed over him as he observed her delicate features. Not far from him, Morgana slept her endless sleep, with no one to comfort her.

*

With each passing day, the path became steeper and trickier. The snow continued to fall relentlessly, but softer than it had been on their arrival.

'It's close to the change of season,' explained Ruxshin.

Knowing how long the march would take, they had rationed the food and drinks to make them last until they reached the Archer, although feeding a fourth mouth meant that there was definitely less to go around. In exchange for using up part of their provisions, Ruxshin proved herself to be a really useful guide, using her experience of the land to pick the path efficiently, avoiding the most treacherous ways. It was her home world, after all, and she was an experienced hill walker.

Day followed night and they carried on for over a week, seeing nothing but snow. Then, on the morning of Wednesday the 1st of October, Ruxshin stopped onto a large flat ridge, and inspected the sky. 'Captain Kelly,' she said eventually, 'this would be a good time to open that tent of yours and that field thingy you use at night.'

'We can't stop now,' replied Skye. 'We just got up.'

'It's the rain,' she explained. 'It's coming.'

Kelly didn't seem overly convinced, but he had no reason not to trust her, so he opened the tent. 'All aboard.'

Once inside they sat, waiting curiously for this famous Mah downpour, and secretly enjoying the unplanned break. After about ten minutes, they heard a heavy *tock-tock* sound on the top of the tent.

'It's starting,' she told them.

Julius looked up, puzzled. *TOCK. TOCK-TOCK.* He flinched, startled by the loudness of it.

Then, as if a waterfall had materialised right above them, the rain came crashing down. It had happened in a matter of seconds.

'What the-' cried Skye, placing his hands protectively against the roof of the tent, as if he expected it to collapse on their heads.

'You should have seen the Arneshians when they got caught in it, last year,' said Ruxshin, with a cheeky smile. 'One of their guards got himself electrocuted when he tried to use his palm weapon on one of us. Black smoke everywhere.'

The thought made them all grin, then laugh out loud; it seemed a strange sound, because it hadn't been heard for a while, but it was definitely welcome.

'Ahh … priceless,' said Kelly, wiping a tear from his eye.

'Are these fur coats waterproof?' asked Skye.

'If you have replicated them well enough, they will keep you dry. Besides, it's only one more night before we reach the statue.'

'That's good news and no mistake,' said Kelly. 'Suit up, people. We're going swimming.'

One by one, they filed out of the tent, while the rain lashed at their visors. It didn't relent until after sunset, when they reached the top of the last hill.

Julius stopped to catch breath, trying to keep his footing in the muddy river that was washing over his boots. 'This place is *dreich* and dreary,' he vented.

'You should feel right at home then, McCoy,' replied Skye.

'Maybe we could camp here tonight,' volunteered Ruxshin. 'The top isn't far, as you can see, but I wouldn't climb up there in the darkness.'

Julius followed her gaze. He could see the summit easily enough, but the rocky slope leading to it was already covered in a shady curtain. The night would catch them in mid climb and, with the rain turning the ground into slush, heading up was too big a risk. Kelly must have thought the same thing, because he began to set up camp.

They were awake at first light. No one spoke as they got ready, but Julius could tell they were all as excited as he was, judging by the scarlet blotches in their auras. It was, of course, still raining relentlessly and Kelly insisted that they walked within grabbing distance of each other, since there was no rope at hand.

At two thirds of their climb, Julius began to feel uneasy, but didn't know why. At first he thought it was the effect of the altitude making his ears buzz, but then his head began to ache; a dull, remote pain, somewhere in the back of his skull.

'Everything all right, McCoy?' asked Kelly, noticing his distress.

Julius stopped and began to scout the grey sky.

'Did you feel something?'

'I'm not sure. There's some sort of interference though. Don't you feel it too?'

Skye shook his head, but Kelly paused for a moment, his eyes closed.

'What's going on?' asked Ruxshin warily. 'Is it the Arneshians?'

In answer to their questions, there was a rumbling from the lip of the mountain behind them. The ground shook under their feet in one single, long growl.

'Oh crap,' said Skye. 'I say we leg it.'

'Come on then,' said Kelly, hurrying them. 'And watch your feet.'

Julius didn't know what the rumbling was, but he also agreed that they needed to reach the top on the double.

They scampered up the slope, boots slipping on the wet gravel. As they climbed to the peak, the path became narrower as the slopes to either side dropped off. They couldn't see the ground below and, powers or not, they wouldn't survive a fall like that. As the noise behind them grew louder, they began to climb faster, a sense of urgency in their steps. Kelly grabbed Ruxshin by the arm and pulled her along with him.

Skye, who was climbing on all fours, had just turned his head back to check on Julius, when his face lit up in surprise. 'It's the Mazda! The portal worked!'

They all stopped and turned, pointing in excitement at the shadow growing over them. The thunderous noise hadn't subsided though, but seemed to be increasing and coming from different directions.

'Why aren't they stopping?' asked Skye.

In answer, five small Arneshians aircrafts shot up from the bottom of the valley, appearing all around them like water jets in a fountain, and converged on the Mazda, firing as they flew.

'Run!' cried Kelly, starting to sprint, with Ruxshin following.

Julius and Skye were right behind them, keeping their heads low and hoping none of the crafts would notice them.

'Mazda, this is Kelly. Do you read me?' he cried over the noise. 'Do you read me?'

The fight intensified above them. Julius could see the enemy crafts crisscrossing each other as they tried to push the Mazda against the rocky face of the surrounding peaks. Just as he was considering opening his shield, a stray hit burst a hole in the ground a foot away from him. He halted just in time.

Thankfully, Elian's voice carried to them through their EMU systems. 'JD, do you read me?'

'Elian?' he answered, relieved. 'Loud and clear!'

Another voice came through on their coms, that of the Grand Master. 'Kelly, make your way to the statue. We'll cover you.'

'Roger that. How many are in pursuit?'

'Seven at the moment, but there'll be more. You must hurry!'

Julius activated his new shield implants, creating a dome-shaped capsule around him and Skye, who in turn opened his own device to shelter Kelly and Ruxshin. In this tight formation they covered the last six-hundred feet, keeping a wary eye on the battle raging above them.

Having scampered, rather than walked up, they didn't see the statue until they were practically at its feet. The size of the pedestal stopped them in their tracks and they took shelter against its grey, wet stone.

'This thing is so big I actually thought it was part of the mountain,' said Skye, catching his breath.

'I had no idea ...' said Ruxshin, her voice trailing off, equally mystified by its size.

The base was extremely wide. Julius had to take a few steps back before he could actually see the whole statue. 'It's at least sixty feet tall,' he said, awestruck. The statue of the Mahini man looked exactly like it had in his dream, from the fur growing on the back of his body, to his cocked arrow pointing towards an unknown location beyond the grey sky.

'What do we do now?' asked Ruxshin, looking at each one of them in turn, an edge of fear returning to her voice.

A stray shot bounced off their shields, making them all jump.

'I'll not be used for target practice,' said Kelly. 'Skye, double up your shield on top of mine. We'll walk around the base to see if we can activate the arrow somehow. Julius, you'll do the exploring, seeing as you know this *guy* better than we do.'

With the protection in place, Julius began to circle the statue, his palms opened flat against the surface, in case of hidden pressure pads. He looked up and down the smooth rock, keen not to miss anything, but also aware that their shields couldn't withstand a direct attack from several crafts. After a couple of frustrating minutes, he looked at Kelly and shook his head. 'Nothing here.'

'You'll need to go up, then,' he replied. 'How much do you weigh?'

Julius looked confused for a second, but quickly realised what Kelly was thinking. 'I haven't had a doughnut in ages.'

'Skye, cover us while I send McCoy on a mini mission,' he said, closing his shield.

'Huh? Where to?'

'I wish Faith was here,' muttered Julius. 'All right, I'm ready.'

As Kelly focused on Julius, Skye caught on to what the captain was about to do and gave a fresh burst of energy to his shield, which was the only active one they had now.

Julius relaxed and focused on the statue's right arm, which was bent, drawing the string of the bow; as Kelly pushed him up with his mind, he began to use his own skills to pull himself towards it. He let his eyes explore the massive limbs in front of him: feet, legs, knees then thighs. The stone looked as smooth as marble, any signs of age washed away by the constant snow and rain. The ascent was steady, thanks to Kelly's experienced mind-skills, so Julius ceased his own mind-pull and used his hands to explore the material, unsure what he should be looking for.

'Kelly!' cried Skye. 'Craft incoming!'

Julius turned his head, left to right, and spotted it. Kelly must have flinched too, because Julius dropped down a few inches. Adrenaline surged through him and he scrambled to try grab the Archer's arm. His fingertips scraped the huge forearm, which was too big to grab for human-sized hands, but a sudden push forced him upwards again. It was just enough for him to reach the top of the forearm, which was pressed flush against the statue's torso, where he quickly hunkered under the folds of its sculpted clothes. He couldn't see Kelly anymore, as he was now stuck a good 30 feet above the captain, with a perfect view of the enemy shuttle making a beeline for the group at the base.

The Arneshian pilot opened fire as the craft made a fly-by of the ground, sending up a spray of debris and water. Stones and water drops ricocheted off their shields. Ruxshin balled up next to the pedestal, while Skye and Kelly stood over her, focusing on keeping up the protective layers.

'Julius,' called Kelly over their com-system, 'we need both shields to keep us safe from that craft. We'll be distraction enough, but you need to activate that arrow on your own and double-quick.'

'I'm on it …' he replied, '… somehow.' He waited for the craft to move out of sight, then straddled the forearm and slowly began to drag himself towards its wrist. He knew the enemy was no doubt veering back to renew its attack. However, it was tricky going, as the pouring rain had rendered the stone too slippery for hurrying. He edged forward, focusing on the statue's cupped hand. He could see the stony feathers at the back of the arrow, clasped within the Archer's thick fingers and palm. A sort of alcove had been created within it, and Julius knew he would have to pass through it in order to go further.

When he reached the base of the thumb, he twisted and stretched his left hand forward towards the fletching, but couldn't quite reach it. He tensed and pushed his body towards it to cover the last few inches. His hand grasped the top line of the feathers, and he dragged himself forward, sliding off the hand. Julius did his best to avoid looking down as he dangled in the air. With his right hand, he grabbed another section of fletching. His nose was almost touching the nock, the little notch in the rearmost end of the arrow - he could see the string, delicately sculpted, passing through it, as the bow was being drawn. The shaft ran between the index and forefinger of the Archer's right hand, creating a gap wide enough for him to squeeze through. Edging slowly, he moved as close to it as he could, before heaving himself up and planting the tip of his right boot on one of the protruding fingertips. There, perched like a bird, he gave himself a moment to look around for anything unusual.

'Captain,' he said to Kelly, 'I'm on the arrow.'

'Anything?'

'Nope. I think I need to move forwa-'

'Damn!' Kelly interrupted. 'He's back.'

Julius looked down, fighting a sense a vertigo, and saw the craft flying toward the pedestal. He tried to lock onto it, hoping to push it away with his mind, but it was flying erratically, and dipped from view just when he thought he had a clear shot. Skye and Kelly were firing blasts of energy at the shuttle, but they weren't strong enough to do any real damage. Only the Ahura could save them at this point.

On cue, Freja's voice came over the com: 'McCoy, what's your position?'

Julius scouted the sky and saw the Mazda surrounded by an increasing swarm of small crafts, in the middle of a frantic battle. 'Precarious, sir,' he replied. 'I'm on the arrow shaft, but there's nothing here that looks useful.'

'We're kiting the enemies for the moment, so they keep focusing on us, but it's a game that can't last too long. We'll have to fire back soon – their number is growing fast.'

It was true, but what was he supposed to do about that? It was a miracle he had reached this spot at all.

'Julius,' said Freja, 'think of your dream. Any detail may help at this point.'

'Roger, sir,' he replied. Closing his eyes, he turned his mind to Eneamar and his visions of it. Whenever he had reached the statue in his dream, there had been someone there waiting for him. Generally, it was Eronan, though Morgana had also been there once. He revisited the sequence of events, but nothing stood out immediately. Neither Eronan, nor Morgana, had touched anything on the statue, yet the beam of light had emitted from the arrowhead every time. 'Yes, but every time after *what*, exactly?' he said aloud.

'Are you talking to us, Julius?' said Skye.

He ignored the question and stayed focused. 'What's the damn constant of all the dreams?' he said aloud again.

'McCoy?' said Kelly, this time sounding worried.

Julius could feel the right memory dancing at the edge of his consciousness. He forced all other thoughts from his mind and took a deep breath, creating an inner space of calm and concentration. As the chaos and anxiety drifted away, the answer appeared to him clear as day. 'The name! They both said *its name* …'

'McCoy, what's going on?' pushed Kelly.

'I think I know how to do it!' he cried, excited. 'Grand Master, you need to pick the team up now. Then get the Arneshians away from here and be ready to do a flyby to get me as soon as I say so.'

'Sure, but …' started Freja.

'Trust me, sir, there's not much time left.'

He looked towards the Mazda and saw it veering their way, with a thick train of Arneshian planes on its tail. He stuck his head between the Archer's fingers and began to pull himself onto the shaft, until he was fully resting on it. The raindrops bounced off the surface, splashing against his visor, making it harder to see clearly. His EMU was supposed to help him blend against the rock surface, making him a less obvious target for the enemies, but unfortunately it was buried under the thick leather coat. As he dragged himself forward, he saw the Mazda coming to a halt between the crafts and the group, before opening one of its lower ports.

'We have a teleportation gate, Julius!' cried Skye. 'We'll come get you.'

'Just go, Skye. Now!' he shouted, shimmying along. The left hand of the statue was right in front of him, with the thick bow secured in its palm and the arrowhead just beyond the fingers. He climbed over the left index and stood tall, with his arms fastened around the bow. He looked down, briefly, and saw that the others had been safely retrieved by Freja. The sky was getting ever darker, not because of rainclouds, but on account of the growing number of Arneshian shuttles.

The Mazda's shields were taking strain from all directions, until one section became fully exposed, allowing the enemy to land a couple of direct blows. Julius saw smoke drifting from the hull, before the ship regained altitude and zoomed away, with the Arneshians in pursuit.

'You're clear, McCoy,' said Freja. 'Whatever you want to try, do it fast.'

'Roger, sir,' he replied. He waited for the group to move completely away, before attempting to activate the beam – the last thing he needed was an Arneshian spectator. When he felt safe enough, he crouched down, holding on to the Archer's finger, and removed his visor. The wind and rain lashed at his face, but he ignored them. Taking a deep breath, he shouted the only word he had ever heard uttered in his dreams with the Archer: 'Mah.'

There was a slow rumbling and the statue began to shake. It felt as if whatever was causing it was rising from the very depths of the mountain. Julius tightened his hold on the bow, to prevent himself from slipping off. Then he looked at the arrowhead, and was gobsmacked by what he saw. The point had become piping hot, boiling the droplets of water on its surface and evaporating any raindrops before they struck it. The grey stone had turned yellow as a result of the intense heat, and Julius tried to shield his face behind the bow, fearing that the rock would explode. The heat converged at the tip of the arrow, where it lingered for a moment, before shooting outward so violently that Julius had to hold on for dear life. The beam pierced the grey clouds, vaporising every drop in its path, and disappeared out beyond view.

'You did it!' Skye said over his com-link. 'Now what?'

Unfortunately, Julius didn't really know how to answer that. 'Can't we just follow it?' he said.

'What, with the Arneshians in tow?'

'Any other ideas, then?'

No one answered him for a while, which wasn't reassuring in the least. Then, unexpectedly, Faith came online.

'McCoy, do me a favour, will you?'

'As long as it doesn't involve me climbing down.'

'Find something to throw – something heavy.'

Julius paused, baffled. But, this was Faith, and he had no reason to argue with that kind of brain. He opened his coat and searched the utility belt of his EMU. There was a spare retractable snap-hook attached to it. 'Got it.'

'I want you to cast it into the beam.'

'What for?'

'Testing a theory. Indulge me.'

'All right then. Here goes nothing.' Cradling the hook in the palm of his hand, he focused his mind on it and slowly lifted it using his mind-skills. The steel carabiner floated up and forward until it was right above the beam. Carefully, he lowered it towards the yellow ray.

At least, that was what he had planned to do. As soon as the object was within a few inches of the beam, it was sucked into it and whisked away by the stream. A millisecond later, he was pulled after it.

THE COUNCIL OF ENEAMAR

He found himself in a conduit that appeared to have no solidity, zooming forward so fast that all he could make out was bright, cold light streaming past him. The speed at which he was moving kept his arms pinned alongside his body; no matter how much he tried, he couldn't shift them an inch. After the first immediate reaction of shock, fear started to force its way into his consciousness, as it dawned on him that he was going to be lost in space until death took him; this seemed to be the only outcome he could see.

Abruptly, he was brought to a halt, as if someone had grabbed the back of his suit at the waist, and held fast. His arms and legs shot forward and the air was forced from his lungs. Sharp pain jolted through his body, wiping all thoughts away, leaving him in a state of clarity.

He was floating in space, a foot away from a blanket of interweaving beams – "energy beams" was the closest description that sprung to his mind. They contained lights and colours, of the same kinds he knew, but in the coldest tones he'd ever seen. Interspersed throughout them was a nebula, a sort of dust that filled the voids of this unnatural tapestry, bestowing it with a kind of sandy appearance. Julius stuck his fingers through one of the beams, but nothing happened, except that the flow of particles – or whatever they were – flowed around the obstacle. There was no apparent pattern he could see, and yet, there was an indefinable order. The problem though was that there was nothing for him to aim for – no planet, or station; nothing that equated to *safety*. Was he even in space, or was this a pocket within it?

Julius turned around, to see if there was something behind him that he had missed, refusing to let panic take over completely. That was when the Ahura Mazda materialised a short distance from him. He screamed inside his helmet, watching helplessly as the massive bulk of the ship ploughed towards him. 'STOP!' he cried with his mind, hoping someone would hear him; but the ship just kept on coming. Julius lifted his arms in front of him, bracing for the impact.

A few seconds passed, and nothing happened, so he dared to open one eye. That was when he saw Faith and a furless Skye behind the glass of the Upper War Deck, banging against it, to try attract his attention. It seemed like they couldn't hear him over his com-link, or even telepathically. Relief washed over Julius. Just like him, it seemed that the Mazda had been halted before it could hit the weave of beams. Faith was motioning for him to wait there, but then stopped, eyes fixed to a point beyond Julius.

'What?' he mouthed. 'What is it?' Faith didn't answer. Julius looked at Skye, who motioned for him to turn around, so he did.

There was a bright spot inside the weave. It illuminated the space around it for a moment, before settling into a more subdued tone. It moved towards them. Julius flinched backward instinctively; he bumped against the hull of the Mazda and began to scamper upwards, until he was perched against the window. To his left and right, his friends, together with Kelly, who was now also furless, and Freja, were mesmerised, witnessing this phenomenon.

When the nebula reached Julius, it stopped, illuminating his face and suit as if it was dawn. Julius stared at it, transfixed. Cautiously, he reached his hand toward it and touched its surface. This made it glow a little brighter. He retracted his hand again.

A face began to emerge from the vapour, one that they all knew well. Soon, Eronan was gazing at them, smiling. He wasn't wearing any sunglasses, as he had been many of the other times they had seen him; in such close proximity, this allowed Julius to really appreciate the peculiarity of his eyes – they reflected the light off the many tiny sections that made up their surface, just like a diamond would. In this way, they didn't seem to have any one discernible colour, except for the dark pupils. Eronan's body began to slowly materialise in front of them, from his red robe to the eerie luminescence around the collar that had puzzled them for so long, but that now made sense. *No wonder he's been around for ages*, thought Julius. *He's incorporeal.*

'I have not seen humans for some time,' said Eronan suddenly. He looked at the Mazda, then at the faces behind the ship's glass, before settling his eyes on Julius. 'And from Zed, no less. Why have you come?'

Julius had to swallow before he could manage to speak – his mouth had gone dry. 'You … you said you can help us defeat the Arneshians … when I was on the Guardian's Trail.'

'A seeker of the crystal, I see.' Eronan seemed pleased.

Julius nodded. 'I'm the one who won it.'

'Then you better come in.' With that, he lifted his arms to his sides, his hands touching the energy beams around him.

As if activated by an unspoken command, the beams started to shift, still surrounded by the sandy dust. They bent and twisted, slowly at first, then faster, until the dust became a whirlwind, eventually obscuring the view like a desert storm.

A sudden gust of wind blew the nebula towards the Ahura. Julius instinctively brought his arms up to shield his face, but he felt no push against his body, as a real wind would have done. He looked up and, to his perfect astonishment, the sand washed away, leaving him and the ship docked on what appeared to be the seaport of a marine city. He looked behind at the rest of the crew, but they were just as hypnotised by the scenery as he was.

A spaceship the size of the Mazda could never have landed on a planet like a shuttle could, let alone dock like a sea vessel. Yet here it was, resting in a huge enclosure filled with ocean water, like a majestic cruise liner. Noisy flocks of seagulls dotted the blue skies over the city, their shapes crisp and defined in the clean air. Tall glass buildings littered the skyline, some of them bent into arches over lower edifices. Parks and green spaces were planted around the city, including numerous hanging gardens that clung to the structures.

Julius was the only one who had seen this city before – albeit only in his dreams – and instantly knew he was in Eneamar. He slid down the front of the Mazda, and landed safely on the pier, then watched as the crew emerged from one of the escape hatches above water level.

'Julius, are you all right?' called Faith, hovering over to him. He wasn't wearing his EMU. 'You have no idea the fright you gave us when you disappeared on Mah!'

'You're telling me. I thought I was done for.'

'Here,' he said, pulling out an injector. 'For your *de-furring* … and remove your suit – we seem to be fine without them.'

Julius did this, and allowed Faith to administer the antidote to the left side of his neck. 'That stings,' he said, as an unpleasant tingling nipped at the areas of his body that were covered in fur. He looked at the backs of his hands and saw that the fur was slowly retracting, as if growing smaller, before disappearing completely. It was as odd a sensation as he'd ever felt.

Freja, Kelly, Ruxshin and Skye joined them shortly afterwards, while the rest of the crew remained aboard the ship.

Eronan, who had just silently stood watching, finally moved towards them. Unsure what to do, they bowed to him and Ruxshin followed suit.

'True Tijarans,' he said, bowing back. 'Welcome to Eneamar. And also to you,' he added, to Ruxshin, 'child of the Mahini.'

'Thank you …' Freja paused, unsure how to address him.

'Eronan will do.'

'I am Carlos Freja.'

'Tijara's Grand Master,' he said, admiring his uniform. 'I am given to understand that you need my help?'

'We do. I'm sure you remember the Arneshians. They must be stopped, and it seems we are losing that fight.'

Eronan regarded him intently before answering. 'Let us go inside.'

It seemed to Julius that Freja sighed with relief at the invitation and could understand why – now they would have a chance to plead their case. These people - or whatever they were - constituted their only hope, so they followed Eronan along the dock towards the city entrance.

'Sir,' said Faith eagerly, 'let me tell you, this place is grand, if I may say so.'

Eronan smiled, but didn't stop walking.

Faith took this as an invitation to ask a few questions. 'Where are we? I mean, I can tell this isn't like our cities, but … how do you do it?'

'Eneamar is a vision, you could say; a construct. Normally I exist as energy, but I can interact with matter. The shapes you see all around you are the forms I choose to assume in order to interact with you. This,' he said, gesturing at the city around him, 'makes sense to you humans, and so I project it for your benefit.'

'So the beams we saw … it was you?'

'Precisely. That is how I exist.'

'You are a network … of one?'

'Yes, you could say that.'

'Wow. And do you have a name? I mean, how do we call your kind?'

'Names of this sort are an enjoyment of Earthlings; I have no need for it. Perhaps *you* can think of something suitable.'

'That would be awesome!'

'This part of the city seems to be empty,' ventured Ruxshin, 'but you're saying it isn't?'

'I *am* the city, young Mahini. There is no need for more than my appearance right now; but rest assured, the whole place is listening.'

'Wow,' said Faith, awestruck at his surroundings. 'So I'm actually hovering *through* you. Just wow.'

'You populated it for Farrah,' said Julius, before he could stop himself.

'She told you, did she?' he replied, amused, but volunteered no further explanation.

Julius didn't think it was the right moment to probe further, so didn't push it, but his curiosity hadn't been appeased. Certainly, Eronan was real and standing in front of them, but he, or *it*, was something unlike anyone or anything they had ever met: the first alien life form they'd encountered. He felt a sense of awe at this long awaited moment.

Eronan ushered them inside a small, cubic glass building. It contained a silver rectangular table surrounded by chairs, with potted plants along the walls. It was illuminated by the sunlight, but it didn't feel hot or stuffy – a cool breeze drifted across the room, even though there was no sign of wind, judging by the stillness of the plants.

They sat around the table, leaving the top chair for their host. Julius could sense hesitation in the Grand Master, as if he didn't know where to start.

It was Faith who broke the ice. 'Are you God, by any chance?'

The fact that no one scoffed at him was sign enough that it was a mighty good question, thought Julius.

'Ah! An interesting word that, is it not?' Eronan smiled inscrutably. 'I'm more of a *custodian* though – you could call me that.'

'Of what? Who are *you*?' Faith was determined to get to the bottom of this.

'I simply am and always was, young Earthling. I choose to make, to watch, to nurture. My dealings with your planet span thousands of years – you have always fascinated me. I have observed you, unseen, encouraging life to flourish in the midst of natural upheaval; gave you ways of surviving when the planet said *stop*. Sometimes it worked, sometimes it didn't.'

'For some people,' said Kelly, 'that would be reason enough to quit meddling.'

Though Freja raised an eyebrow at his son's tone, Eronan didn't seem offended by the implication; on the contrary, it brought back his enigmatic smile. 'You could say that I enjoy directing humanity towards improvement – and I say *directing*, not forcing. With every attempt, I change the circumstances, but leave you free rein as to what to do with it. I offer my help, without assuming it will be accepted. You're a very adaptable race.' Behind his head, a picture formed, similar to a holographic representation. It showed the North Pacific Ocean, with an unfamiliar feature: what looked like an island, surrounded by four smaller ones.

'Um ... where is that?' Skye wasn't the only one looking confused at the image.

'Or you could ask, *when*? Earth was young then. This was my first project and, although it didn't work out quite as planned, it served its purpose. It brought you Marcus Tijara as a matter of fact. But that is another story.'

'So the fact that you keep coming back means we aren't improving very much, right?' Kelly still felt the need to dig deeper.

'Yes and no. I found it fascinating that a species such as yours survived despite the limitations of your physical bodies and your propensity for self-annihilation. However, in the twenty-first century, it became clear that, in order to avoid extinction, you would need to expand outside the boundaries of your planet. I decided to help the humans once more, starting with *her* people,' he said, pointing at Ruxshin. As he talked, a new image appeared.

Immediately Julius, Skye and Faith sat up, recognising the scene as the one they had found in the archives of Ahriman. It was 2020, and Eronan was shaking hands with Captain Gorghinian, surrounded by families and their suitcases.

'Mahin Space Enterprise,' he continued. 'They were eager to leave, so I helped them. I believed that one day they could provide a safe haven for their mother planet.'

'I don't look like those people,' said Ruxshin, observing the hairless features of the families in the scene.

'I gave them modifications once they were on Mah,' answered Eronan. 'Your planet was the closest habitable one available. Its atmosphere was chemically similar to that of Earth, only colder and damper. I had no choice but to introduce some genetic mutations into the colonists, like the fur. After that, the colony settled down and a new life began. Hopeful, I moved on, but not before leaving them with a means of getting in touch.'

'The Archer,' said Ruxshin.

'Precisely. It was to be the duty of your leaders to pass on its secret to their successors.'

'Hmm … I think that part didn't come out so well,' observed Kelly. 'A *Chinese Whisper* problem.'

'You are here, no?' replied Eronan, satisfied. '400 years after the Mahin mission left, it was evident that Earth was heading towards a slow, painful death with no space expansion to speak of.'

Julius knew what he meant, as he had studied this in his History classes: the complete breakdown of society had exacerbated deeper unresolved issues; drought, famine, depletion of resources; wars and diseases had worsened, leaving Earth on the brink of collapse.

'The people of Mah,' continued Eronan, 'had surprisingly reverted to a lower level of technology than the one they had left behind and were in no shape to become the rescuers I had envisioned. That is why I came back, to save your people from themselves.'

'And how exactly did you do that?' asked Kelly.

Eronan looked at Freja, who stared back in anticipation. 'It was agreed that the only way out was to help you become more … efficient, and better equipped to overcome your technological setbacks. I gave you the White and Grey skills, creating people like Marcus and Clodagh. And they did it; they brought the change.'

'But *how* did you give them those skills?' urged Kelly.

'It happened as a result of the Chemical War; that is how I gifted you.'

'*Gifted us?*' said Kelly, sitting up. 'You killed 12 billion people. How is that a gift?'

'JD,' began Freja, putting his hand on his son's forearm.

Kelly motioned for his father to wait. He wasn't finished by a long stretch. 'And who allowed this to happen?'

'Some of your own people did, on behalf of the human race. It was their intelligence that put them in charge.'

'Sorry to burst your bubble, Eronan, but humans aren't always renowned for their intelligence, otherwise we would not have needed your help.'

'So what are you renowned for then, Captain?'

'Our heart. Our *goodness*. That's how we function, and that's what has kept Earth from extinction for billions of years.'

'Alas, your time will come.'

'Then why help us? Why help Marcus?'

'Because sometimes, just sometimes, the odds are tipped by the smallest improbability, with the power to affect the whole universe.'

Freja gripped Kelly's arm again, and this time he did settle back in his chair.

Julius' felt his very soul stirred by Kelly's questioning of Eronan, along with the answers he'd received; he could see the others had been similarly affected. The War obviously had a whole hidden story behind it that he would never know about. But another question needed to be asked: 'I saw you when I was on the Trail. You told Tijara that you could reverse the effects of the Chemical War.'

'And why would you wish me to do that?' he asked calmly.

'The Arneshians strive to become the most evolved group there is, no matter how, or what it costs. Besides, you said it yourself: they could be *the smallest improbability with the power to affect the whole universe*; they could tip the odds.'

'And what is wrong with that? Isn't their victory survival also?'

Julius was about to tell him what they had witnessed of Michael's new abilities, back on Mah, but the Grand Master was ready to have his say.

'The skills you gave us worked for the majority of people, but not all. You know that the Arneshians went rogue from the time of Marcus and Clodagh. Centuries later, they are still bringing death;

only, this time, in another system – yours. You said you *nurture* life, but it *has* to matter what kind of life you allow to flourish. My son is a hothead,' he said, placing his hand on Kelly's shoulder, 'but he said it right: it is humanity's goodness that has kept us alive for so long. No more, no less. And I think you know that, Eronan.'

'You're partly correct,' said Eronan. 'You think it is goodness that defines your race because you are good people – or at least as close to this as the concept of goodness allows – however, it is adaptability that has allowed humans to survive; your greater ability to evolve and tame the world around you. Good and bad are relative concepts and so don't define my choices.'

Freja pressed on: 'We could argue semantics all day, but your trail of *interventions* on Earth speaks for itself – you've always helped the *right* sort of people, the ones willing to bring *improvement*. The land of Mah that you created is no more. Arnesh has seen to that. Her people,' he said, pointing at Ruxshin, 'are enslaved as we speak, dying under the Arneshians' fists. And Zed isn't strong enough. They've reached a point that puts them beyond our grasp, creating an invincible leader for themselves. That's why we're here. That's why we risked everything to find you. It was based on Julius' dream and his memories of the Trail, but it was all we had left. Now, you said you can help us, like you wanted to help Marcus. You built the Trail for Gelar Ganan, to protect Marcus' legacy and you planted the information in the crystal for the right seeker to find – otherwise, why show Julius those conversations? Tell me I'm not right.'

Eronan stood and went to stand by the window overlooking the dock and the Mazda anchored in it. 'Yes, the Ocluths were my doing. They got out before it was too late, unlike Tijara, and accepted becoming the guardians of his powers. And yes, there is *always* a solution,' he said, finally facing his guests, 'but it could be worse than the problem itself. Are you sure you want to hear this?'

Julius nodded and so did the others.

'Purification,' he said. 'I deactivate all the pearls, permanently. A complete reset.'

'You don't mean another "Heart" machine, do you?' said Julius, alarmed.

'No. I can remove the skills once and for all – the pearls are all linked to my … network, for want of a better word – I can shut them all down at once, although the Arneshian leader will require something extra, I wager.'

'Hey … we have pearls too,' said Skye, getting worried. 'You don't mean *us* too, do you?'

'As I said, all the pearls, *permanently*. It would cause a levelled restart to all.'

Julius' jaw dropped, and a heavy silence descended on the room.

'Once their leader is defeated,' continued Eronan, 'I can begin with the humans on Mah – the Arneshians are a priority, you would agree. Then I would move on to your system. In my pure form I can purge all human habitats, even simultaneously if you wish me to.'

Along with trying to cope with the absurd finality of the plan, Julius' mind kept returning to the *defeat of the leader* part - did he mean killing Michael right before handing over all his powers for a second time? There was no way he could go through with that.

'If this is all you can offer us, it is an important decision to make, Eronan,' said Freja eventually. 'Unlike my ancestors, I cannot speak for humanity. I will need to bring it to our people. We will need a referendum.'

'You can't be seriously consid-' began Julius, stupefied, but Freja raised his hand, motioning for him to be quiet.

'I understand,' answered Eronan. 'I can help you return to your system, unhindered and unseen.'

'How much time will you give us?'

'How much time can *her* people hold out?'

Freja nodded and stood. 'Give us a month, then,' he said.

'It's too long!' complained Ruxshin, visibly unhappy.

Freja ignored her though. 'We shall return with an answer.' He beckoned for his crew to follow him outside, leaving Eronan within.

Julius looked at Skye and Faith. He really didn't much care about Ruxshin's feelings just then – she'd never had mind-skills and so wouldn't know the difference they made. How could they give it all up? The others stared back at him miserably, like animals in a cage, trying to look for a way out that wasn't there.

THE FORUM SPEAKS

Julius observed the people in the Mazda's ready room as they quietly talked to each other in small groups. Freja was deep in conversation with the GMs of Tuala and Sield, Roland Kloister and Edwina Milson, while Kelly sat to one end of the table with the Earth Leader, Paulo Trent, and the Curio Maximus, Aldobrando Roversi. He looked deeply upset, and with more grey hair than ever.

First, Freja had to explain the importance and impact of Eronan's actions on human space history, and the improbable, yet real, form of existence of the alien: a being of pure energy. His hand reached far, and he had proven to be a trustworthy ally to Earthlings. Then Freja broke the news in the clearest possible way, explaining how Eronan's solution came with the heaviest price tag any of them would ever have to pay. Just like Julius, their reaction was one of incredulity. Eventually, considering Eronan's knowledge of Earth's history, and confirmation from the Ocluths that he had indeed been responsible for their settlement, they were convinced that he truly intended to help them.

'I need to return to Earth,' announced Trent to the room, at the end of the consultation.

'Very well, Paulo,' replied Freja. 'We have agreed to hold the referendum on Friday the 31st of October – it should give us enough time to inform the people and organise the voting.'

'I will send an envoy to the five members of the Federation,' added Roversi, 'and when this is over, we shall add another star to our new flag, for the Mahini.'

'So let it be,' said Milson.

'So let it be,' echoed everyone in the room.

The meeting ended then and, as he was walking past, Freja stopped by Julius. 'You will need to assemble the Forum. Once the information is out, you must be there for them, and so must Shanigan. You will leave tomorrow at noon. Miller and Ruxshin too, if they wish to join you.'

Julius didn't feel particularly excited at the prospect, which didn't escape the Grand Master.

'What is it?'

Julius had been quiet throughout the conference, but he could not leave the room without speaking his mind. 'Permission to speak freely, sir.'

'Granted.'

'Quite frankly, I find it baffling that everyone went right ahead with the referendum without considering other options first.'

'Such as?'

'How about fighting the Arneshians without giving up who we are, for example?' He was aware that his voice was rising slightly, and he tried hard to keep it at bay. 'All of you in this room have had less than four days to digest the news. Yet today you all voted for the referendum. You told Eronan that you couldn't decide for the race, but don't you see that today's call to vote has already set the wheels in motion? You have decided for us all.'

Freja pondered his words. 'I cannot live with the alternative, Julius,' he said eventually. 'Removing the choice from our people altogether is essentially deciding for them. I'm sorry.' And with that, he left the room.

Faith and Skye walked in as soon as the coast was clear, but one look at Julius' face told them all they needed to know.

'When?' asked Skye, downcast.

'The end of the month. And Faith, we are off to the Forum tomorrow. Freja says you and Ruxshin can come too, Skye.'

'Back to Ahriman then, huh? I can't imagine what else I would do here, anyway,' he said.

Faith's expression, on the other hand, improved visibly and Julius knew why. 'Siena will be happy to see you.'

'When did she move there?' asked Skye.

'Her post started on the 1st of October,' replied Faith. 'She's Junior Assistant to one of the Curiates: the Vietnamese De Bui. So yes, at least I'll get to see her this month. What about you, Skye? Any news from Valentina?'

'Nah,' he said, sounding quite chilled. 'Distances don't agree with us very much. We'll probably have clandestine affairs until old age takes us and we can't boogie anymore.'

'Amen to that,' said Faith.

Ruxshin was quite excited at the prospect of landing on a new planet. Deep down, Julius could understand this: a plan to rescue her people would shortly materialise, while she was travelling to Funesto, where she would meet new people and even have access to some of her own Mahin history. But, for some reason, tiredness being one of them, her happiness ticked him off, until he could no longer restrain it. 'Hey, Ruxshin,' he said, just before they landed.

She looked up, smiling.

'You know that you will have to vote too, right? As a representative of the Mahini, no less.'

Her smile faltered. 'I … I guess so?'

'And I'm guess you'll vote a big fat Yes too.'

Skye and Faith turned to him.

'What are you doing, Jules?' asked Faith. 'It's not her fault, you know?'

Julius knew this, but he still felt like he needed to vent a bit more. 'All you ever wanted was for your people to be free – that's why you came to us, right? And if it takes all we have to help *you*, then so be it.'

Ruxshin looked away, growing visibly uncomfortable.

'She has no skills; why should she vote?' he continued.

'That's a fair point,' said Skye, stepping in, 'but still not her fault. Bring it to Freja - the first feedback

for the Forum.'

Julius sighed, and finally let it rest. He knew it was petty, but he felt better for having said it; a little payback for her using Morgana against him like she had, back on the Mazda. He was slowly discovering that a little bit of coldness went a long way when releasing stress. No one else seemed to care about what really mattered, so why should he?

Just like the first time they'd arrived there, Milan Todorov welcomed them on the landing pad. He stood there in his usual obsequious manner, but he faltered a little when he saw Ruxshin's fur.

'He's the Secretary of the Curiates,' Faith explained to her quietly. 'A bit bonkers, but nice.'

Todorov was too well trained to betray more than the smallest hint of surprise. He took them to their quarters, before showing them the Forum room, which was accessible from the main courtyard of the Halls. Just as they were about to enter, Siena called out to them.

'Hey! You made it!'

Faith welcomed her with open arms, followed by Julius and Skye. Julius was always happy to see her, perhaps because of the close connection she'd had with Morgana.

'You must be Ruxshin,' she said, giving the Mahini a hug.

Ruxshin was taken aback by the gesture, but the kind expression on Siena's face relaxed her immediately. 'Hello,' she ventured.

'Come inside, guys,' she said, opening the door. 'The preparations are already underway.'

The Forum was shaped like an amphitheatre, with marble steps descending towards a circular inner floor. Large screens were dotted around the room, positioned at different heights.

'It reminds me of the Hologram Palace's waiting area,' said Skye. 'I like it.'

'I've been assigned to liaise between you and the Curiates,' Siena explained. 'I shall pass on all orders to Julius, as the Forum Leader, and to you Faith, as one of the people's experts.'

'When do we start?' asked Julius, stepping down to the lower floor.

'A full broadcast has been sent out to all humans one hour ago and you can expect the delegates to arrive from as early as tomorrow.'

Julius turned and looked up at her, surprised. 'So soon?'

'With a decision like this to make, you'll have a full house. And the press, of course. I suggest you spend today getting familiar with the issue, because people will come to you for advice.'

'Well, that's easy enough,' said Skye. 'He'll just tell them to vote *No.*'

'Even more reason to be prepared. There will be some who would prefer a reset for everyone – especially those who have been jealously wishing they had mind-skills.'

Julius knew she was right. 'Sure. Send me what you have and I'll get ready.'

That afternoon, while Todorov escorted Ruxshin on a tour of the complex, Julius, Skye and Faith lay sprawled across the steps, poring over the videos and the communications that had gone out to the

GFE that morning. Whoever had written the reports had managed to stay neutral, stating the facts as plainly as possible – even Julius had to admit that. Every so often, one of them would ask a question, pretending to be a *Yes* voter, and they took it in turns coming up with convincing counterpoints.

Around 20:00 hours, Siena took them for dinner in the Curia's social complex, a more relaxing place than the daily canteen used by the workers. It was the kind of place where visitors and diplomats could be seen, as well as the off-duty officers. It had several areas, from bars to cafes to different food outlets – it wasn't as big as Satras, but it had enough choice. They opted for a pizzeria and it wasn't until they sat down that they realised Ruxshin didn't know what they were talking about.

'Pizza?' she asked, curiously eyeing the large wood-fire oven.

'I think the best way is to just try one,' said Siena, showing her a menu. 'What do you like?'

Ruxshin looked at the list of ingredients, completely baffled, and had to admit defeat after a minute or so. 'You couldn't order for me, could you?'

'I'll take care of it,' said Skye. When the waiter arrived, he asked for a margherita with extra mozzarella and a glass of beer. 'Let's start simple,' he said. 'You'll like it.'

And of course, he was right. The pizza had a thin and crispy base, with slightly charred edges, courtesy of the wood fire. The smell of oregano and cheese wafted to Ruxshin's nostrils, making her stomach gurgle. She took up the beer tanker, aware of the little cold droplets covering the outside of the glass. Hesitantly, she brought it to her lips and took a sip.

Julius, like everybody else, was watching her, waiting to see her reaction. When she looked up and smiled, he couldn't help but grin, at least for a few seconds. He had decided to be mad at her, and he wasn't done yet.

They stayed at their table for a couple of hours, discussing the situation. Siena wanted to know everything about Eronan and, only after hearing it all, she allowed Faith to take her away for a walk. Julius had half a mind to ask Ruxshin what had happened between her, K'Ssander and Michael, to make her so frightened, but changed his mind. He had enough reasons to hate them as it was; besides, he didn't need to take on her problems too, on top of those of her whole planet. With that in mind, he also took his leave, but not before sending Skye a mind-message reminding him about what might happen to any illegitimate *kittens*.

Siena had been right: the first delegates began to arrive from the early hours of Tuesday morning. Todorov was busy ushering them all inside, first to their rooms and then to the Forum, logging their presence in the central system, so that Julius would know exactly who was there and where they were from. By lunchtime, Todorov had to enlist the help of several colleagues, because the number of people landing had shot to the stars in a way they could not have anticipated.

'Schedule the first meeting tonight at 16:00,' Siena advised Julius. 'You'll need two a day until the referendum.'

And so Julius did. He scheduled one for that evening, then a morning slot, from 10 to noon, and a later one from 16:00 to 18:00. He knew that, as they got closer to the vote, he would need more time, but this would do to start with.

That afternoon, the Forum was officially declared open and a stream of people entered the room, sitting down on the steps until there was no space left. Siena was seated at a table on the lower floor, ready to take notes and moderate as needed. Julius stood next to her, looking around calmly. He had reminded himself that, in order to win the referendum, he would need to use his weight as a White Child, so he needed to look assured and credible – no space for stage-fright. He waited for the last of the delegates to arrive before motioning to Skye to close the doors.

Julius had decided to begin the meeting by replaying the broadcast they had all received. He knew people had seen it already, but it was essential that Eronan's solution, proposed by the Curio Maximus, was understood thoroughly. When the video ended, the assembly turned in his direction.

'Welcome to the Forum of the Galactic Federation of Earth,' he began, his voice steady and clear. 'I am Julius McCoy and I have been appointed as leader of this assembly. Thank you all for coming.'

The crowd murmured its assent and a few shouts of "Hear, hear!" echoed around the room.

Heartened, Julius continued. 'It seems that the first decision this council will discuss may very well also be the last; because, rest assured, a *No* vote will bring consequences that none of us can foresee.'

'And what would you recommend?' called a voice from the crowd.

Julius looked around until he found its owner: a male in his twenties, wearing civilian clothes.

'Can you state your name, please?' called Siena, professionally, but firmly.

'Alano Tirosky, from Colonial 2.'

'As a civilian from one of the Earth colonies, I assume you have no mind-skills, correct?' he asked him, trying to sound non-confrontational.

'I am. Is this a problem?'

'Not at all, but your situation gives me the opportunity to raise the first question of this meeting, and I would ask each and every one of you to take it back to your people tonight.' He cleared his throat, gathering some courage. 'Should non-skilled people be allowed to vote?'

Immediately, thick chatter broke out in the previously quiet room, which pleased Julius.

'Order, please,' called Siena. It took a minute but, eventually, she was able to give the floor back to Julius.

'The Referendum has two choices,' he continued. 'A *Yes* vote will see a permanent removal of all mind-skills from this solar system. Now, for half of our people, there will be no tangible difference to their lives, except that their DNA will be altered in such a way that passing on the mutation will become impossible. For the other half of humanity, life as they know it will disappear in an instant. All they fought for, all they worked hard to study and master, will be gone. And never mind all the technology that will become useless, because it requires mind-skills to be operated.' He looked around, wanting to strike up a connection with those in front of him. 'Since the establishment of Zed and the development of White skills, we gave ourselves a fighting chance against all threats, a chance that can still be guaranteed by a *No* vote. The countless lives that have been lost protecting and defending Earth, and humans across our galaxy, will be honoured if you choose *No*. Anything else would be an insult to their memory; to what they lived and died for.'

Applause broke out around the room; not from everyone, but it was something, thought Julius. 'You may think that my position is an obvious one, given that I have skills but, trust me, I do believe that a purge would drag us all backwards, and nowhere near an end to the war with the Arneshians, nor prevent future threats.'

As a new wave of applause died down, a female voice piped up: 'I'm not so sure, Julius.'

Julius looked up to the top tier, scouting the crowd – he knew that voice all too well. Sitting beside a dejected Bernard Docherty was Kaori, Morgana's sister.

'Kaori Ruthier, Earth,' she stated for Siena, standing up.

She looked tired, but she was resolute in her gaze. It was the look of someone who had finally made a hard decision. Julius didn't like that.

'I used to believe,' she began, 'that life without skills was nothing. I used to think that if I trained hard enough I would put a stop to the fighting and the war. In all these years, nothing of the sort has happened, except death upon death of friends and family members. I believed in that so much that I convinced my entire family of it. When my little sister was old enough to join Zed, I convinced her too. And now, the most important person in my life … has gone. She died because of it!'

Julius felt his heart shrink in his chest, completely unprepared for her words and the emotion of them.

'It is crucial to remember,' continued Kaori, 'that the Purge will remove every single mind-skill, from the Arneshians *and* us. Once it's done, we will *all* be equal and, although we will still need to fight, it will be a fair fight; an equal fight. And we can win it, because we have our hearts in the right place; because we are the righteous!' She looked around the crowd, parts of which appeared to be incensed by her words. 'I am willing to give up *my* way of life and *my* way of being for the greater benefit of humanity.' She turned back to Julius. 'Can you say the same?'

Applause rippled around the room, this time louder than ever.

Julius wasn't sure he could talk, let alone reply to her.

'*End the meeting,*' said Faith telepathically.

But Julius didn't trust himself to speak and was glad that the

146

applause was protracted.

Faith hovered over to the middle of the room and did it for him. 'The Forum will remain open until 18:00. Feel free to stay and continue the discussion among yourselves. Don't forget to bring the first point back to your groups: should non-skilled people be allowed to vote? Thank you.'

The delegates stood up almost immediately and milled about, forming clusters with people of similar views.

Julius' eyes were still on Kaori, who was looking straight back at him. He moved forward and climbed the steps to her tier but, as he did so, she turned and left the room. Docherty's hand shot out as he passed by and stopped him.

'Not now, Julius,' he said.

'What's going on?' he asked, feeling frustrated. 'Of all the people … Why?'

Bernard slumped down on the step, crestfallen. 'She's been like this since Morgana died. She's changed: blaming Zed … our mind-skills …'

Julius sighed and sat down next to him.

'I thought it would just be a matter of giving her some time - you know, to move on. But when the news came out yesterday, she totally flipped. She told me that this was the best thing that had ever happened to us and that I was a fool not to see that.'

'So you don't agree?'

'How could I? I'm a Solo champion, Julius,' he said, with a tired grin.

Julius nodded. 'I'm sorry, man.'

'I love her, Julius, but this referendum is going to break us up … I can feel it.'

As he sat there beside Bernard, he wondered what Morgana would have said to her sister. Somehow, he knew in his heart that she would never have voted *Yes*.

*

One day followed another, faster than Julius could ever have anticipated. The Forum meetings had become the most intense parts of the day, around which everything else revolved. The gatherings began to stretch well over the designated starting and closing times as the number of delegates increased, and the issues to discuss multiplied. The Curia ran out of accommodation and the visitors had been confined to sleeping in their ships, which were docked in orbit. To allow for all visitors having a chance to physically enter the Forum room, they had to assign particular days to the delegates. He had tried to find Kaori so he could speak properly with her but, every time he went looking, she was never available. Julius knew she was avoiding him, but there was nothing he could do. He actually felt particularly sorry for Bernard, who was facing the possible end of more than just one important thing.

Together with Siena, Julius was always on his feet, replying to requests, relaying decisions back to the leaders and generally making himself present and available. Faith and Skye gave all the help they could, and even broke up a few fights when tempers rose. Ruxshin, meanwhile, eagerly listened to all the arguments that were being made, trying hard to make up her mind about something that really had nothing to do with her or her own life experience. She understood why Julius didn't want people like her to vote but, since she was about to become a part of this new Galactic Federation of Earth, she figured she might as well be prepared for what was to come – that is, if they managed to defeat the Arneshians.

On Monday the 27th of October, Julius entered the Forum to find an unexpected addition. Overnight, a large interactive screen had been fitted to the central wall, showing different maps and locations.

'Would you look at that?' remarked Skye, his head raised.

Faith, on the other hand, hovered up to it, and observed it as if he was standing in front of an art piece, tilted head and all. Julius stopped halfway up the steps, to get a good vantage point. Earth was fully displayed according to its political map, with all five continents shown. To its right were the colonies, their names beside them, one above the other: Earth Colonies and Zed Colonies, including the Lunar Perimeter; next was Buruwang.

'Where's Mah?' asked Ruxshin, perplexed. 'I thought you said I might get to vote too.'

'Technically the vote is secret,' explained Siena, 'and since you are the only voter from Mah, you'll probably be counted with Earth.'

'If at all,' added Julius. 'We still don't know if they'll let people without skills vote.' Julius hadn't meant it to sound churlish, but it was the truth – they still hadn't confirmed who would be eligible to vote.

'Ahriman is in the Federation, but it's missing too,' added Skye. 'Probably because no one has been born here since *the War.*'

'Except for Arneshians,' added Faith.

Julius' stomach closed a little. It was going to be a tense week and he wasn't looking forward to the outcome. In all honesty, he had purposely avoided talking about the reality of a *Yes* victory with the others as if, by doing so, it would make the threat less real. Even though he had lived without powers once before, this was different. Back then, he had chosen to give up his powers, for what he believed to be the greater good of all – now he would be *forced* to do that. And there was no turning back.

The newly erected screen became one of the main topics of conversation within the Forum, given that voting instructions hadn't yet been released. They had to wait until Thursday night, when a galaxy-wide communication was broadcast. Julius took his seat on the steps, between Faith and Skye, and waited for the news with bated breath.

At 8PM that night, Iryana Mielowa came online for what was the most important broadcast of her career.

'Gosh, I've never seen her quite so fidgety,' said Siena. 'Still, her hair is immaculate as ever.'

'I'd be fidgeting too with that lot behind me,' added Skye.'

Julius knew what he meant and couldn't have agreed more. While Mielowa did some introductory chit-chat, he could see that, behind her, was a long table occupied by a serious line-up: Kloister, Milson and Freja, followed by Roversi, Trent and Daku Derain. 'They look as tense as I feel, funnily enough.'

Mielowa ended her introduction and turned to the panel behind her. 'The Curio Maximus will address this meeting tonight,' she said, moving out of frame.

The Curio Maximus cleared his voice before speaking. 'Thank you, Iryana. Citizens of the Federation, it is with a heavy heart that I am here tonight. We have chosen a live transmission in order to be with you all, on the eve of the most important day we have faced since the Chemical War. By now, you have had many days of discussions and, I am sure, quite a few sleepless nights. I know I have. After listening to your feedback and, after much deliberation, we are now going to lay down the two eligibility criteria for the vote.'

Julius tried to read Freja's expression, but the Grand Master just stared ahead impassively.

'The vote is open to all human beings from the age of 11 upwards,' he said.

A murmur spread around the Forum, as people expressed their feelings on this to one other.

'I like that,' said Skye, nodding. 'If we're old enough to train on Zed at 11, then we're old enough to vote.'

Julius agreed – it was a good start.

'The second criterion has been the hardest, and it concerns the eligibility of voting for those without skills.' Roversi shifted in his seat. 'When the Chemical War happened, no one could foresee the repercussions. As the years passed, some of us began to display the mutations that would eventually be developed by Marcus Tijara and Clodagh Arnesh, with results that are familiar to us all. No citizen was asked if they wanted these mutations or not – chance made that decision, affecting their lives and that of their descendants. We all had to get on with it, on Earth and in space. The people who live outside of planet Earth have all been affected by these mutations, - that is, except for the humans on Mah.'

Julius saw the eyes of the Forum shifting in Ruxshin's direction, making her aura turn red from the embarrassment of suddenly being the centre of attention.

'The Mahin Space Enterprise left Earth many years before the War broke out, avoiding contamination. It is because of this that Ruxshin, as representative of her colony, will not be allowed to vote in this referendum.'

Assent spread through the room at that. Julius was satisfied; for some reason, he also believed that Ruxshin would be relieved too at not having to make the call on behalf of her people. Sure enough, her aura took on a tinge of green, confirming Julius' suspicions.

'As for those humans without mind-skills,' continued Roversi, 'it is the will of this council that you be allowed to vote.'

A cacophony of noise erupted from the crowd, some cheering

and some yelling in protest. Julius looked at the others in frustration - he knew that full participation could very well change the result; and not necessarily in their favour.

'It's not over yet,' said Faith. 'You'll see.'

Roversi's voice hushed the room once again. 'Voting will take place tomorrow at noon, standard time throughout the Galaxy. It will remain open for a one-hour window and will be accessible from all personal terminals and PIP screens. The Federation map will show the results live, and each territory will take the colour of the majority vote: yellow for *Yes* and blue for *No*. The colour will continue to shift until 13:00 hours, when the voting will close. We have one last night to think about our choice; our own *personal* choice. I can only advise that you look into your hearts, examine your lives and think of the repercussions that each vote will bring. Ask yourself, if my choice wins out, can I live with that? Humans, I bid you goodnight.'

The transmission ended just as Freja was beginning to stand. Julius did the same and stretched. There was nothing else for him to do that night. He only hoped that his vote would count.

*

After a sleepless night, Julius met the others for breakfast around 09:00. Siena didn't stay long, and returned to her office with the promise of joining them at noon. They were all nervous but, with nothing else to do, they went to the Forum to try gauge the overall feeling.

It was obvious that most of the delegates wanted to watch the results together, although the room was far too small to accommodate them all. When they saw Julius arriving, they immediately asked him to create a similar space elsewhere and he set to work eagerly, glad to have something to occupy him for a few hours. Together with Todorov and his colleagues, they managed to transmit the feed from the Federation map to a new temporary screen in the main atrium of the Halls, where large numbers of people could assemble; then, to make sure that no one would miss a beat, they tuned all screens in the social areas in to show the map in the Forum. Only when everyone seemed to have settled down somewhere, did Julius allow himself to take a seat on the steps with Faith and Skye. At

11:50, Siena and Ruxshin arrived, and sat behind them.

Julius noticed that Bernard and Kaori were at the end of the row to his right. He nodded towards Docherty, who greeted him back. Knowing that it was too late now to change Kaori's mind, he opened his PIP and selected his mail inbox. He saw that he had a new message from home. Anxiously, he opened it first. A video recording of Rory and Jenny showed the pair of them on their sofa smiling. "We are voting NO, Julius! And so is Nana! You'll have our support!" Julius couldn't refrain a grin at that. Immediately, he typed a big thank you, followed by a string of *NOs*, before hitting reply. His eyes then went to a message from the Curia; the same one that had been received by all humans. It contained the link to the online ballot and he re-read the instructions one more time, just to be sure. His stomach was now completely closed and his mouth dry. He kept cracking his knuckles distractedly, watching as the seconds ticked down.

When noon arrived, a wave of silence fell over the Halls of Ahriman and no one spoke.

Julius saw the link on his mail turn from red to green and he pressed it quickly. The new screen showed the ballot paper with only one question. Julius forced himself to read it again, afraid to make a mistake. It said: "Do you agree to the complete, final and permanent removal of mind-skills from all human beings belonging to the GFE?" Below it there were two boxes, one yellow saying YES and one blue with a NO on it. 'Do I agree to the end of my life as I know it?' Julius asked himself. 'No, I certainly don't.' As he pressed his thumb on the NO box, a message appeared, confirming his identity via print authentication and delivered a receipt to show he had indeed voted. The ballot paper disappeared from the screen and, with that, he closed his PIP.

'Look at the screen,' said Skye. The areas on the map were shifting colour from blue to yellow as the votes came in.

'It's interactive,' said Faith, linking his PIP to it by scanning the map on his hand device. 'Shall we check what our own people are voting?'

'Start with me then,' said Siena excitedly.

Faith's PIP showed a projection of Italy, with two columns representing both outcomes. At the moment they were moving up and down erratically, making it impossible to predict results. Faith then checked Ireland, Scotland and finally Terra 3, but it was still too early to predict where the majority was going. Ruxshin, in the meantime, was looking around mystified, fascinated by people's reactions.

Julius' eyes were darting from one end of the main screen to the other, following the changes in colour of all the different places. At 12:20, the area representing Buruwang seemed to have stopped on the yellow colour. 'Damn,' he growled.

'I thought they'd stick with Marcus' people,' said Skye.

'Actually, they left Earth because of all the fights caused on account of mind-skills,' remarked Siena. 'I'm not surprised in the least.'

As the minutes ticked by, tensions continued to rise.

'Terra colonies are blue!' cried Skye, pointing frantically at the screen. 'I knew they wouldn't let us down!'

'Come on, Zed Colonies,' said Julius. 'Show me some more blue love.'

'Come on, Zed … come on …' urged Skye.

When the remaining colony shone an unchanging blue, they all jumped to their feet. Faith and Siena hugged each other excitedly.

Julius threw a glance towards where Docherty was sitting and saw him grinning back at him with his thumbs up. Only Earth was left now. He sat down again and waited.

A new graph appeared to the left of the screen, showing the overall percentage of votes in two columns. At the moment, the *No* vote was winning, strengthened by results from the colonies, but the *Yes* was also slowly rising.

'Faith,' called Julius, 'can we see what the individual continents are voting?'

'Sure,' he replied, before selecting a new link. 'Oceania is gone, I'm afraid.'

Julius looked and, sure enough, he saw the continent tinted yellow. Europe, however, had turned blue. He looked up at the overall screen and saw that the No vote was still holding. Five minutes later, America had also turned dark, to their delight.

'This is killing me,' said Skye, rubbing his face in his hands. 'Come on!'

Suddenly Africa stopped shifting hues and solidified on a bright yellow shade. The Yes column in the overall graph shot up, overtaking the No, and Julius' heart sunk. They had one last chance now – the fate of their skills rested with the people of Asia.

Julius sat down, not realising that he had brought his hands up and cupped them in front of his mouth, as if he was warming them up from the cold. His eyes were focused on the shape of the Asian continent, his mind blank. Then all the noise around him disappeared and the crowd blurred away. It was as if he was staring along a tunnel at the shape that lay beyond it. There was light there: a bright, yellow light. Julius closed his eyes in despair.

ERONAN'S CHOICE

Julius was standing in front of a screen, waiting for the video-call to start. Behind him, and to the left, were Skye, Faith, Siena and Ruxshin. It was eight o'clock at night and the Forum was empty, now that the delegates had returned to their homes. He shifted from one foot to the other, vaguely remembering that he still needed to pack his belongings, as few as they were. He would have time to do that afterwards – Kelly wouldn't arrive until midnight.

Finally, the display came to life, with the screen split into two halves. On the left side of the screen stood Freja, from the Ahura's ready room; to the right was Roversi, who was travelling back to the Halls from Earth.

Julius bowed to them, barely able to keep his face free from the disappointment of that day.

'McCoy,' said Roversi cordially, 'a job well done with the Forum. You have our thanks.'

'Only doing my duty, sir,' he replied.

'Be that as it may, it was an important job. And now that the people have spoken, we know what to do once the war is over.'

Julius couldn't refrain a "*hmph*", which didn't go unnoticed.

'Is something the matter?' asked Roversi.

Julius looked at Freja briefly, before answering. 'Actually there is, sir, if I may speak my piece.'

'You may,' replied Roversi, leaning back in his chair.

'It is obvious that you wouldn't want us to fight without mind-skills. Useful things, aren't they? I wonder what's going to happen next time we're threatened. Are we planning to call on Eronan when that happens?'

'Julius!' cut in Freja.

'Leave it, Carlos,' said Roversi. 'I understand exactly how you feel, McCoy, but Eronan's help comes at this price. We had a choice to make - all or nothing - and our people feel that *all* is better. We will just be ourselves after the purge, as we were intended to be; no more, no less.'

'*Intended?* And what about adaptation and evolution? We are who we are because of our capacity for hanging on, no matter what. What if we don't take Eronan's help? What if we fight *our* way?'

'Unfortunately, I don't think we have that option anymore,' answered Freja. 'I do believe we can beat the Arneshians without powers, but not Michael. You told us about the machine he created and the testing that went with it. And that was weeks ago. Your brother will be several stages ahead of us once the Arneshians have finished shaping him into their perfect vessel and, to stop him, we would need your powers, along with any other help Eronan could give us.'

'I agree with Freja,' said the Curio. 'Once this is over, we will initiate the purge throughout our race and start again. Granted, *some* of the technology will become obsolete, but we have resourceful people among us - we will succeed in the end.'

'Sir, it isn't just some technology. All the ships rely on our skills to function. It would cost us less to do away with the entire fleet than to replace the individual war decks. The Cougars, on the other hand, will be ready for Pete's graveyard.'

'Yes, McCoy, I am aware of that. As too am I aware that our current FTL and hyperjump functions will receive the hardest knock.'

Julius shook his head. 'After all we've been through - the effort; the deaths - it would be a choice worse than the one that caused all this in the first place. It's who we are! You can't be serious.'

'The people have spoken, and that vote has won.'

'Of course it did,' continued Julius. 'The skill-less are many more than we are, and they're all jealous. I bet they were delighted at the chance to get even. How is this fair? We are the good guys!'

'Even if I agreed with you, Zed belongs to Earth and its colonies - it serves them - and their decision is binding. Zed will continue to exist, training people for space exploration and expansion, but in a natural way; a real, human way.'

Julius groaned. 'But what is *real*? I am a real human being, just the way I am! Please don't do this to us!' He was pleading now, but he didn't care. It was all he had left.

'Enough,' said Roversi firmly. 'McCoy, you have this mission to see to; the most important thing you'll ever do. Don't worry about matters outside of your control.'

'*Back down,*' said Faith in his mind.

'We'll dock in a couple of hours, McCoy,' said Freja. 'Make sure you're ready to leave.'

Julius stared back at the two men, then bowed. 'We will be ready, sir.'

*

Arriving in Eneamar the second time wasn't as traumatic for Julius from inside the safety of the Mazda. He was able to appreciate the tapestry of colour in all its grandiosity and vastness as they slowly approached it. This time, as soon as the hull touched the energy beams, the transformation was immediate, and they found themselves anchored at port, in Eneamar's impossible ocean.

Eronan was waiting for them on the pier, his countenance serene. Freja took Julius and Kelly to meet him, leaving everyone else on-board.

'Eronan,' said the Grand Master, bowing.

'Do you have an answer for me, Freja?'

'We do. Our people have spoken: the purge has been authorised.'

Eronan nodded. 'Follow me then.' He led them inside the familiar small building they had used before; only, this time, the table had been replaced by a large 3D map of Mahin, split into two layers: above ground and beneath.

If Julius thought that their reconstruction on the Mazda had been good, this was ten times better. Every building was perfectly detailed and, when he touched one, it grew larger and opened up to show the internal layout. Faith would have had a fit at the sight of it.

'Are these … Arneshians?' asked Kelly, pointing at tiny figures moving around the streets.

'Indeed they are. And look, there goes the Ambassador,' he said, pointing at a little shape of a man, moving from building to building.

'How is this possible? Are they real?' said Julius.

'Oh, they are very real,' answered Eronan, with a hint of a smile. 'Mah has been under strict observation for the last month. They obviously don't know about it.'

'I must say,' added Freja, 'knowing that it is still doable to pull one over on these people fills me with confidence.'

'Is Mah Gira still in prison?' asked Kelly.

'He is. They haven't harmed him.'

'Ruxshin will be pleased to know that.'

'I think she would be happier to find out where her friend Khavar is,' commented Julius.

'I'm not sure who that person is,' said Eronan, 'but I have seen a group of Mahini sneaking suspiciously in and out of this building.' As he said that, the top layer of Mahin lifted, fully revealing the underground. Eronan tapped on one of the dwellings, causing it to expand in size.

'That's Mah Gira's house!' said Julius. 'I bet anything Khavar's got back inside it and is using the secret tunnel.'

'I saw the tunnel being used, yes,' confirmed Eronan. 'It is possible they are using the house as a meeting place.'

'When we saw Mah Gira,' said Julius pensively, 'he asked us to move a black stone he kept in his courtyard.'

'That's right,' said Kelly. 'He told Skye to move it to the left, under the bench. Can you tell if it's still there?'

Eronan manipulated the hologram of the building until he pinpointed the bench. There was a small black spot in the left-hand corner. 'Maybe it was a signal.'

'It was, yes,' said Kelly.

'This building here, at the end,' continued Eronan, pointing at a house by the cliff, 'is the focal point of the map. The Ambassador and one of his men visit it daily, but, worryingly, I cannot see inside. I can only assume the Arneshian leader to be there.'

'Sounds plausible,' said Kelly. 'What do we do now?'

'Julius' job is to deal with the Arneshian leader and I will help him prepare for that. Yours is with the soldiers.'

Freja walked around the map, observing it intently. 'We will need to keep the troops occupied.'

'And stun them,' added Kelly. 'When we're done, I want to leave behind a stream of sleeping Arneshians, ready to get their medicine.'

'That is right, Captain,' continued Eronan. 'Once their leader is down, and you are safely in orbit, I will begin the purification of the planet. It won't have any effect on the Mahini, but anyone else carrying a pearl will be immediately purged. Do you understand?'

'Trust me,' said Kelly, 'we'll be well out of range. If I have to be purged, I'd rather be among my own folk.'

'What will happen to the Arneshians afterwards?' asked Julius.

'What you do with them is your business,' replied Eronan.

'We can't leave them there, can we?'

'You could consider relocating them to Arnesh, and get rid of their fleet altogether. They'd be stranded for a long time. Or you could relocate them and then destroy their world, once and for all.'

'Wow,' said Kelly. 'You don't mince your words, do you? I like it.'

Freja threw a sideways-glance at his son, obviously not quite as keen on that plan.

'Be that as it may, it is your choice to make. Shall we start?'

'Very well. I will leave the Curia to decide on the aftermath. May I use this graphic to plan our attack? We have nothing quite as sophisticated.'

'It has already been transferred to your ship, Grand Master.'

'Thank you. Julius, I will see you later then. Good luck.'

Julius bowed, and waited for Freja and Kelly to leave before turning to Eronan unenthusiastically. 'I'm all yours.'

Eronan waved his hands once, making the room instantly disappear. Julius tried to hold on to something, but even the ground had vanished under his feet. He thought he would fall into darkness; instead, he found himself seated in a reclining chair, not dissimilar to a dentist's. Lights and machines appeared all around him, almost masking the fact that there was still no floor and no walls around him. Julius looked down, but he had to turn away, as a hint of nausea crept over him.

Eronan approached the chair and sat on a stool by his side. 'Freja has explained to me the true nature of their leader-'

'Michael,' cut in Julius. 'His name is Michael.'

Eronan nodded. 'Michael. Truly a remarkable technological miracle. I did not expect Clodagh to set up such a machine: a treasure of knowledge, instantly accessible to all its followers. Still, for all its greatness, this device contains the same pearl all humans have and, once you remove the distilled powers that Farrah gave him, Michael will become vulnerable to the purge, just like everyone else, rendering his knowledge useless.'

'Go on.'

Eronan waved his hand again and a 3D human shape appeared in front of them. 'Farrah's knowledge has been distilled into a tiny package which has attached itself to Michael's pearl, using it as a medium to express itself. The package may have been absorbed,' explained Eronan, 'but it's still a foreign body to Michael, so we can build a vaccine to debilitate it.'

'And how do you make it so that it attacks the right bit?'

'That's where you come in handy. See, the package comes from Farrah – it has her genetic code in it - and you and her share a portion of the same DNA: Marcus Tijara's.'

Julius' eyes widened. 'She's his daughter and I have his powers – I drunk that liquid when I won on the Guardian's Trail.'

'Exactly. Using the DNA introduced into your body by the Buruwang crystal, I am creating a vaccine so that it finds Tijara's DNA within Michael. Once it has locked onto it, it will be destroyed.'

Another thought occurred to him then. 'How come Farrah could see you?' he asked. 'In fact, why was I able to dream of you too? Neither of us had ever been here.'

Eronan seemed to be lost in thought for a moment. 'I had hoped Tijara would follow me,' he said eventually. 'I left an imprint in him about Eneamar; a vision to recall at will. He must have passed that imprint on to his daughter.'

'And since I essentially *drank* part of Tijara, I also got it. Is that it?'

'It certainly looks like it,' he replied.

Julius was trying to determine if there was more – he had a feeling Eronan wasn't telling the whole truth. He was about to ask one more question, when Eronan changed the subject.

'Do you know how to locate the pearl, young man?'

'I don't.'

Eronan opened up an image of a brain and rotated it until the lower side was facing them. 'See the four lobes of the brain? It is right at their centre. The mutation brought about by the Chemical War creates a bridge between them which grows into the pearl.'

Julius' moment of hope faltered slightly. 'Hold on; am I supposed to walk up to him and *inject* him in the head?'

'If he refuses, you'll need to find another way. That is *your* task.'

Julius closed his eyes and lay back in the chair, leaving Eronan free to work. *Another way*, he thought. He couldn't really perform open surgery now, could he? 'It won't end well,' he muttered disconsolately.

*

Eronan took the whole morning and the best part of the afternoon to create the vaccine. He made several doses, in case Julius needed extra. Each one was encased in a metallic container, ready to be loaded into a syringe. How he would get close enough to inject them into Michael was anybody's guess though.

At sunset they returned to the Mazda. Julius halted before boarding, and watched the sun disappear into the sea. 'Eneamar System,' he said. 'Faith has named this solar system the Eneamar System. And your species is now known as the *Dathannach*. It means multi-coloured in Irish.'

Eronan looked genuinely touched. 'Thank him for me. The name will be mine from now on.'

Julius nodded. 'So … you said that you *choose* to nurture. Why help humans? At all, I mean.'

Eronan stared at the horizon for a while. 'Eternity alone is a mighty long time, if you must know.'

For the first time, Julius noticed a hint of sadness in his features, and he could partly share this sentiment. The prospect of the years to come without Morgana by his side made him feel extremely lonely. And, in truth, even losing Michael had deepened that feeling. 'Did you know that the Arneshian leader is my brother?'

Eronan looked at him inquisitively. 'I did not. For some reason though, I sense that this is not why you are full of anger right now.'

'That obvious, huh?'

'Tell me.'

Julius thought about it for a moment, then decided to talk straight. 'I hate this. You know what I went through to get Tijara's crystal and win my skills back. It's all been for nothing and it isn't right. I am who I am, and I have no intention of changing. They can't make me. No one can.'

'I offered Marcus a way out once,' he replied. 'You were there with us in his office when it happened. To you, and anyone who would follow you, I could offer another path – this system is small and exhausted - there is nothing for you here. However, it does hold the door to a new one. You could leave all you know behind after this, with your powers intact, and head out into the unknown.'

Julius remembered when Ben Hastings had offered him the same thing. At least this time he knew that Eronan's offer was genuine though. 'Is … is there more to see? More life?' he asked hesitantly.

'Are there stars in the universe?' replied Eronan, with an enigmatic smile. With that, he turned back towards the city.

*

Over the next four days, the crew of the Mazda worked hard to organise the mission. Most of the fleet was moved into Mah's system, thanks to Eronan's advanced relay junctions, which sent Faith into a tizzy. At one point, he tried sneaking up to one of them to see if he could draw its schematics. It was only after Kelly promised he would ask Eronan to send these to him that he was able to be dissuaded from boarding one.

Julius sat in the ready room, observing the comings and goings of the officers, without saying much. Although he would land on Mahin with the others, his only job was to get to Michael and deal with him. He had hoped that his friends would join him - Kelly too - but at the moment they were being assigned to other missions.

As he sat in his chair, tucked away in a corner, he kept thinking about Eronan's words. Could he really defect? Because that is what he was contemplating. His mind turned to the samurai of feudal Japan. He had loved and read so much about them that he knew what they would have done in his place. A samurai was loyal to his master; the order of committing *seppuku* – taking one's own life - would have been embraced on the spot, without any second thoughts. Disobedience was not an option. No self-respecting samurai would have challenged the Curia's order. 'Hmph. I guess I'm not a samurai after all,' he muttered to himself.

On Thursday evening, the eve of battle, the mess hall was filled with hushed voices and a sombre atmosphere. Freja had retired to his quarters early, to go over the attack one more time, while Ruxshin stared at Eronan's map of Mahin with renewed interest. Since finding out that it showed her city in real time, she was taking it all in, checking on her friends and family and, most of all, trying to discover if Khavar was still alive. Julius sat at a table with Skye, Faith, Elian and Kelly, staring at his food.

'Eat something,' Elian told him. 'You'll need your strength tomorrow.'

'What is it, Julius?' asked Kelly eventually. 'You've been acting very weird lately, and I mean more than usual.'

'Like he doesn't have a reason,' said Elian, but Kelly kept looking at him, ignoring her remark.

Julius glanced around, to make sure they were out of earshot. 'It's something Eronan said,' he told them quietly.

The others leaned in a little.

'After this is over, he could help us escape, powers and all. Would you do it?'

Silence descended on the table, as everyone looked at each other hesitantly.

'Tempting,' said Kelly, after a minute. 'But not for us. We have a kid now. Living as fugitives isn't exactly a great legacy for Savannah.'

Skye and Faith looked at each other, but couldn't think of any reply.

Julius was disappointed at their lack of enthusiasm. 'What's the matter? I thought you two at least would understand.'

'It's … deserting, Julius,' said Faith. 'It never really occurred to me as an option.'

'I mean, it's Zed we're talking about,' added Skye. 'Our family and friends. We would never be able to come home again.'

Julius bit his lip and backed down. 'Sure. Let's forget about it.'

Kelly stood up, and grabbed his tray. 'It won't be easy, Julius, for any of us, but we'll need to make do together.'

'Focus on your mission now,' said Elian, following her husband. 'If we fail, we'll have far worse scenarios to deal with.'

*

Around 2AM, Julius got out of bed, unable to sleep. He took a wander around the Mazda, relaxing among the engine noises and the general quiet. There were people still milling around, but no one paid him much attention. When he passed through the canteen, he stopped to grab a cup of hot chocolate and, with it, he resumed his stroll.

Without realising it, he found himself in engineering, on one of the upper gangways. He put his cup on the floor and sat down, letting his legs hang out. One of the engineers looked up and gave him a wave, before returning to his work. There were many reasons why he couldn't sleep that night, the latest being a sense of disappointment at being let down by his friends. It was obvious that they all had something worth staying for, and he wondered what Morgana would have done. She had been his partner in crime, so to speak, many times, and he felt sure she would have gone with him; even to the edge of the universe if need be.

At that moment, a figure appeared to his right, interrupting his thoughts. He looked up and saw Freja. 'Grand Master,' he said, surprised.

Freja smiled and slowly, using the bannister, lowered himself down next to him. 'I don't think I've ever sat on a walkway before,' he said, sounding as surprised as Julius was. 'Can't sleep?'

Julius shook his head and finished the last sip of his chocolate.

'I never sleep well the night before a big battle,' Freja told him. 'Granted, I didn't see that many battles until *you* joined Zed.'

That made Julius smile. 'That bad, huh?'

'It's okay to be scared, you know? A little fear keeps things real. This battle, humans against humans, is our responsibility. I can't promise you it will be the last time, but it is *our* battle. I can understand that the thought of facing Michael is daunting, but-'

'I'm not really worried about tomorrow, sir,' cut in Julius. 'At least not now. It's the rest that bothers me; being robbed of my identity, and you know that.' *You started this*, thought Julius defiantly.

'A true White Child,' said Freja kindly. 'You want to talk about *after*, so let me tell you about it. The world will need a leader; someone to take the GFE forward; a man of his time. Tijara was the man that brought us into the space era, and you will be the man to take us into a new one. A symbol to unite the systems of the Milky

Way; an explorer and ambassador for the human race.'

For a moment, Julius felt warmth in his heart, as if the sun had come out from behind a cloud. There was hope in Freja's words of what things could be like, and that brought a sense of peace. Then he saw Morgana's body, lying in sick bay covered in blood, and the sun was obscured once more. 'I don't think I care.'

'But you *have* to care,' replied Freja, more urgently. 'When our powers go, people will still look to us for guidance and safety. We must make that transition smooth and seamless. A White Child is the hero of our times and you need to rise up to that challenge. That's what maturity is – facing up to facts. If Morgana was here …'

Julius glared at him.

'… If she was here,' continued Freja, unperturbed, 'you know what she would say to you. Deep down, in that stubborn heart of yours, you know what *she* would want you to do.' With that, he pulled himself up and walked away.

Julius felt like screaming. Maybe that was the problem, he thought. No matter how much he tried, he couldn't tell what Morgana would have done anymore. He felt more alone than ever.

THE SIEGE OF MAHIN

Julius was standing inside a Stork, holding on to the handrail, waiting to jump out. There was a reinforced inner pocket concealed inside his suit, where the vaccine had been stored, and his hand kept going back to it, to check it was still there. Skye, Faith and seven other soldiers were standing next to him, ready for launch. The fleet had arrived in Mah's orbit ten minutes before, counting on the element of surprise. Julius knew that, without Eronan's technology, this would not have been possible. The alien had boosted all their basic shields and cloaking devices, as well as improving their Exoskin suits. Most importantly, he had introduced a special device into the Gauntlets to heighten the effect of the stun setting, so it would induce a deep sleep in the target.

'Are you sure these boosters will work?' asked Skye, touching the two cylinders attached to either side of his Exoskin belt.

'If you three halted a falling shuttle just by using your hands as outlets,' said Faith, 'those two thrusters will be way more stable.'

'We'll soon find out, won't we?'

'Just be glad that they didn't see us coming.'

Julius couldn't have agreed more. The element of surprise was all they had. As soon as the Storks released the infantry, the Cougars and Herons would enter the fray to deal with the enemy crafts and lend aerial support to the ground troops.

'One minute to launch,' said the pilot.

'This is it, guys,' said Skye to his friends. 'Let's make it count.'

'For Morgana,' said Julius, putting his hand forward.

Skye and Faith placed theirs over his, briefly giving rise to green wisps in their otherwise red auras.

Julius' heart was heavy, but he couldn't allow himself to worry about the Curia's decision now. His mission was to find Michael and bring this war to an end.

The emergency light over the hatch flashed and Julius activated the helmet on his Exoskin. They were high above the ground, but not enough to need their EMUs. When the door slid open, he felt someone pat his shoulder a couple of times. He took a deep breath and jumped.

He stretched his body fully, cutting through the air like a bullet. In a few seconds Skye, Faith and the soldiers from their shuttle were at his side. In that moment, everything below him was still peaceful and, as he flew to meet the ground, he saw hundreds of Zed soldiers all around him, falling to Mah like silent spears amidst the raindrops. A storm was falling on Mahin.

The first anti-aircraft gun opened fire a few seconds later. Julius had no desire to slow up just yet, so he opened his shield to full, creating a protective bubble around him. The rain pelted against it to either side.

Skye pointed at a turret, where Arneshian soldiers were firing at them, and fired up his boosters. He changed course immediately, swerving to the left and soaring parallel to the ground. As he drew closer, he shot at them from his Gauntlets. Faith followed, while Julius aimed for the portion of ground directly below the enemy. He activated his boosters at the latest possible second to break his freefall, creating a thick wave of jet-stream around him and causing a puddle of raindrops at his feet to fly off in every direction, as if he was landing on the sea. Once on the ground, he tore down the turret's entrance door with a burst of energy and marched in, taking the steps two at a time. When he reached the top, one of the soldiers was lying on the floor, while the other shot at Skye and Faith, who were hovering above his head. Julius stunned the first man unconscious, just as Skye and Faith laid out the soldier who'd been firing at them. Julius strode forward and obliterated the artillery gun with a mind-push.

Skye and Faith landed by his side and crouched down. As per orders, they quickly sent their personal co-ordinates to mission control, confirming they had landed safely.

'That was a welcome-party and no mistake,' commented Skye, drawing breath.   Julius looked at the city below the turret. The infantry had all landed now and bursts of lightning and energy flashed all around. At the same time, Cougars were performing dangerous flybys over the offensive positions, demolishing the Arneshian guns with their shots. With the enemy crafts tight on their tails, though, this wasn't the easiest thing to do. Troops of soldiers poured from the various lift shafts like ants from a hill, spreading over the ground, hunting their attackers. Among them were Mahini prisoners, some still in shackles, fleeing the crossfire and seeking shelter. Soon there would be no safe place left.

Faith used his PIP to activate a holographic display of the layers of the buildings in front of him. This was linked to Eronan's live map and so capable of showing exactly what each building was and how many people were in them. He moved around, trying to identify their mission hotspots. 'Right, so, Mah Gira's prison is straight ahead, below that shaft,' he said, pointing at his screen. 'Kelly and his team are in charge of that. We're heading east, past T'Rogon's office – over there.'

'Let's go then,' said Julius, not wanting to stay out in the open much longer. Using his boosters, he leapt from the tower and landed safely on the ground. 'Quickly!'

Shields up, they advanced, skirting whatever shelter they could find, staying out of sight as much as possible. The collapsed greenhouses were the best hiding places along their path, so they cut through them as they ran to their goal. Faith made use of his hovering skirt whenever he could, warning the others of possible dangers. Aided by the power of his boosters, he was able to zoom back and forth quicker than usual, helping Julius and Skye overwhelm the small groups of Arneshians along their path.

'To the right!' cried Faith, as they approached one of the largest gardens.

Julius whirled in, Gauntlets blazing, even before he had laid eyes on the enemy. As he turned a corner, three guards sprang out in front of him, but were repelled by his shields. As the guards retreated, Faith and Skye moved behind them and shot them in their backs with powerful mind-pushes, propelling them against what remained of a nearby support wall. They were knocked out cold.

'In here,' shouted Faith, leading them inside the ruins.

Shards of broken pots were strewn across the floor, at the feet of dead stubs that had once been living trees. Fallen leaves lay scattered over the ruined tables, whose wooden tops were rotting away in the pouring rain.

Julius edged around the room, wary of any guards waiting in

ambush. As he moved, he heard a rustling noise over the sound of the rain, coming from a large wooden container, that was possibly an old compost bucket. He stopped and gestured for the others to halt, and pointed to the source of the noise. Skye immediately moved to its side, blocking any escape route.

Slowly, Julius locked his eyes on the lid and began to raise it open with his mind. The cover moved a few inches before slamming back down again. Julius hadn't expected that. He aimed his Gauntlet at the box, and pulled; this time the wooden top flew off to the left.

A frazzled Ambassador T'Rogon jumped up like an overgrown jack-in-the-box. 'You can't shoot me!' he cried, red-faced.

In all truth, Julius was too stupefied to even speak. Of all the things he had been expecting to see, the Arneshian ambassador was the least of them.

T'Rogon must have sensed Julius' surprise, because he recomposed himself and assumed his more familiar, controlling persona. 'You should not have come here,' he said. 'Putting yourself in the path of Arnesh is neither sensible, nor wise. Your brother will destroy yo … ooooh!' He managed to say that much, before slumping to the ground unconscious, courtesy of a right hook from Skye.

Again, Julius' mouth fell open. 'I did not see that coming either,' he said.

'I'm sorry to spoil the moment,' said Skye, massaging his hand, 'but I've heard quite enough from that pompous prick.'

'Way to go, Miller,' said Faith, hovering over to the Ambassador and checking that he was still breathing. He grabbed the hem of T'Rogon's tunic and ripped a piece off, before using it on its owner as a gag. 'Let's put this Jack back in his box.'

Julius looked around the greenhouse and spotted several small lengths of rope hanging to one side. He pulled them towards him with his mind and tied T'Rogon's feet and hands. Once this was done, Skye lifted the Arneshian and placed him back inside the container.

'Move over,' said Faith. With a quick gesture, he used his mind to scoop up dirt and leaves from the ground and poured it into the box, all around and over the man, leaving only his face sticking out.

'That's the ugliest cabbage I've ever seen,' said Faith, patting the soil down around the Ambassador.

T'Rogon opened his eyes groggily and, when he realised his predicament, he tried to scream, but managed only a few incoherent, muffled wailings, thanks to the gag in his mouth.

'Say *cheese*!' said Faith, taking a picture with his PIP. 'Freja will love this one. In fact, the whole fleet will; let me just send it since we're here. It's sure to go viral.'

'MMMMMM!' protested T'Rogon.

Julius strode up to him and stared into his eyes. 'You have no idea how lucky you are to be breathing right now.' With that, he slammed the lid shut over the prisoner. 'He cannot get out, understood?' he said to Faith.

'I'll take care of him,' he replied, plonking himself down on top of the crate with his full shield on. 'Freja is on his way. I'll join you soon.'

Julius nodded and motioned for Skye to move forward. They hopped over a wall and onto the street beyond, advancing swiftly through the rain.

When they reached the outskirts of the city, they stopped in the shadow of a crumbling shelter. Skye opened his PIP and used the map overlay to get their bearings. There was only one building remaining, before the face of a high cliff. There were guards outside, watching the unfolding battle not too far from them. Eronan's map identified the building as Michael's Chamber.

'Get down,' said Julius, pulling Skye with him. 'There's a vehicle coming.'

To their right, a small, open-topped hover-car skidded through the rain, aiming for the building's entrance. Next to its pilot, K'Ssander stood tall, holding on to the top of the windscreen, oblivious of the rain lashing at his face. The car had barely stopped before the Arneshian jumped out effortlessly, but didn't head inside. Instead, he jogged back towards the city, and entered a smaller, newly built home to the left.

Julius experienced a surge of hatred so strong that he could feel his powers seeping out through his fingertips, inside his Exoskin suit. The noise around him had faded. All he could hear was his heart, pounding furiously inside his brain.

'… lius … Julius …'

It took him a minute before he was able to focus on Skye's voice. He turned.

'K'Ssander is mine. You have your mission,' Skye told him resolutely.

Julius knew this, but all he could see was that horrible moment: Morgana crumpling to the floor; K'Ssander fleeing. The person who had taken everything from him, and he was right there within his grasp.

Seeing that Julius was obviously considering disobeying orders, Skye placed his hand on his friend's shoulder and looked him straight in the eyes. 'He tried to kill me,' he said. 'He killed Morgana. Do you think for one moment that he will see the end of this day?'

Julius mulled over those words, weighing his options. The aura surrounding Skye was the darkest shade of red he had ever seen - he meant business. Julius backed down. 'Make sure that he doesn't.'

'If it's the last thing I do,' replied Skye, full of determination, before leaving the shelter and disappearing through the maze of ruined buildings.

Alone, Julius focused on the guards patrolling the Chamber. He needed to distract them if he wanted access to his brother. He left the safety of his hideout and moved to the right, giving it a wide berth before heading toward it again. He used the rocks, the trees and his Exoskin in camouflage mode, so that they wouldn't be able to see him. He even closed his shield, in case the raindrops bouncing off it gave him away. It took him almost five minutes before he reached the side of the building, and stopped by a large boulder to catch his breath.

On the other side, where Skye had followed K'Ssander, all was quiet – maybe his friend was also waiting for the right moment. Julius looked around and, when his eyes settled on the hover-car, he realised that it could act as the diversion that would help them both. He focused on it, simultaneously creating a fireball. When he felt he had accumulated enough, he lifted the vehicle, making sure the guards would see it; then, with a jerk, he threw it in the direction of the building and the house, followed by his fireball, which set it on fire in mid-air, causing it to explode. The guards recoiled, then recovered and ran to investigate the burning wreckage. Using the distraction, Julius fired up his boosters and flew to the roof of the

Chamber, where he landed on it, like a cat. He scampered to the edge, looking for an entry point below the eaves of the roof. There was a window cut into the top floor, so he activated his boosters again and hovered down to it, before kicking the glass in and swinging into the room. His entrance surprised a guard, who had very little time to react, but still managed to shoot a bolt of energy at Julius. He ducked just in time, and flung himself head-first into the man's midriff. They grappled on the ground, each fighting to get the upper hand. Finally, Julius managed to strain and get his Gauntlets up to the man's head, where he unleashed enough power to stun him. Julius lay motionless for a minute, listening for any footsteps coming his way, but all seemed calm. Then a second explosion shook the entire building. He staggered to his feet and steadied himself against a nearby wall, hoping the explosion was one of his own people's doing.

When he was sure that the coast was clear, he stepped into a corridor beyond the room he was in. There were no other areas on this level, so he moved quietly downstairs. The main entrance was wide open and unguarded, with another exit opposite it. Julius selected the camouflage setting again, activated his full shield and moved towards this secondary door. It was closed firmly and, when he tried to push, it didn't budge. Finally, he noticed a thin pressure pad running alongside the right hand side of the frame. *Here goes nothing*, he thought, and pushed it. He heard a click beneath him and looked down, but too late; the trapdoor had already swung open, leaving Julius to tumble into a dark hole.

BROTHERS

He fell into a conduit, and was unable to stop himself bouncing from side to side as he slid downwards; the only thing he had managed, as an instinctive reaction, was shielding his head with his folded arms. After a few seconds that felt more like an eternity, he found himself freefalling. Instinct kicked in and he flipped on his boosters, just in time to halt his fall.

He looked around and saw that he was hovering in the middle of a huge, circular, iced cave, its roof lined with stalactites. When he looked down to the ground, a range of razor-sharp rock-shards jutted up from the surface of a frozen lake – without his boosters he could have fallen to his death. By all accounts, this natural opening had been turned into a trap of sorts, to keep out intruders. There were no openings in the ceiling that he could see but, somehow, light was creeping in, allowing him to see a little of his surroundings. There was a frozen lake below him and a suspended ice bridge in the middle of the cave. Carefully, he lowered himself onto it, turning the boosters off as he landed, for fear of melting the ice. He found his footing and waited to see if the structure would hold his weight. It creaked a little, but didn't break. Using the light on his Gauntlet, he explored the cavern, looking for a path. There was nothing leading off from the lake below, except for a narrow slit in the rock for the water to trickle through. He checked the two sides of the bridge, but the exits at both ends had caved in long ago. Lastly, he looked at his PIP, hoping to identify his coordinates but, not only were there none, he couldn't even send a signal out.

'Damn,' he muttered, creating a sudden, eerie echo in the room, while his breath spread out in a white cloud. There was clearly no one here and nowhere else to go – Julius' only choice seemed to be to use the boosters to try to make his way up the conduit he had fallen from. He looked up, trying to gauge its position and, just as he was about to lift off, he noticed an alcove.

Excavated within one of the walls was a large recess of smooth brown rock. It was pretty dark but, with his torch, Julius could just make out the beginning of a path. He flew over to it and landed, feeling the temperature rising immediately. Cautiously, he followed the path and was soon descending along a spiral tunnel. A few times, his feet stumbled, but he always managed to steady himself against the rocky walls. He was getting worried though, wondering whether he was going in the right direction, or if he had just fallen into a new trap.

Eventually he reached the bottom of the passageway, where an arch, protected by a film of energy, led into a sophisticated control room. He stepped inside, unhindered by the field. The new room was clean and well lit, its walls functioning as computer terminals. It reminded him immediately of the hideout where they had found Farrah, only this time there was no floating tank in sight, or Nuarn bodies. As he moved around the place, he became aware that even the air around him was coated with green cyphers and bits of code scrolling in every direction. The only way he could explain this to himself was thinking of a glass of salty water: the glass was the room, containing a mixture of some sort, with him in the middle of it. He had the feeling that, if he poked his tongue out, he might even be able to taste it, but thought better of it. He reached toward a random spot in front of him and, as he touched it, hundreds and hundreds of tiny letters and numbers flocked to his fingertips, swirling around his hand and arm, as if attracted by curiosity. If it wasn't for the seriousness of his mission, Julius might have found it enchanting – Faith surely would have fainted from excitement.

'I thought I recognised you,' said a male voice suddenly.

Julius instantly knew it was Michael's. He raised his Gauntlet, and spun round. No one there. He jerked back in the other direction again, but there was no trace of his brother.

'Can't you see me?' Michael taunted.

Julius didn't like this – how was it possible? He could have sworn Michael had been behind him! And his voice … it sounded so innocent; childlike.

'Can't you feel me?' he continued.

Julius turned again, and saw nothing but the exit. *This won't do,* he thought. He made an effort to calm himself, and took a proper look around. 'Where are you?'

'All around you.'

There was a hint of playfulness in his voice, but what really hit Julius hard was that he hadn't heard that particular tone in his brother's voice since before Zed – no malice, or hate; just his little brother. 'What do you mean? I can't see you, Michael.'

Suddenly, a cluster of letters and numbers began to assemble in front of Julius, and formed into the outline of a man. The shape lifted its hand. 'Here I am.'   Julius stumbled, stopping only when his back met the wall. His heart was racing. Was this the real meaning of the Arneshians' knowledge? 'What did they do to you?' he asked shakily. It didn't matter that his brother was now the leader of the Arneshians because, right then, Julius had even forgotten his brother's betrayal, seeing only a child who had fallen prey to ruthless enemies.

The Michael-shape shrugged its shoulders. 'I've evolved, Julius. I am the people. I'm their legacy, you see. It's *all* in here,' he said, tapping his head with his finger. 'And I feel great!'

'This … this can't be. It isn't natural, Michael. You've given up your identity to become these people's vessel!'

'I don't understand why you're so upset about it, Julius. Had I stayed in my corporeal form, like you, what could I have accomplished? My life would have ended in a few decades time, leaving virtually no trace of my existence behind. In this way, not only have I carved my name in the history of my people – I have become their future.'

Julius' initial shock began to wane, leaving in its place a slowly rising sense of anger and frustration. This didn't bode well at all. How was he supposed to inject the vaccine now? Was the distillation from Farrah even there anymore? Without a physical body to interact with, Julius didn't think he could win this battle. He had to find another way; he had to know more. 'Will you listen to yourself?' Julius said, changing tactic. 'Actually, Michael, scrap that. I bet you *can't* listen to yourself, because there's nothing *left* of you to begin with!'

That seemed to irk Michael, who stopped and suddenly dissolved into the air again. 'That is not nice,' he said, his voice coming from all around.

Julius kept his gaze fixed ahead – there was no point in looking for a source that didn't exist. He was pleased, however, that his words had shaken him a little. Maybe there was more Michael left within than he had initially thought. He needed to use this to his advantage and pry him out again. He moved forward, and strolled around the room, as if window shopping. 'So,' he said, 'is this your new home then? I mean, do you actually live under this frozen mountain?'

'For now,' he answered. 'The heat in here allows me to change state; it keeps me fluid and efficient, and my chamber can be moved.'

'What's the fun in that? No more swimming; no running about; no dating! What kind of a life is this?'

'I'm past those needs, brother. Although, if I really wanted to, I could do all those things – I'm not a prisoner; I'm the King of Arnesh.'

Julius made a mental note of that; what did he mean by *fluid*? The thought that the Arneshians had mastered chemical transformations to this degree was alarming as well as mind-blowing. His mind conjured up the earlier vision of a salty water mixture within a glass. Pretending to ponder what he had just heard, he turned towards the exit and observed the door. The energy field in its frame needed to go; without it, he could draw Michael out. He could short the mechanism, or at least try.

'What do you want from me, Julius?'

'I guess I'm here to convince you to stop this nonsense. Even Clodagh saw the error of her ways, or have you forgotten what we saw on the Trail?'

The particles in the air slowed.

Julius took advantage of the silence and continued. 'Clodagh was the ultimate Arneshian, and she said, *enough*. It was someone else's greed that brought centuries of hostilities upon us. But we can stop it! We have the power to do it, you and I.'

'It's too late, Julius.'

'No, it isn't. Help me set things right and be my brother again.'

'It's too late! I know too much,' he said, in anger and frustration. 'You don't understand. I don't need you anymore. You are no match for the King - stop bothering me!'

Those words were like ice water to Julius, and he flinched. Whatever pity he had felt before had now been pushed aside, and replaced by a welcome coldness of thought. 'You lost on the Trail because you were thinking like an Arneshian. You're right: you're not one of us and you're certainly not fit to have anyone's powers; not Tijaras, or mine.' With that, he made straight for the door.

'Wait … where are you going?' Michael sounded outraged. 'How *dare* you walk out on me?'

'Come and get me then!' he shouted over his shoulder. As he crossed the threshold, he discharged a full blast of energy into the sensor grid, sending sparks everywhere and shorting it. The field disappeared with a crackle and Julius turned. The room had gone quiet and nothing moved. The little letters and numbers were nowhere to be seen. *Come out, Michael*, he thought.

A whooshing sound filled the air as the cyphers appeared again, circling the room in a whirlwind. The maelstrom expanded until it was bigger than the doorframe, before changing into the shape of a man again. Michael faced the exit and lunged forward, rushing at his brother.

Julius couldn't see much more than a green, code-filled shape coming his way, but his instincts told him to run. He scampered up the path, unsure what to do next. He could feel the wind behind him drawing closer, so he fired up his boosters enough to stay ahead of it. The whirlwind continued to give chase, until it was almost on him. Julius veered left and out into the rocky alcove. Just as he emerged into the cave, the wind propelled him forward and slammed him down onto the icy bridge. Sharp pain jagged up his leg, from just above the ankle, and he cried out. He was panting, his breath drifting from his mouth in a mist. With difficulty, he sat up, sure that he had broken something. Meanwhile, the whirlwind had left him and was now hovering above the lake.

'Come on, coward! Are you afraid to show yourself?' he said, trying to goad his brother. Michael's shape appeared again at that, this time almost to perfection. Julius couldn't see a face as such, but he could tell it was his brother's from a lot of little details. However, there was something odd about the way he moved. As Michael flew at him, Julius realised two things: the cold was making him less fluid in his mobility and, secondly, if he could draw him into the snow, he was sure this would accelerate the process.

Before Michael could reach him, Julius rolled off the bridge, fired up his boosters and flew directly at his brother. The two clashed in mid-air and tumbled towards the ground. Not wanting to use the boosters too much, in case they heated the air around Michael, Julius instead had to use his mind-skills to cushion their fall. He doubted that Michael would feel any pain in that form if they crashed, but Julius might not make it out in one piece. He managed to break their descent just enough, but his wounded ankle jarred against the floor, and a fresh burst of pain shot up his leg. They rolled along the ground, Michael becoming increasingly tangible as the cold took effect. Julius used all his strength to roll him along the snowy floor – it had turned into a wrestling match, as if they were two young brothers again, just messing about.

But there was nothing playful about this contest. The change from code to a flesh-and-blood version of Michael happened so quickly that Julius was caught off guard. As his brother fully materialised, he planted his feet against Julius' chest and levered himself away. Julius saw Michael rushing back for him, so he opened up his boosters and flew from his grasp at the last second.

'Come down where I can get you,' snarled Michael, glaring as his brother hovering above him. 'Don't make me change shape.'

'I don't think you can, actually,' replied Julius. 'You're too cold for that, and now that you're just a little boy again, you can't even fly back to the alcove.' Michael's expression changed from one of rage to uncertainty, no doubt realising the truth in Julius' words. 'Are you ready to listen now?'

Michael looked around frantically, like a caged animal trying to find a way out that didn't exist. He paced up and down near to the icy walls, searching for any kind of opening.

'I brought you a vaccine,' said Julius. 'If you let me use it, I can cure you and you will be Michael again.'

'This is not a virus,' he growled. 'I am not ill. Don't you dare speak to me like I'm any different from you!'

'Soon, we'll really be exactly the same, Michael, more than you can imagine.'

His brother stopped and looked up. 'How?'

'The being that gave us our Grey and White Skills is ready to purge us all, and turn us back to norm- to the way we were before. The Curia held a referendum and every human in the system has voted on it. We'll all be stripped of our powers.'

'It's a lie,' he said, incredulous.

'I wish it was.'

'Even more so then, I have no intention of standing down. You'll have to find another way.' He turned suddenly, shooting two lightning beams from the disks in his hands.

Taken by surprise, Julius managed to veer to the side, but one of the shots brushed his back and he felt a surge of heat searing his skin. He gritted his teeth and focused again, knowing he couldn't afford to let Michael use the disks on the surroundings, or he would be able to heat the air and change shape once more. He veered down at him, but Michael was too quick and fired off a barrage of shots as he ran along the snowy banks around the lake. Some of the stray rounds crashed into the stalactites high above, and they rained down and smashed onto the frozen water, causing several cracks in its surface. It took every ounce of dexterity and reflexes that Julius possessed to avoid being struck by his brother's weapons or the falling shards of ice.

He spotted a protruding rock and quickly hovered behind it, catching his breath. 'I'm going to ask you one more time, Mickey,' he shouted. 'Stand down and come back to us.' It occurred to him that Freja had been right after all: blood was thicker than water, and he couldn't bring himself to deny Michael one last chance.

There was silence, then a shot skimmed his right thigh. He fell the couple of feet to the ground and landed painfully on the ice. He could hear Michael running towards him, and realised that he couldn't allow him to get hold of his boosters and escape. There were no excuses left for his brother anymore. He rolled on to his side, stretched his hand forward, and pushed Michael back with his mind, giving enough of an opening to heave himself up. Keeping the weight off his broken ankle, he focused all of his mind on the young man in front of him. All White Skills worked through balance – he had learned that in school. Right now though, Julius needed *imbalance*. He was going to try something new, something drastic, and he needed the right fuel. He needed to fill himself with righteous anger. He thought of all the faces of the fallen, their pain and anguish, suffered at the hands of the Arneshians. To top it off, he filled his mind with the image of Morgana lying dead on the hospital bed, her dark hair matted in blood; the hole in her stomach; the cold lips that would never kiss him again. It worked as a powerful catalyst, toppling the towering rage building inside his mind. When Michael squared up to him, Julius brought his hands forward and *unbound* his brother.

The world had suddenly stopped, leaving them enveloped in the cold stillness of the cave. Where before was nothing, now countless small red clusters floated in the air, revolving gently like tiny frozen pebbles. Julius stood there, the realisation of what he had done too great to handle. His eyes darted around the room, staring at the molecules that made up his little brother. No hair, or entrails – he didn't see eyeballs or floating ears either - this particular *Twist* had gone well beyond that. He was too petrified to move; if he tried to grab the vaccine, he could lose his grip, and Michael would be killed. There was no way out that he could see. He was stuck. For want of a better plan, he waited, trying not to move a muscle.

He wasn't sure how much time passed as he had stood there, ignoring the searing pain in his ankle, but he did know that he was really cold. He tried to open his mouth, but his jaw was stiff and he wondered if his lips were turning blue. What if he passed out? Would Morales be able to put Michael together again? Just as desperation was beginning to seep into his mind, Julius heard a noise, nothing more than a faint echo, but a noise nonetheless. He jammed his broken ankle on the ground, using the sharp pain to wake himself up. He screamed hard, but he felt better; vigilant.

He heard a second noise, like a padded explosion, and the cave shook; debris fell to the ground. The noise grew in intensity: a whooshing sound that echoed around the cavern. It was coming from the opening in the ceiling; the very conduit that Julius had fallen down. He listened carefully, making sure not to let any part of Michael drop from his field of focus. The echo became ever louder as whatever the source of it was drew closer; he began to think there were voices in the midst of it. Could it be …

'Julius!' Skye's voice exploded into the cave.

Julius allowed himself to breathe out, relief washing over him. The sound of boots landing on the ice belonged to more than one person though. In a flash, he was surrounded by his friends, along with Kelly and Freja.

'What are you doing, McCoy?' asked Faith, hovering towards

the cluster that was Michael.

Julius forced his jaw open and cried, 'Don't touch them!'

There was enough desperation in his voice that Freja stepped forward. 'Stay where you are,' he told the others. He moved closer to Julius, observing his stance and the way his eyes were focusing so intently on the particles floating in the air. Then he turned and slowly approached them. He allowed himself to take it all in, before turning back to Julius. 'Is this who I think it is?'

Julius nodded slowly.

'What are you talking about?' asked Kelly.

'The vaccine is in my p-pocket, sir,' said Julius, teeth chattering from the cold.

Freja looked shaken, but he went ahead and closed Julius' Exoskin, in order to retrieve the little box, before activating it again. Inside was the injector with a few samples of the vaccine.

'You need to find the pearl and inject it,' explained Julius.

'Why would the pearl be among those fragments?' asked Faith. 'I mean, only people have pearls, right?' The silence coming from Freja told its own story, and his eyes widened. 'Crikey, McCoy! Did you Twist your brother?'

'Mr Shanigan, please!' said Freja nervously. 'I need your help, all of you.'

The others stepped forward to join Freja.

'You're something else all right,' mused Skye as he walked past, with a mixture of admiration and incredulity.

'I don't know what a pearl looks like,' said Freja truthfully, 'because I've never seen one, but we're going to learn today.'

Julius watched anxiously as they moved cautiously among his brother's parts, trying to identify the right cluster. He was beginning to feel weak and wondered how long he could last in this cold.

Beyond everyone's expectations, Freja called them to him after only a few minutes. 'Over here,' he said. 'This particular clump has an odd growth to its side – not organic, I don't think.'

They gathered around him as he pointed at it; even Julius was able to get a glimpse of it. From afar, he could only make out that the pearl was off-white in colour and that it shimmered in the light; he watched as Freja injected the vaccine into it, trying not to touch it with his fingers. As soon as it had been administered, the odd growth fell to the floor and, to everyone's astonishment, shattered as if it was made of glass - the freezing temperature had done its job. Immediately, the cluster turned black and shrivelled, like a rotten fruit.

Freja moved away from the dead pearl and ushered everyone back with him. 'It's time to fix this, Julius,' he said gently. 'He cannot harm anyone now.'

Julius didn't respond for a moment, toying with the possibility that he wouldn't be able to put his brother back together.

'I know you can do it,' said Faith, reassuring him.

'Not like this,' replied Julius. 'It's too cold.'

'Leave it to us,' said Kelly, stepping forward and directing the others into a circle.

They positioned themselves around the area where Michael was and created fireballs in each of their hands, until the clusters were surrounded by a circle of fire.

Even Julius benefited from the warmth, as some of the heat touched the skin on his face.

The ice began to thaw quickly and the clusters to lose the shine they'd been given by the crystallised liquid. There were no drops of water falling to the floor though, as the clusters were still very much encased in the hold of the Twist.

'Whenever you are ready now,' Freja told him calmly.

Julius dearly hoped that all the training he had gone through wouldn't let him down now. He bent his will on the particles in front of him and, with one single click of his mind, he willed them back together, just like he had done countless times before on inanimate objects. He feared it wouldn't work, but it was the only way he knew how.

There was a snapping sound, instantly followed by a *whoosh*, and Michael appeared in front of them, looking dazed and with much shorter hair. He swayed for a moment, not looking at anyone in particular, then fainted.

Julius lowered his arms and fell to his knees, exhausted and unable to stand any longer.

'Excellent job, Julius, but you cannot rest yet,' said Freja, lifting him up with the help of Skye and Faith. 'We need to leave, or we'll be caught in Eronan's purge.'

Julius was tempted to ask why that mattered anyway, but let it go. He bent over and massaged his ankle with a grimace.

Noticing this, Skye moved back to his side to support him, taking most of his weight on himself. 'Get those boosters on; I'll take you up.'

Julius didn't move at first, but merely looked him in the eyes, wanting to know what had happened to K'Ssander. Skye's upper lip was split and his right eye was on the way to turning black; he also had several spots of dried blood on the front of his Exoskin.

He opened his mouth but, before he could talk, Skye cut him off. 'It's done,' he said quietly, so only Julius could hear him.

Julius tightened his grip on his friend's shoulder and nodded gratefully. It was all he needed to know.

Freja went ahead, followed by Kelly, who was carrying Michael. Next came Skye and Julius, with Faith last. They zoomed back up through the chute and emerged in the foyer of the home; Julius took note of how they had made the trapdoor chute much larger – in fact, it was fair to say that they had blasted half the floor away. They must have taken some serious power tools to the conduit. Julius grinned.

The group exited from the house, into the twilight, and waited by a boulder for a Stork to pick them up. Julius stood on one foot, his arms on Faith and Skye's shoulders for balance. He didn't think he needed all that support in reality, but he guessed that they too were keen for some closure - the remaining Skirts, standing together. Warm rain began to fall and he turned his face up to it, letting it wash away the memories of his last fight, not quite fully appreciating that it was all over. He could feel blood pumping through his veins, reminding him he was still alive. He had fought and won and, although the future was hidden, he knew that something important in him had changed. The detachment he had experienced towards an increasing number of things - situations, people, even emotions themselves – hadn't quite left him, even now, at the end of it all. It was as if the icy cold of the cave had escaped with him – *inside* him – and, without the warmth of Morgana to melt it away, Julius knew it was there to stay.

He looked at his brother, resting against the rock, fast asleep. It would take a while to explain his new predicament to him, and he was glad to not have that task. Prison was the most likely ending to his story; it would break their parents' hearts, but he couldn't see any other solution. One thing that war taught was how to handle yourself in order to survive. Michael had obviously lost that fight the moment he forgot who he really was.

Julius' gaze turned to the city of Mahin; it was quiet again, and there were bodies on the ground as far as the eye could see - he didn't believe all of them were merely stunned. Zed officers were uplifting the surviving Mahini; at least until Eronan had performed his duties on the planet. Once this was done, they would be allowed to return home and start afresh, while the purged Arneshians awaited their fate in the holding cells of the fleet. Perhaps taking them back to Arnesh wouldn't be such a bad idea after all.

The Stork landed ten minutes later, and shuttled them all to the safety of the Mazda. Mahin had witnessed the end of an era: the long-standing conflict between Arnesh and Earth was over.

A NEW BEGINNING

'It seems that the Mahini's Winter Gardens are one of the most successful exhibitions at this year's Mid-Winter Festival in Oslo,' said Iryana Mielowa, wearing a fur-lined hood and full-length snow-coat. 'Mah Gira has invited us all to see them in their natural environment, on Mah. I, for one, intend to accept that invitation.'

Julius, who was getting dressed, stopped and looked at the screen. Mah Gira was standing next to the reporter, surrounded by Ruxshin, Khavar and a couple of Norwegian delegates. They seemed to be having a great time, eating new food and learning new words. As it turned out, Kelly had had an easy job during the Supreme's rescue. The black stone Skye had moved on his behalf, back on Mah, had alerted a few selected Mahini, including Khavar, to organise a full scale insurrection. When Kelly had arrived at the prison cell, he practically had no choice but to join a large number of hunters, bent on making the Arneshians' lives a misery. Mah would certainly benefit from being in the federation, thought Julius. And maybe Ruxshin and Khavar would take on roles in the Forum, as spokespersons.

'As a symbol of unity between Earth and the Mahini, a memorial has been erected at the feet of the Archer, to preserve Morgana Ruthier's coffin. Without her arrival on Mah, things would have been very different.'

Julius had already been told of that decision. Perhaps housing her on Mah was the best way to protect her from further dangers. He didn't like to think about it though, so he focused back on the screen, ignoring the feeling it stirred within him.

'In other news,' continued the anchorman in the studio, 'After the successful purge of the GFE, Zed readies itself for the purification session this afternoon. Zed is the last remaining place in the Federation where skills are still active.'

Julius watched as images of the previous purges flashed across the screen. The nebula that was Eronan appeared and surrounded the planets. The phenomenon lasted for almost thirty minutes before the beams slowly dissipated into the atmosphere, leaving all pearls deactivated.

'There are still tickets available to watch the Zed Purge. Purchase is possible through MoonBee box office. And now, the weather …'

'Like a bloody circus,' he muttered, turning the screen off. He moved to the mirror and finished adjusting his suit. They had been asked to wear their white ceremonial uniforms to mark the occasion; something he found completely unacceptable and in poor taste. He had tried to change the Curio's mind one last time, after leaving Michael in his custody, but to no avail – the world had already moved on, leaving him behind.

His PIP beeped and he opened the vid-screen. His parents smiled at him, but he could see their eyes were red and puffy. The news about Michael had not been easy to digest.

'Hello son,' said Rory. 'Are you all set?'

'Almost, Dad,' he replied, continuing to adjust his jacket.

'You look so handsome,' said Jenny.

'Indeed, our little guy is now a man. We are so proud of you, son.'

Julius felt a lump in his throat and couldn't speak.

'You'll always be our White Child. Walk with your head held high, son. It isn't an honour bestowed on many.'

Jenny couldn't hold back her tears and Rory hugged her to him. 'Write soon!' he said, wiping the corners of his eyes.

'I will.' He looked up at them, a sense of finality on his heart. 'I love you.' He didn't know if he would ever see them again in his lifetime. Eventually, he closed his PIP, taking a last look around the room. Nothing would ever be the same again.

He took the lift back to the Tijaran promenade and headed right. There were several students milling about, since all lessons had been suspended. Some, like him, had already changed into their uniforms, waiting nervously for the afternoon. He saw a few of his former classmates, huddled together chatting in the garden, but had no real inclination to talk to anyone, so he kept on walking. He passed the technician's den where Mister List had fitted him with the infamous Holopal, the infirmary where Nurse Primula had patched him up countless of times, and the mess hall, where Felice Buongustaio was shouting orders to his chefs around the stoves, as per tradition.

When he reached the main entrance, he headed swiftly for the stairs that led to the school's hangar; he didn't want to attract the attention of Mister Leven, or the security guards. Still, he paused on the first step and looked up. The sign, "TIJARA – HANGAR ACCESS" looked exactly the same as it had six years ago, when a much shorter Julius, along with Morgana, had seen it for the first time. *"That'll be my bedroom, then!"* she had cried out enthusiastically. He sighed and moved on.

A couple of officers walked past him, and nodded in his direction in greeting. It looked like they were about to say something so Julius nodded in return, but didn't slow and they didn't call after him.

When he arrived in the hangar, he couldn't help but notice an eerie quiet - all Zed personnel and students had already arrived and no one was scheduled to leave the perimeter until the evening, after the purge. Julius took the stairs down unchallenged, floor after floor, and eventually reached the lowest deck.

As he stepped onto the runway, he looked for his shuttle, dreading the possibility that something had gone wrong, and that there might be no one waiting for him.

'Come on!' called Skye suddenly, standing in front of a Stork's hatch with Faith. Behind them, he could see Siena plus a couple of other people he couldn't quite make out. They were all wearing their white uniforms. 'We thought you'd changed your mind!'

Julius beamed. 'No chance.' He began to move towards them, when two figures emerged from the shadows to either side of him. He saw Skye and Faith's expressions freeze and he was instantly glued to the spot.

'Mr McCoy,' said Master Cress. 'Going somewhere, are we?'

A look of panic spread over his face. They had been caught. With a last glance at Faith and Skye, he turned, preparing himself for a fight. Surprisingly, Freja was wearing a familiar enigmatic smile and his aura was bright green. Whatever the Grand Master had come to do, it wasn't to stop him.

'It seems that, the next time we meet, I will have to arrest you for deserting,' he said jovially.

'I'd like to see you try that, sir, without your powers,' he replied with a grin.

Freja and Cress smiled. Julius could tell though, despite their efforts to appear relaxed, that they were both visibly emotional about this last farewell.

'Are you sure you don't want to join us?'

'And leave Tijara?' said Cress. 'Thank you, McCoy. I'm sure we'll have plenty chance to regret this, but we've decided to stay. We taught you well,' he said, gesturing to him and the group by the Stork, 'and you've learned well. You'll make us proud, no matter where you go. In your heart ...'

'... Tijara,' Julius said, his right fist touching his own heart. 'Always. I will not forget you, Master Cress. I will not forget you,' he said, bowing low. Then he turned to the Grand Master, who was smiling, though his eyes were teary. For the first time Julius saw an older man, rather than the Tijaran GM, burdened by everyone else's troubles, not least Julius'.

'Take care of my granddaughter, White Child,' he said.

'Wha- Kelly?' he asked, delighted.

'And Elian. The Mazda is waiting for you at Eronan's, with a few other ... escapees.'

Julius' pleasure at this news was written all over his face. He straightened up for a final salute, his heart swelling with pride, just like the first time he had met him. "It has been an honour serving with you, sir.'

The Grand Master stepped forward unexpectedly and hugged him tightly. 'Good luck, son.'

Julius felt tears welling in his eyes. At this moment, in Freja's arms, he felt as if Rory and Jenny were also there holding him, and he didn't want to let go.

It was his mentor who eventually stepped back, bowing to him along with Cress.

Julius bowed gratefully, then turned and ran to the Stork, joining Faith and Skye on its steps. For one last moment, the three remaining Skirts stood there staring at each other, almost as if to check that they were really going ahead with their plan. After a final glance at their former teachers, they disappeared inside the shuttle.

They took off without delay, aiming for the black hole that would lead them to the Eronan System and, from there, to a new life beyond.